The Internet

& World Wide Web

THE ROUGH GUIDE

There are more than seventy Rough Guide
travel, phrasebook, and music titles, covering
destinations from Amsterdam to Zimbabwe,
languages from Czech to Thai, and musics from
World to Opera and Jazz.

To find out more about Rough Guides, and to
check out our USA titles on HotWired's
Worldbeat site, get connected to the Internet
with this guide and find us on the Web at:
http://roughguides.com/

Rough Guide to the Internet Credits

Text editor: Mark Ellingham

Design and lay-out: Henry Iles

Production: Susanne Hillen

Proofread by Ellen Sarewitz

This first edition published Nov 1995 by Rough Guides Ltd
1 Mercer St, London WC2H 9QJ
375 Hudson Street, New York 10014
Internet: mail@roughtravl.co.uk

Distributed by The Penguin Group

Penguin Books Ltd, 27 Wrights Lane, London W8 5TZ

Penguin Books USA Inc., 375 Hudson Street, New York 10014

Penguin Books Canada Ltd, 10 Alcorn Avenue, Toronto, Ontario MV4 1E4

Penguin Books Australia Ltd, PO Box 257, Ringwood, Victoria 3134

Penguin Books (NZ) Ltd, 182–190 Wairau Road, Auckland 10

Printed in the United Kingdom by Cox & Wyman Ltd (Reading)

320 pages; includes index

A catalogue record for this book is available from the British Library

ISBN 1-85828-198-9

The Internet

& World Wide Web

THE ROUGH GUIDE

by

Angus J. Kennedy
of **Internet**

Contents

Preface

There's nothing worse than feeling left behind. When everyone is talking about something, but it just doesn't gel. The Internet has had this effect over the last year or so. Everything you pick up. Internet this, cyber that. But, unless you've been connected, you'll still be in the dark. If you find it daunting, don't worry. It might be a steep learning curve, but it's a short one, and it won't take long to master. This small guide is crammed with nuggets of practical advice, troubleshooting tips, step-by-step tuition, and addresses of the places you'll need to go. It aims to make you a Net guru in the shortest possible time.

Internet books generally fall into two categories: the type that tell you far more than you want to know in unimportant areas and not enough on shortcuts; and the patronizing, simplistic ones that make it look easy in the bookstore, but aren't much use once you start having problems. And, if they're written before mid-1995, they should be filed in the ancient history section.

This guide gives it to you straight. We think the Net is a pushover. If you can figure out how to use a word processor, you can master the Net. But we know you'll have problems, so we show you how to solve them and where to go for help. Rather than compile everything there is to know about the Net, we give you the basics and tell you how to make use of the Net itself to find out more. Since the Net and its associated technology change almost daily, it's wiser to get your information from where it's always fresh.

What's more, we'll show you how to get the best deal on Internet access, how to find all the software you'll ever need for free, how to become an expert in the most important Internet programs, and how to locate anything, anywhere, on the Net without having to learn any difficult commands. Or, if you're really impatient, you can wing it and go straight to our guides to surf through the star attractions on the World Wide Web, or find hundreds of like-minded souls on one of the special interest Newsgroups.

Well, what are you waiting for?

basics

Frequently Asked Questions

Before getting into the nitty gritty of what you can do on the Internet – and what it can do for you – here are some answers to a few Frequently Asked Questions (or FAQs, as acronym-loving net users call them).

What is the Internet?

The Internet is an international computer network. The core of the network consists of computers permanently linked through high-speed connections. To join the Internet, all you have to do is connect your computer to any of these computers. Once you're online (connected) your computer can talk to every other computer on the Internet whether they are in your home town or on the other side of the world.

What's it going to do for me?

Having the Internet at your disposal is like having 30 million expert consultants on your payroll. Except you don't have to pay them. You can find answers to every question you've ever had, send messages across the world instantly, transfer documents, shop, sample new music, visit art galleries, read books, play games, chat, read the latest news in any language, meet people with similar interests, obtain software, or just surf mindlessly through mountains of visual bubblegum.

The Internet will become as integral to business as the telephone and fax machine.

Who's in charge?

Various bodies are concerned with the Internet's conventions and international congruence. Foremost among them are the *Internet Network Information Center* (*InterNIC*), which registers domain names, and the *Internet Society* which, amongst other things, acts as a clearing house for technical standards. No-one, however, actually "runs" the Internet. As the Internet is, in effect, a network of networks, most responsibilities are contained within the local network. For instance, if you have connection problems, you would call your connection supplier. If you object to material located on a Japanese server, you'd have to complain to the administrator of that server.

While it certainly promotes freedom of speech, the Internet is not as anarchic as some sections of the media would have you believe. If you break the laws of your country and you are caught, you will be prosecuted. For example, suppose you publish a document in the USA outlining the shortcomings of a military dictator in Slobovia. It might not worry the US authorities, but it could be curtains for any Slobovian caught downloading it. The same applies to other contentious material such as pornography, terrorist handbooks, drug literature, and religious satire.

But isn't it run by the Pentagon and the CIA?

The Internet was conceived in 1969 in the USA, as the American Defense Department network (ARPAnet), and its purpose was to act as a nuclear attack resistant method of exchanging scientific information and intelligence. But that's old history in Internet terms.

In the 70s and 80s several other networks, such as the National Science Foundation Network (NSFNET), joined, linking it to research agencies and universities. It was probably no coincidence that as the Cold War petered out, the Internet became more publicly accessible and the nature of the beast changed totally and irreversibly. These days, intelligence agencies have the same access to the Internet as everyone else, but whether they use it to monitor insurgence and crime is simply a matter for speculation.

Is this the Information Superhighway?

The Internet is often called the Information Superhighway by the popular media. And no wonder. The concept of a Global Information Infrastructure or Information Superhighway envisioned by US Vice President Al Gore, and talked up by Microsoft's Bill Gates and associates, has a very similar structure.

The Internet is the closest thing we have to a prototype. It has huge capabilities for cheap, global, and immediate communication; it may grow to dominate areas of education; it is already providing an alternative shopping mall; and it will almost certainly make inroads into banking and customer services.

But unless the existing, relatively slow telephone lines which link the network are replaced with fiber optic cables and digital technology, it will never have the capacity for features like video on demand. The real digital revolution is still on hold.

What is electronic mail?

 Electronic mail or email is a method of sending text files from one computer to another. You can send messages across the world in seconds using Internet email.

Who pays for the international calls?

One of the Internet's proudest claims is to make distances and political borders irrelevant. For the most part, it succeeds. Suppose you're in Boston, and you want to contact a friend in Bangkok. You just compose your message, connect to the Internet in Boston, transfer the message to the Boston host, and then disconnect. The Boston host then looks at the message's address to determine where it has to go and passes it on to its appropriate neighbor, who follows the same procedure. Each computer in the chain ensures that the message makes its way to Bangkok and not Bogota. The message should only take a matter of seconds to reach Bangkok even though it may have passed through any number of computers to get there.

Apart from your Internet subscription costs, you'll only have to pay for a local call to the computer in Boston. Your message will pass through many different networks, each with its own method of recouping the communication costs. But don't worry, adding to your phone bill is not one of them.

What are Internet Servers and Online Services?

Any computer that allows you to connect into it is known as a **server** or host, even if you are connecting through several other computers in between. There are hundreds of companies – as well as educational and business establishments – that operate as servers. Most of these **Internet Service Providers** (ISPs – also known as Internet Access Providers or IAPs) do little more than hook you into the Internet, but there are also some much larger companies, like CompuServe, America Online, IBM, and Microsoft, which provide both Internet access and "private" commercial networks, offering their own forums, services, and shopping malls. These operations are commonly referred to as **Online Services**. We deal with both approaches in this book.

And how about Internet Clients and Browsers?

The software you use to connect to the Internet is called a **client**. A World Wide Web client is a piece of software that allows you to browse (or "surf") the **World Wide Web (WWW)**, the hugely popular, magazine-like area of the Internet – of which more later. This kind of software is also referred to as a **Web browser**.

What is full Internet access?

As mentioned above, you can access the Internet through several channels, but not all methods will let you do everything. Most of the Online Services started out offering access only to their own networks, along with email into the wider Internet. This is changing fast, however, and by early 1996 full Internet access is likely to be a standard feature.

The World Wide Web, IRC, FTP, and Telnet – the main areas of the Internet, which we'll deal with later in this book – require full access from one of the Online Services or what's called an **IP (Internet Protocol)** account with an Internet Service provider. You'll encounter a choice of IP accounts, which may include **SLIP** (Serial Line Internet Protocol) and **PPP** (Point to Point Protocol) for standard modem dial-ups, ISDN, and various types of direct connections. Regardless of what grade IP access you choose, you'll be able to do the same things, though at different speeds.

What are IP addresses?

Every computer which is permanently connected to the Net has a 32-bit unique **IP (Internet Protocol) address**, so other Internet computers can find it. A typical address looks like this: 149.174.211.5 (that is, four numbers separated by periods).

Your computer will be allocated an IP address when you get full Internet access. If it's a SLIP (Serial Line Internet Protocol) connection you'll get a fixed address; if you access with a PPP (Point to Point Protocol) connections your host will allocate a new one each time you log in. The good news is that, other than when you first get connected, you'll probably never have to use these numbers. Why? Because there's a different system for humans called the **Domain Name System (DNS)**.

OK, then, what's the Domain Name System?

People don't like using numbers. Isn't it easier to remember a name than a telephone number? With this in mind, the Internet uses the **Domain Name System (DNS)** parallel to the IP number system. That way you have the choice of using letters or words, rather than numbers, to identify hosts.

Domain names look somewhat confusing at first meeting, but they soon become familar. Indeed, you can often tell a lot about who or what you're connecting to from its address. For example, let's consider the email address: `marvin@easynet.co.uk`

As all Internet email addresses are in the format `user@host`, we can deduce that the user's name or nickname is Marvin while the host is easynet.co.uk. The host portion breaks down further into subdomain, domaintype, and country-code. Here, the subdomain is easynet (an Internet Service Provider), its domain type "co" means it's a company or commercial site, and the country code "uk" indicates it's in the United Kingdom.

Every country has its own distinct code, although it's not always used. These include:

au	Australia
ca	Canada
de	Germany
fr	France
jp	Japan
nl	Netherlands
no	Norway
se	Sweden
uk	United Kingdom

If an address doesn't specify a country code, it's more than likely, but not necessarily, in the USA.

Domain types are usually one of the following:

ac	Academic (UK)
com	Company or commercial organization
co	Company or commercial organization (UK)
edu	Educational institution

gov	Government body
mil	Military site
net	Internet gateway or administrative host
org	Non-profit organisation

What is a BBS?

Once upon a time **BBSs** (Bulletin Board Services) were like computer clubs, allowing members to dial in and post messages and trade files. However these days, the definition is far fuzzier. All of the online services, such as CompuServe and Microsoft Network, are technically speaking BBSs. That is, they have a private network or file area which is set aside out of the public domain of the Internet. The big online services are not what most people refer to as BBSs, though. The term is usually taken to mean a small network which primarily acts as a place to download and trade files.

There are well over 100,000 private BBSs in the USA alone, most often devoted to particular or local interests, and in some cases access is free. They customarily have areas to play games, chat, use email, post messages, and sometimes get limited access to the Internet through their own private network connections. Many business organizations also operate their own BBSs to supply product information, support, or useful data.

Can I shop online?

It won't be long before you can buy anything you want via the Internet. There are already hundreds of online "stores" but net shopping has yet to take off in a big way. It suffers from the usual reticence people feel toward mail order as well as much publicized (and to be honest, inflated) concerns about credit card security.

At present, numerous companies are working on methods of secure payment through encryption and cash alternatives, so it can only be a matter of time before it gains mainstream acceptance. The launch of Microsoft's own secure network – planned as an add-on to Windows 95 and avowedly commercial in outlook – is likely to provide a major boost to Net shopping.

How can I make money out of the Internet?

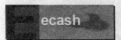

Would you like to set yourself up **selling products** through the Internet? If so, you're not alone – it's an almost universal reaction to the present Net-frenzy. It can certainly be viable, but spend a couple of months getting to understand how the Internet works before diving in. Unless you have a unique and brilliant idea, selling on the Net will involves hard, labor-intensive work, long hours, and very low margins. In other words, it's not easy money.

One thing you should dismiss straight away is any idea of applying traditional **direct response marketing**, either by means of email or especially on the non-commercial Usenet newsgroups. If you try, you will find yourself cyber-assassinated (or "flamed" in Net jargon). If you want to see what that means, just post an urging advertisement in Usenet . . . and wait for the response!

The main commercial area of the Internet right now is the **World Wide Web**, whose magazine-like pages are proving a draw for every kind of company, from book publishers (Rough Guides among them) to coffee suppliers. The main problem here is not how to get your advertisement online, which is pretty straightforward, but how to get people to look at it. It's wiser to incorpo-

rate a World Wide Web presence within your overall marketing mix, than to rely on it alone.

So is the Net still basically a geek hangout?

There's no doubt about the Internet's geek-pulling power. There's stuff for Star Trek geeks, investment geeks, political geeks, music geeks, movie geeks, health geeks, gardening geeks, sporting geeks, and every other sort of geek imaginable. Face it, geek is hip.

Yes, but what about deviants?

More than 30 million deviants worldwide have Internet addresses including the American President and Vice President, Bill Gates, Madonna, Prince, Courtney Love, the Mexican Zapatistas, journalists, university students, stockbrokers, scientists, doctors, and real estate agents. That number is exploding at a growth rate of over 10percent per month. It may eventually come close to merging with the telephone. Of course, there may be perverts, gangsters, and con artists as well, but maybe not as high as the percentage who shop at your local supermarket.

Will I make friends on the Internet?

It's certainly easy to meet people with common interests, and if you read the computer features in newspapers – or check out Douglas Coupland's wonderful new net-world novel, Microserfs – you'll be regaled with stories of email romance. One fascinating aspect of email communication is its anonymity. This can make it a startlingly intimate means of communication, and its ease of access and scope mean you can get in touch with literally hundreds of people with interests similar to your own.

Translating email pen pals into the real world of human contact is a whole different ball game. There is no way of knowing what your e-pal posting messages as John or Adrienne looks like, whether they're six or sixty, or indeed what sex they are. It's an Internet cliché, but an awful lot of people on the Net use the name of the family dog or cat as their email "nickname."

What if children discover pornography or drugs?

Children will find what interests them, pretty much whatever anyone else does about it: Face it, they're a computer generation. Many educative bodies have taken steps to limit access to contentious matter, and some commercial companies have been working on programs that deny access to material containing sexually explicit or drug-related key words (see the "Kids" section in our World Wide Web guide). However it's impossible to filter the Net completely, and perhaps just as well, because it's not the Internet's place to preach morals.

If you are worried about kids becoming perverts on the Internet, comfort yourself with the fact that less than one percent of the Internet "Newsgroups" are devoted to sex, and an even smaller percentage of the World Wide Web pages. How does that match up to the shelves of your local news store?

And take the time, also, to reflect on the thought that children exposed to the Internet might mature faster and learn to think more freely and independently. What they see of things like drugs, sex, and religious cults will usually be through first-hand interactive debates and discussions. If someone posts an article in a news-group advocating crack as an easy way to make money and friends, it might attract twenty negative postings in response. By following the trail of responses, children can understand the structure of reason and form their own opinions based upon evidence.

Will I need to learn any computer languages or UNIX?

A basic knowledge of computer languages can enrich your Internet experience, but it's by no means essential. If you can work a word processor or a spreadsheet, you'll have no difficulty tackling the Internet. You will have to get familiar with your Internet software, but in most cases it isn't too hard. The biggest problem most people have is in setting up for the first time, and with the "Internet made easy" packages available these days, that's no longer too much of an issue.

Once online, most people access the Internet by means of a graphical "icon-based" program, not too different from the way you use a Macintosh or Windows. And on the World Wide Web – the most popular part of the Net – you won't even need to type: everything is accessible by a click on your mouse.

The only time you may need to use **UNIX** commands – the traditional "language" of the Internet – is if using Telnet to remotely log on to a UNIX computer. This can be a useful too, but most Internet users have never needed to use it.

Can I use the Internet if I can't even use a computer?

As mentioned above, even if you can't type, you can still use the World Wide Web – all you have to do is point your mouse and click. That's about as far as you'll get though. If you've never had any contact with computers, consider the Internet your opportunity. Don't think of computers as daunting modern technology. They're just a means to an end. There is only one way to learn how to use a computer – get one and use it.

How do I get connected?

Good question and worth a whole chapter. Read on.

Getting Connected

There are all kinds of ways to gain access to the Internet. You don't have to hold any privileged position. It's very likely that within the next year, you'll be able to use a Net-connected terminal at work, college, school, or maybe even your local library or coffee shop. If you're not in that position already, you don't have to wait. It's possible to get everything you need to be up and running within a few days. The good news is it's no longer expensive and complicated, and it's getting cheaper and easier by the day.

You don't need to be a computer expert

The most common barrier to getting connected is technophobia or more specifically fear of computers. That's understandable, because the Internet requires an almost symbiotic relationship with your computer. However, it's not that demanding. In fact, most people find it fun, once they've started. Internet programs are nowhere near as complex as the latest series of word processors. Even if you've never used a computer, you'll be able to figure out how to surf the Web within minutes. Finding your way around is another matter, but you're at an advantage – you have this guide.

Although it's relatively simple, things will go wrong. You will have to understand the temperament of your operating system. Be prepared for a month or two of modest confusion, and you will soon learn the ropes. Hang in there. Everyone goes through it. The online community is always willing to help, as long as you direct your queries to the right area. Before long, you'll be sharing your newly found expertise with others.

What you'll need

Before you can get connected, you'll need three things: a **computer** with enough grunt to handle the software; the fastest **modem** you can afford; and a reliable and full **Internet connection**. How you connect to the Internet can make the difference between pleasure and frustration. You don't necessarily need state of the art computer gadgetry, but no matter what you have, you'll find a way to push it to the limit.

Computer power

It's possible to access the Net in some way with almost any machine you could call a computer, but if you can't drive your browsing software seamlessly with your mail program and graphics viewer in the background, you're going to get frustrated. To drive browsing software comfortably, you'll need at least a 486 SX25 **IBM compatible PC**, with 8MB of RAM, or a **Macintosh** 68030 series, again with 8MB of RAM, or the equivalent power and memory on an Atari or Amiga.

If you want to listen to the Web's **music samples** and sound effects, or use the **Internet Phone**, you'll also need an internal sound card, microphone, and speakers or headphones. Standard Macintoshes come with reasonable sound capability, but with PCs it's usually an extra. Unless your primary purpose is to create professional quality music, buy a **Sound Blaster** compatible card as it will work with almost everything.

Without special **video hardware**, you may be disappointed with the Web's short movies as they will only appear matchbox-size on your screen. If you'd like to improve the drawing time, quality, and size of your downloaded images and movies, you should consider graphic upgrade options such as accelerator cards, RAM additions, and MPEG movie cards.

If you're on a network at work or college, don't attempt to connect to the Net without your systems manager's supervision. Networked PCs and Macs can use the same software mentioned later in this book, but they sometimes connect to the Net in an entirely different manner.

Throw away that old modem

A powerful computer won't make up for a slow connection to the Internet. Get the fastest one you can afford. Unless you're hooked up through a network, you'll need a **modem** to act as an interface between your computer and the telephone line. There will be a similar device at the other end.

Modems come in three formats: internal, external, and PCMCIA. Each has its advantages and disadvantages.

The cheapest option is usually an **internal modem** – unless you have a portable, for which internal modems are often comparatively pricey. It can be installed inside your computer by plugging it into a slot called a bus. It's not a difficult job, but does require that you take the back off your computer and follow the instructions carefully (or ask if your computer store will do this for you).

Because they're hidden inside your computer, internal modems don't take up desk space, clutter the back of your computer with extra cables, or require an external power source. They do, however, generate unwanted heat inside your computer, place an extra drain on your power supply, and lack the little lights to tell you if or how the call is going.

An **external modem** is easier to install. Depending on its make, it can simply plug in to your computer's serial, parallel, or SCSI port making it easily interchangeable between machines. External modems require a separate power source, which in some cases can be a battery. Most external modems give a visual indication of the call progress through a bank of flashing lights (LEDs).

The credit card-sized **PCMCIA modems** are a mixture of both. They fit internally into the PCMCIA slots common in most modern notebooks but can be easily removed to use the slot for something else such as an external CD ROM drive. They don't require an external power source. They are expensive, though, and don't like being dropped.

Whatever type of modem you choose, the major issue is **speed**. Data transfer speed is expressed in bits per second or bps. It takes ten bits to transfer a character. So a modem operating at 2400 bps would transfer 240 characters per second. That's about a page of text every eight seconds. At 28,800 bps, you could send the same page of text in two thirds of a second.

A **14,400 bps (V.32)** modem is considered entry level for the World Wide Web. But if you can afford it, get a **28,800 bps (V.34)** modem. It is a little more expensive but it will reduce your online charges, or at least give you twice as much for your money.

Finally, make sure whatever you buy will work with your particular computer. PCs need a high speed serial card with a 16500 UART chip to be able to process any more than about 9600 bps reliably. Most modern PCs have them as standard, but check anyway. They're not an expensive upgrade.

Can I just plug in and get on with it?

Getting on to the Internet is not as straightforward as plugging in a cable and taking off. First you have to decide how you are going to access and how much of what's available you want.

This book is unapologetically geared to full Internet access. If you want to look at what's on the World Wide Web, that's what you'll need. On the other hand, if you're only interested in email and maybe Usenet, there are many options of various merit. You could even find a local BBS who'll transfer your messages to and from the Net, a few times per day, for a very small fee. You probably won't know what you want until you've tried it. But be warned, once you've had a full connection to the Internet, you won't want to give it up.

So, how do I get a connection?

To connect to the Internet, you'll need someone to allow you to connect into their computer, which in turn is connected to another computer, which in turn . . . that's how the Internet works. Unless you have a working relationship with whomever controls access to that computer, you'll have to pay for the privilege.

A firm in the business of providing Internet access is known as an **Internet Access Provider (IAP)** or an **Internet Service Provider (ISP)**. Once, Internet access was available only to the echelons of research and defense. Now, it has become a lucrative business for clever entrepreneurs. As with the businesses of all entrepreneurs, they can go broke and leave you with no access. You'll have no trouble finding a new account, but will probably acquire a new email address. If that could threaten your commercial credibility, choose your ISP carefully.

You also have the option of subscribing with one of the major **Online Services** – CompuServe, America Online, IBM, Microsoft, and the like – which have recently introduced full Internet access at increasingly commercial rates. In reality, most of these commercial giants offer two separate services: access to the Internet and access to their own private network. On the Internet front, they can be appraised in the same way as any other ISP, and are reviewed in the following chapter.

How much is it going to cost?

Since the gates to the Net have fallen into the hands of small business, a highly confusing array of access providers – and pricing structures – has emerged.

The biggest issue is whether you have **time charges**. Where calls are fixed or free, as in North America, Hong Kong, and Australia, providers have to either restrict the number of access hours included in the monthly charge or charge by the minute. Otherwise you would stay on the line all day and keep others from using it. In countries such as the UK where local calls are timed, lengthy connections mean hefty phone bills.

This means that in the **UK** charging is quite simple. It's common just to pay a single monthly fee of as little as £10 or an annual fee of £100. In **North America** and **Australia** there are commonly time charges of some sort. For example, in the USA, you might pay $20 per month for the first 40 hours access and then $2 per hour thereafter. It can get complicated as almost every provider has its own policy and there is often a large disparity in charges.

In America, if you don't have a local provider, or you have to call your provider from another state, it may offer a free **1-800 number** with a flat fee of about 15¢ per minute which includes the cost of the call.

Wherever you are based, it pays to shop around aggressively and look for the optimum combination of price, service, availability, and extra features. After you've been online for a couple of months, you'll have a better idea of what your usage demands will be and which plan will work out cheapest and most convenient for you. Finding an ISP is easy, but getting a cheap, trouble-free, fast connection is harder.

To help with your quest, we've provided a **list of providers** at the end of this book. Inevitably, given the huge number of operators, it's far from complete, but it will get you started – and you can always change later on, exploring the Net itself to see what's on offer in your area. You could also check the computer classifieds in one of the proliferating Internet magazines. Most of these provide guides comparing local providers' prices, services, and **points of presence (POPs)**. The points of presence are crucial: they are the local dial-up numbers. You will need an ISP with a local POP, and if you travel around you may want a range of access numbers, otherwise you can run up some serious phone bills.

In general, the best idea is to get started with someone who will give you all the start-up software and cheap access for the first month. Ring several free call numbers and ask them to send you their latest information pack and access software. Alternatively, look in at your local computer store and pick from one of the packages offering easy-to-install software pre-programmed with a call-up to a local provider.

When shopping around, ask as many as possible of the following questions:

Can I access for the price of a local call?

If you have to pay long distance rates, it's going to cost you more. Many providers give you the option of dialing a toll-free national number and charging you back. Get a local provider if possible. Ask if there is a range of points of presence (POP).

Do you offer 24 hour support?

It's not essential to have 24 hour support, but it's a bonus to know someone will be there when you can't get a line at 11pm.

What is your start-up cost ?

Avoid paying a start-up cost if you can. If you want to switch providers after trying them out, you lose that money.

What software do you supply?

Avoid paying for start-up software. Some providers recommend commercial packages such as *Chameleon* and *Internet in a Box*. For some people, that's good advice. But if you are reasonably confident with your computer you may prefer to try a free software alternative first. Spending more money is no assurance of long-term higher standards or simplicity.

What are your ongoing monthly charges?

Most providers charge a monthly fee, with some that's your only cost. This is common in the UK where local calls are charged by time. Elsewhere it usually forms a base rate with certain time constraints.

What are your usage time charges?

In most countries where local calls are free or untimed, you'll be charged for the amount of time you are actually online. In many cases your monthly charge will include a number of free hours per month or day.

Are there any premium charges?

Premium charges are one of the main drawbacks with the Online Service giants such as CompuServe which provide quality

commercial databases as well as Internet access. Having to pay
extra to use certain services is not necessarily a bad thing, but you
don't want to have to subsidize something you don't use.

When are your busiest hours?

If you can get a free trail, go online during the busiest periods –
early evenings – to see how well the service copes with traffic.

Is it cheaper to access at certain times?

In an effort to restrict traffic during peak periods, providers may
offer periods with reduced or no online charges. Think about when
you're most likely to use the service. Try the service during the
cheap period. If you can't connect, it's slow, or you would rarely use
it during that period, then it's no bargain.

Can you support my modem type and speed?

Modems like talking to their own kind. When modems aren't happy
with each other, they reduce the negotiation speed and connect at
a lower rate. It's not much use if your 28.8 kbps modem can only
connect at 14.4 kbps. Ask what connection speeds the service
supports. If it's lower than your modem's top speed, look
elsewhere.

What is your user to modem ratio?

You might not get a true answer to this question, but it's worth
asking to make providers aware of your concern. If it doesn't have
enough modems per user, you'll often get a busy signal when you
call. There's no rule about what is too high or low, but it's worth
comparing responses. No matter what they answer, ask them if it's
going to improve. It'll keep them on their toes.

Do you offer full access, that is a SLIP or PPP connection?

If you want to surf the World Wide Web, you'll need a full
connection to the Internet. You may be offered SLIP or PPP access.
Choose PPP if available, it's quickly becoming the Internet standard
as it supports error correction and compression. It's also easier to
set up. If you only want email and Usenet, you could ask for a
UUCP or shell account which are usually substantially cheaper. Each
provider will have several alternatives, at different prices, just ask.

What will my email address be, and how much do you charge to register a domain name?

You should have the option to choose the first part of your email address. You might like to use your first name or nickname. This will then be attached to the provider's host name. Ask if your name is available and what the host name would be. You don't want a name that could reflect badly on your business plans, nor do you want a number. For instance, if you register with the UK service provider Demon, your email address will end with *demon.co.uk* That may not be the ideal choice for a priest. If you want your own domain name, your provider should be able to register your choice for you. For instance, if John Hooper trains ducks to use computers, he could register *duckschool.com* and give himself the email address *john@duckschool.com*. Then it would be easy to remember his address, just by thinking about who he is and what he does.

Do you carry all the newsgroups in Usenet? If not, how many do you carry and which ones do you cut?

Usenet has more than 15,000 groups and it's still growing. That's 95% more than you'll ever want to look at in your lifetime. It's common for providers to carry only a portion of these, but it's still usually over 60% of them. The first ones to be axed are often the foreign language, country specific, provider specific, and the adult (alt.sex and .binaries) series. If you particularly want certain groups, your provider can usually add them, but if it has a policy against certain material it may refuse. Unless you're concerned that particular groups could have a negative influence on whomever is using your connection, get as many groups as you can. You never know what you'll uncover.

How much does it cost for personal Web page storage?

Many providers will include a few megabytes of storage free with your monthly charge so you can publish your own Web page – something you might think about doing once you're hooked on the Internet. In general, if you go over that megabyte limit there'll be an excess charge.

Once you've done your calculations, drawn your shortlist of providers, and received your start-up software you should be ready to dial your first provider. If you've done your research well you should have come across at least one free introductory period. Take up those free offers first.

Free offers

Be careful with free offers. You'll often have to supply your credit card details and join before they'll let you in. Make sure the offer really is free and doesn't have any hidden costs. If you give your credit card details, check your statements closely to see you haven't been charged. If you've been overcharged, complain. If you don't get action, tell your story in Usenet.

Those reservations aside, free offers are usually bona fide, but can still give an inaccurate view of the provider. If the free offer is part of a major publicity campaign, the service may become swamped with callers and hard to access. You might get the impression that this is the way it will always be. If you have difficulties getting connected, ask why. If it's likely to continue, try another provider.

What problems am I likely to have with my ISP?

Think of Internet demand like a toll bridge. If you suddenly erect a shopping mall on the other side of a river, people will want to cross it. If there's only one bridge, it's going to be a slow trip. However, as money comes in from the toll, repairs can be made and eventually the bridge can be widened to carry more traffic. If that expansion is done before traffic becomes heavy, people will continue to use the bridge. Otherwise they may seek an alternate route.

In real terms, ISPs will go through cycles of difficult traffic periods. If they have the resources and the foresight to cope with demand, users won't notice. As it is a low margin business, they're more likely to stretch resources to their limits. If you have troubles with your provider, call them and ask them what they're doing about traffic demand. If they're not already in the process of upgrading, find another provider.

The most common problem you're likely to encounter is the **busy signal** when you dial, or **connection failure**. If and when this happens (and it's common to just about all ISPs and Online Services) just keep trying until you do connect. Even though you only dial a single number, there are several modems attached to it at the other end. When no modems are available, you won't be able to connect.

Once you're hooked up, the next two most common problems are **slow transfer rates** and **not being able to get on to the Net**. If you can't get on to the Net at all, your provider's line may be down. Call and find out why, and when it will be back online. Slow transfer rates are caused by bottlenecks between where the file or Web page is stored and your computer. If transfers are slow from all locations, the problem will lie closer to home. One reason could be that your provider has too many users connected to it, and the bottleneck is forming between it and the Net. In this case your provider needs to increase the size (or bandwidth) of its connection. Report the problem, and ask if it is upgrading. You know the rest.

By calling your provider when you have problems, you'll get to know what's going on and where it's headed. If it doesn't treat you with respect, no matter how trivial your enquiry, take your money elsewhere. There's a prevailing arrogance within the computer industry. Don't tolerate it. You're the customer, they're not doing you a favor.

Connection software: TCP/IP

It's standard practice for access providers to supply the basic **connection software**. There may be a charge for this, but with the competition around, most bundle it free as part of the sign-up deal. However, no matter how good the starter kit is, you'll soon want to replace or add components – the Internet is constantly evolving.

The basic kit

What you get from a provider, or from buying a start-up kit or disk in a computer store, varies from the bare minimum to dial in and establish an IP connection, to a full Internet toolkit. At the heart of every Internet package is the **TCP/IP software** which enables the computer to talk to the Net. All your Net software, such as your newsreader, Web browser, and mail client, relies on it to converse.

Once this TCP/IP software is correctly configured to your provider's details, you can pick and choose all the other components as you see fit. If you switch providers you just have to alter a few details in the TCP/IP configuration. Your provider will have no problem telling you what to change or will supply you with the TCP/IP already configured.

Windows 95, OS/2, or Mac?

If you're running **Windows 95**, IBM's **OS/2 Warp**, or **Macintosh System 7.5**, you already have all the TCP/IP software you need. And setting it up to dial its respective Online Service is just a matter of following menu commands. But, if you want to connect to another provider, you'll need their help. Your provider will either supply you with the configuration settings on a file or give you instructions on how to set up. Once that's done the rest is easy.

Earlier systems

If you're using an earlier version of Windows, or a pre-System 7 Mac system, you'll need to either upgrade your operating system or obtain a TCP/IP program.

Of the several TCP/IP programs for the PC, the most popular is **Trumpet Winsock**. It's available freely on the Internet and used as the core of many ISP's bundles. It's not actually free, though. If you want to use it after a trial period, it requests that you pay the author. Its dial-up scripting takes a while to figure out but once you have it going, it's rock solid and works with everything. Next most popular PC choice is Netmanage's Chameleon sampler, the free and best part of its commercial package. Because it's easier to configure, and has a less daunting interface, it's probably the better choice for new users.

Macintosh users need look no further than **MacTCP** which can be obtained separately from most access providers or from your Apple dealer.

Dialing different providers

Once your connection software is set up you should be able to forget about it, unless you have to dial different providers.

This is where problems can occur on PCs. When you install the TCP/IP software, it deposits its own version of a file named winsock.dll into your system path. If you install two TCP/IP packages you could have two such files in different directories, but both in your system path. Make sure this doesn't happen as it can cause conflicts. If you change providers and you already have a

TCP/IP program on your machine, or if you are running Windows 95, OS/2 Warp, or a Macintosh, ask your new provider's advice on configuration.

Dialers

The other essential piece of connection software, is the **dialer**. It is often integrated into the same software that enables the TCP/IP connection. The dialer is the place to enter your user details, password, and provider's telephone number. After it's configured all you should ever have to do is click on "connect", or something similar, to instruct your modem to dial. If it's useful, get a dialer that enables you to enter several providers' details and alternative phone numbers. The Chameleon sampler is one such free package.

Did you get all that TCP/IP stuff?

If you didn't understand a bar of the last couple of pages on getting connected, don't worry! Internet connection and TCP/IP configuration is your **Internet access provider's specialty**. It's in their interest to get you up and running, so if things go haywire, or you're just plain confused, do things the easy way – give them a call.

Right – is that it, or do I need more software?

The TCP/IP and dialer combination is the bare minimum amount of software you can expect from your provider – and it is enough to get you connected to the Net. You'll probably get much more. The only thing you'll definitely need, however, is an **FTP client**, so that you can download all the best Internet software from the Net itself, for free. If you've been given the **Chameleon sampler**, **Winftp**, or **Fetch**, you're ready to start.

Your next step will be to get yourself programs to handle mail, read Usenet, use IRC, browse the Web, view graphics, encode and decode files, and do whatever else you desire. Don't worry, they're not hard to find with the whole Internet at your disposal – and they don't have to cost you a penny. For more on how to do it, just read on.

CONNECTING FOR THE FIRST TIME

The best exercise for your very first connection is to get the latest Internet software.

First, **install or configure your TCP/IP**, **dialing**, and **mail software** to your provider's specification. If your provider has done its job properly and supplied you with clear instructions, this shouldn't be a problem. You'll also need an **FTP program** (see the chapter on File Transfer) which shouldn't require configuration, although it can be handy to set your email address as its default password.

Next, **connect your modem** to the phone line, and instruct your dialer to call. When you're connected, your modem will make all kinds of mating noises, similar to a fax machine. Once the connection has been negotiated, these sounds cease. At some stage you'll have to **enter your user name and password**. It's possible that this could be a once-off event if it's incorporated into your dial-up scripting, or you might have to do it every time. Keep this password private – anyone could use it to rack up your bill or, perhaps worse, read your mail. You may also need to enter a separate password to retrieve mail. Your provider should instruct you on this.

Once you've logged on, you can verify that you indeed have an IP connection by performing a **DNS lookup**. This is the process whereby a designated host computer converts the domain name into an IP number. You will have specified a Domain Name Server in your TCP/IP set-up. The easiest way to do this is by using Ping (see the Net Tools chapter). Just key in any domain name such as *www.microsoft.com*, or *www.ibm.com*, or *www.demon.co.uk* If Ping fails on all attempts, it either means that your Domain Name Server is not working or that your provider's connection to the Net is down. If that happens, call up, report it, and ask for instructions.

If you haven't been given Ping, just skip that test and go straight to your **FTP program**. Now it's time to build your software collection. Just take your pick from the **Software Round-up** (see p.247–260). The latest version of **Netscape** would be a good choice, but be warned it's big so it could take up to twenty minutes to download (if your modem is 14,400).

Once you've successfully downloaded something from the Net, and you've verified it works, you're ready to launch into the World Wide Web, Usenet, or pretty much everything else on the Internet. Give yourself a pat on the back, the hardest part's over.

Online Services

It's important to make the distinction between the major commercial Online Services and the previously discussed Internet Service Providers (ISPs). While the Online Services covered in this section can provide an access point to the wider Internet, they also maintain their own premium-rate networks. These "private" networks, accessible only to subscribers, are in a sense like micro-versions of the Internet, maintaining a variety of forums, news and information services, and secure-payment shopping malls. They are reassuringly well ordered and regulated, which is good if you're new online. However, they are more expensive options than the ISPs, and they can have certain limitations.

Until early 1995, most commercial Online Services were essentially closed networks, with links to the wider Internet only through email and a limited range of Usenet newsgroups. These days they all offer full access either as a separate option or as part of membership. Nonetheless, although you can access both the Internet and the private file area from the same telephone number, they are in fact mutually exclusive networks.

Apart from the specialist features of their private networks, the primary advantages these Online Services offer as Internet providers are easier connection set-up and superior geographical presence. CompuServe, IBM, and Microsoft, for example allow local dial-up virtually worldwide. If you travel around a lot and want a connection, this can be a big plus point. You can dial up a local number, virtually worldwide, and surf the Web, or pick up your email just as if you were home.

One further presence, on the Internet periphery, are the smaller **BBSs or Bulletin Boards**. These for the most part remain closed, local networks, which you can dial direct, and which only offer limited email and Usenet access to the Internet, if any at all. Each BBS has its own personality and range of facilities, and there are thousands of them worldwide. Even if you have full Internet access you may find they have something extra to offer at a very low price. They can be, for example, a centrally organized, more extensive, and cheaper source of shareware and games than the Internet. To find out about specialist BBSs, check your newsstand for titles like *Online Access*, or look at the larger BBS ads in the main PC magazines. Alternatively, once you're online, you can just dial in to any BBS and search for a BBS directory file listing activity in your area.

Following are brief summaries of what's on offer from the **major Online Services**. Even more than usual with the Internet, the comments carry a "sell by" warning: they are all in a state of flux, and, at time of writing, the Microsoft Network, potentially the largest of the lot, is in operation only on a trial basis.

CompuServe

CompuServe is the granddaddy of all online services. It has points of presence in more than 150 countries, over three million members, and a range of references and databases second to none. It has support forums for just about everything supportable, online shopping, news wires, professional forums, chat groups, magazines, software registrations, program patches, sports news,

finance, flight reservations, and more services than you could look at in a lifetime. It's also the world's first truly international full Internet access provider. A major attraction for world travelers is that no matter where you join, you can dial in to any of its international numbers to browse the Internet or pick up your email. Registration is simple, too, and it bundles all its software free, including Spry's Mosaic browser for access to the **World Wide Web**.

There are, however, two disadvantages. First, unlike regular ISPs, CompuServe gives its members a number (now up to ten digits) rather than a name. So you can't opt to call yourself hilary@whitehouse, but instead have to settle for being a multi-digit. This is regarded as uncool on the Internet – if such things matter to you. More seriously, it makes your email address difficult to remember.

The other drawback is **cost**. CompuServe is expensive, and its billing is complex. It charges a flat monthly fee, a timed rate, an extra charge for extended, premium or executive services (which include most of the more interesting forums – like travel), a tariff on excess mail, and prime time penalties.

It's worth noting, however, that CompuServe's prices have been dropping sharply, and will continue to drop farther as competition increases. It has just announced two reduced pricing plans for Internet access only: a flat monthly fee of $9.95 for seven hours; or $19.95 for the first 20 hours. Additional hours for both pricing plans will be charged at $1.95 per hour.

To **subscribe** to CompuServe, call: 1-800 848-8199 in the US; 0800 289-378 in the UK; 1800 025-240 in Australia.

America Online

America Online has long been CompuServe's chief rival in the USA, where, to date, it has confined its sphere of operations. A current 20¢ per minute surcharge for users outside the 48 contiguous United States pretty much rules out its use elsewhere – and makes it little use for travel purposes. The network does, however, plan to install some kind of mirror operation, based in Germany, some time in 1996.

AOL (as it's commonly referred to) has a reputation for being a little funkier than CompuServe, both in its more graphical interface and in its forums. It provides a user-friendly, unpretentious, wholesome environment of databases, shopping, games, mail, chat, forums, news, and product support, and features magazines like *Wired*, *Time*, and *Omni* at premium charge rates.

The service beat CompuServe to the starting line, by several months, in offering Internet access to Usenet groups, although with mixed results. AOL members, used to their own forums, flooded Usenet with questions already addressed, and some well-publicized, unsound articles. This led to a marked feeling of resentment toward AOL from some of the Net's self-proclaimed guardians. And hundreds of billing complaints in the newly formed alt.aol-sucks newsgroup didn't help to bolster that image. To its credit, however, AOL included this group in its newsfeed.

AOL currently has Internet access limited to email and Usenet, but it recently purchased **Global Network Navigator**, a well-respected World Wide Web site, and it should be offering full Web access by the time this book reaches the printers.

To **subscribe** to AOL, call 1-800 827-6364. Charges are about $10.00 per month for the first five hours and $2.95 per hour thereafter.

IBM Global Network

A Spring 1995 newcomer in the online world conquest stakes, **IBM Global Network** already offers full Internet access in 190 cities in 23 countries – and that number is growing monthly. Connection is simple through IBM's new OS/2 Warp operating system, and all Net software is made easily available. Online registration, dial access, and Internet applications are bundled with IBM OS/2 Warp, and a Windows package is in the pipeline.

As well as offering the full range of Internet services the Global Network acts as an information center for IBM's range of products; however you don't need an IBM branded computer to use the network.

While IBM is more expensive than most access providers, you're less likely to get a busy signal and it's still likely to remain substantially cheaper than CompuServe. It also works seamlessly with the OS/2 Warp operating system, whose superb multi-tasking capabilities make the Windows 95 hype look like so much hot air.

IBM Global Network **access numbers** are included in the OS/2 Warp operating system.

No matter what you think of Microsoft and its monopolistic tendencies, you'd have to concede its online service, the Microsoft Network, is pretty impressive. Joining couldn't be easier – you simply click on a hard-coded icon in Windows 95. Once connected, the Network seamlessly pops up as another drive on your PC. You can then drag, drop, and launch files from the Network as you would from a floppy. It is expected that the forthcoming Macintosh version will blend in similarly.

Like CompuServe, Microsoft offers an internal private network, as well as full Internet access, with points of presence in almost every country in the world. But, unlike the other major services, outsiders can come in from the Net as well. This means content providers will not be denied Web traffic.

Many commentators suspect that Microsoft intends its Network eventually to supersede the Internet. It's certainly more organized, integrated and user-friendly, so it's likely to attract those who find the Net too chaotic. Some businesses may also appreciate its accountability, professionalism, and commercial facilities. For example, Microsoft can monitor traffic, provide user demographics, handle billing, and place advertisements in opportune locations. And the eternal online payment dilemma is solved by lumping purchases onto the subscribers' monthly billings.

Although its Internet Explorer browser has a few features that even Netscape could learn from, Microsoft, at this stage, is clearly more interested in creating an alternative to the Web. Blackbird, its sophisticated multimedia content authoring tool, makes HTML programing look decidedly archaic. However, such technical merits come at a high price. And that's not just exorbitant online charges and commissions, it's freedom and independence as well. Microsoft can monitor your movements and profile your preferences, raise charges and introduce tolls as it sees fit, litter your route with advertising, censor, and even tell if you've registered the software on your hard drive. It's about as far removed from the free-wheeling spirit of the Net as you can get.

The one other issue the jury remains out on is whether Microsoft's forums, news, and library services will match the standard of its engineering. Its launch content was extremely limited, offering little of interest beyond Microsoft's own Encarta encyclopedia, and its future direction is likely to be solidly commercial, at least over the next year, with a focus on shopping and business support. In some respects, though, perhaps the content of the Network itself doesn't matter, for subscribers also get full Internet access – and if its own Network fails to reach Microsoft's expectations, it can always fall back on its Internet service. Either way, it can't really lose.

To join the Microsoft Network, follow the instructions on your Windows 95 program. At time of writing, charges for US subscribers are $4.95 a month, including the first three hours of access, with additional hours billed at $2.50. UK (and other international) subscribers pay around 50 percent extra: £6 a month, including just two hours' access, plus £3.25 for each additional hour.

Prodigy

Prodigy is another exclusively North American Online Service, notable mainly for its shopping opportunities. Its graphical interface employs the great American shopping mall theme right down to the escalators and muzak – and ads along the bottom of your screen.

But it's not all shopping. There are plenty of commercial databases, news and weather alerts, travel booking services, stock quotes, reference libraries, magazines, entertainment listings, and discussion groups. There's even a special section for kids and a student research feature called Homework Helper. And there is the option of full Internet access, including an easy interface which allows you to put your own pages on the Web.

To order Prodigy's free software and find your local US number, call 1-800 prodigy. The service charges a regular monthly fee, although like CompuServe and AOL some services cost extra, including full Internet access, which costs about $10.00 for five hours.

Apple E-World

Apple introduced its own network, **E-World**, in 1994, to mixed reviews. As you would expect from the creators of the world's most intuitive and user-friendly computers, it looked very pretty and was very easy to use. The trouble was, Apple didn't do a great deal in the way of promotion, and nor did they take the Microsoft approach of bundling it with their operating systems. So E-World swiftly became dubbed "Empty World": the town of good-looking buildings and no population.

That's not to say that E-World doesn't have its devotees. It is a well-designed network which allows you to send and file email, and attach documents, with the greatest of ease. But to survive and prosper, E-World will need to offer global POPs, and full Internet access. Meantime, its use remains limited.

Delphi

Rupert Murdoch's **Delphi** network has extensive databases, shareware archives, special interest groups, stock and portfolio analysis, financial news, multiplayer games, and many other services. More impressively, it also offers full Internet access in North America for as low as $1.00 per hour for the first 20 hours and $1.80 per hour thereafter. Unless you live near Boston, you need to access through SprintLink or Tymnet, but this is a simple enough operation, and provided you call between 6pm and 6am, connection is free.

To **subscribe** call 1-800 695-4005 in the US, or 0171-757 7080 in the UK, where Delphi currently has a rather limited Internet access presence.

Netcom

Apart from a range of news wires, Netcom primarily supplies Internet access. It offers a number of choices including a dynamic compressed SLIP access called Net-Cruiser, available for both PC and Mac. The Netcruiser software bundle has been acclaimed for its simple installation, minimal software maintenance, and high quality programs. These even include Vocaltech's Internet Phone, though at present you can't use this to dial other providers.

Netcom has local access in most major US cities. To find your local US number, call 1-800-353-6600. It charges about $20.00 per month for the first forty hours, and $2.00 per hour thereafter.

Email

If you need one good reason to justify hooking up to the Internet, email should suffice. Once you become accustomed to conversing by email, and build up a base of contacts with email addresses, you'll soon turn to it as a first choice of communication. You will write more letters and respond a lot quicker – and that means you'll probably become more productive.

Why email is better

Email is such an improvement on every other form of communication that it will revolutionize the way and the amount you communicate. You can send a message to anyone with an email address anywhere in the world, instantaneously. In fact it's so quick that it's possible they could receive your message sooner than you could print it. Sending a message is as simple as keying the recipient's address, or choosing it from your email address book, writing a brief note, and clicking "send". No letterheads, layout, printing, envelopes, stamps, or visiting the post office. Once you're online you can have your mailreader automatically check for mail at whatever interval you like.

Email is also better than faxing. It's always a local call no matter how far you're sending it, you never get a busy signal, and you receive the actual text and not a photocopy, or an actual image file and not a scan. So that means you can send color. You can send a message to a part of the world that's asleep and have a reply when you get up the next morning. That means not having to synchronize phone calls, be put on hold, speak to an answerphone or a receptionist. You don't even have to tell some busybody who's calling. With email, you take the red carpet route straight through to the boss.

Sending letters is not email's only use. You can attach any file to a message. This means you can forward things like advertising layout, pictures, spreadsheets, assignments, or programs. And your accompanying message need only be as brief as a Post-it note or a compliments slip.

Challenging the establishment

One of email's great breakthroughs is its inroads into the stiffness of business correspondence. Some of its limitations have proved to be its assets. Because email messages are simply text files, there's no need to worry about fonts, letterheads, logos, typesetting, justification, signatures, print resolution, or fancy paper. It distils correspondence down to its essence – words.

But it has even gone farther than that, it has encouraged brevity. This could be the result of online costs, busy users, or just the practical mindset of the people who first embraced the technology. Whatever the reason, it's good discipline and it means that you're able to deal with several times more people than you could ever manage before.

In contrary, but equally positive, fashion, email is also putting personal correspondence back into letters rather than phonecalls. Almost all new users remark on this – and its possibilities for a surprising intimacy.

Managing mail

If you're charged by the minute to stay connected, whether by the phone company or your provider, it's wise to **compose and read your mail offline** (ie, when you are not connected by phone). That way when you are connected you're actually busy transferring information, and getting your money's worth.

If you only have a mail and Usenet account, it's worth considering using an offline reader such as **WinNet Mail** which incorporates a dialer, newsreader, and mail client in one package. It connects, downloads your mail and newsgroups, uploads your mail and postings, and then hangs up. Then you're free to read, write, and configure at your leisure. The email services provided by the major Online Services discussed in the previous section all incorporate their own offline mail creation and reading programs.

Filing

In the same way that you keep your work desk tidy, and deal with paper as it arrives, you should also keep your email neat. Most mail clients (programs) let you organize your correspondence into mailboxes or trays of some sort. It's good discipline to use several for **filing**. You should always have an in-tray and an out-tray. If your setup gives you the option to keep copies of outgoing messages, choose it so you can keep track of what you've sent.

Filtering

Some mail programs offer automatic and manual **filtering** abilities to allow you to transfer incoming mail into designated mailboxes, either as it arrives or on selection. Automatic filtering can detect a common string in part of the incoming header, such as the address or subject, and transfer it directly into a mailbox other than the default in-tray.

This can be useful if you subscribe to a lot of mailing lists (see p.56), but these apart, it's better to use the manual option. This way, you leave messages in the in-tray until they've been read and dealt with, and then you can transfer them into archives for later reference.

Etiquette

As regards **etiquette**, it's common courtesy to reply to email promptly, even if just to verify receipt. After all, it only needs to be a couple of lines. Leave email in your in-tray until you've responded. That way you can instantly see how much you have to do.

As email is quick, and people tend to deal with it immediately, if you don't get a reply within a few days you then know what to follow up. Once you've received your reply, you can archive or delete your original outgoing message.

Sending Mail

Despite what they might look like when you first see them, **Internet email addresses** aren't so hard to recall. CompuServe numbers apart, they're a lot easier to remember than telephone numbers and street addresses. However, there's no actual need to memorize them, nor do you have to type in the whole address every time you want to write to someone.

There are two common shortcuts: one involves using a previous message, the other setting up a shortcut or nickname (an "address book" entry).

To **use the address from a previous message**, simply select it and then if it's one you've sent, choose "send again", or if it's one you've received, "reply". You'll then have the option of including the contents of the previous message. You can delete that and also change the subject heading if you want.

The **nickname or address book** option is equally straightforward. All email programs allow you to set up an address book of your email correspondents, and to select these as message recipients.

Forwarding

You can also **forward or redirect** a message to somebody else. Forwarded messages are tagged like replies whereas redirected messages are transferred unaltered. You can add your own comments or edit the messages, if you want.

Carbon copies (cc)

If you want to **send two or more people the same message**, and you don't mind if they know who else is receiving it, you have two options: One address will have to go in the "To:" field, and the other addresses can also go in this field or in the "CC:" (carbon copy) field.

If you don't want recipients to know who else is getting the message you're sending them, put their name into the **"BCC:"** or blind carbon copy field. They will then be masked from the other recipients.

Subject

Once you've worked out who is to receive your message, let them know what it's about. Put something meaningful in the **"Subject:" heading**. It's not so important when they first receive it – they'll probably open it even if it's blank. However, if you send someone your resume and you title it "Hi," two months down the track when they're looking for your talent, they're going to have a hard time weeding you out of the pile.

Filling in the subject is optional when **replying**. If you don't type anything in, most email programs will retain the original subject and insert "re:" before the original subject title to indicate it's a reply. Pretty clever, huh?

Signatures

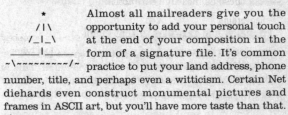

Almost all mailreaders give you the opportunity to add your personal touch at the end of your composition in the form of a signature file. It's common practice to put your land address, phone number, title, and perhaps even a witticism. Certain Net diehards even construct monumental pictures and frames in ASCII art, but you'll have more taste than that.

Replying to mail

Another great email feature is the ability to **quote from received correspondence**. When you want to reply to incoming mail, you simply click on "reply" and – in most email programs – you automatically have the original message duplicated, addressed back to the sender. This message will appear with defining tags (>>) prior to each line, and you have the option of including part or all of the original message – or deleting it all. So when someone asks you a question or raises a point, you can include that section and answer it directly underneath. This saves you having to type it in, or them having to refer back to the message they sent.

If your email program doesn't offer this automatic duplicating and tagging option (as with CompuServe), you can do pretty much the same, copying the text from the letter you want to reply to, selecting "reply," and pasting it in. You can then edit accordingly, indicating which sections have come from the previous letter by typing defining tags (>>).

Whichever system you run, don't fall into the habit of including the entire contents of the original letter in your reply. It wastes time for the receiver and its logical outcome (letters comprising the whole history of your correspondence) hardly bears thinking about.

Attaching non-text files to your email

Suppose you want to send a **picture**, **spreadsheet**, or **word processor document** to someone via email. This is quite feasible, and although it involves a bit of tweaking at both ends, most mail programs do the technical part of it for you.

It works like this. Messages sent via Internet email can be no larger than 64kb and are automatically configured into plain, 7-bit ASCII text (ASCII is a plain vanilla text format that all computers understand). So to send anything other than text, and anything larger than 64kb, it has to be processed first. Your mail reader knows this and offers you a menu option to choose **"send attachment"** or **"attach file."** It then converts the binary file into 7-bit ASCII and chops the message into units less than 64kb. The receiving mail reader recognizes the encoding, reconstructs the file, and drops it into the designated download directory.

Sending and receiving attachments is simple, but there's a catch. There are various encoding techniques, and they are all incompatible. The most popular methods are **UUencode**, **Binhex**, and **MIME**. UUencode is most commonly used in PCs and Binhex in Macs. MIME is becoming a standard across all platforms. Before sending someone an attached file, make sure you use a common encoding method. Some software packages like

Eudora Pro support all three, whereas others support only one. If your recipient only supports MIME and yours is Binhex, you've a problem.

You can tell if someone has sent you an encoded file and it hasn't decoded. It will look like it's been written by a Klingon and can carry on over a few messages all with the same subject heading and sender. If that happens, have it sent it again using a coding method that your mail program can understand. The easiest way to ask is just to choose the "Reply" option when you open the sent message – and tell them it's no good.

Error-free attachments should be high on your list of priorities when choosing mail software. If you have trouble automatically decoding received attachments, get another program, even if it means buying one. **Eudora Pro**, for example, is worth the expense, just for this reason alone.

Microsoft Exchange

Microsoft Exchange, which is built into Windows 95, goes one step further than other mail programs. You just drag and drop documents into the mail window and it looks after the rest. Exchange will probably herald a new generation of email, with the ability to add formating such as color, fancy fonts, and logos. It's by far the most advanced of all packages, so if you have Windows 95, there's no real reason to look for anything else.

Collecting from the road

If you intend to pick up mail "on the road," rather than just from your own computer, through your own regular Internet service provider, you may want to consider the benefits of **POP3 (Post Office Protocol)**.

When using a POP3 mail client like Eudora, all you have to do to send and receive mail is establish an IP connection with the Internet. It doesn't matter whether you dial in to your own account or someone else's, or whether your mail is held in Iceland and you're calling from Tasmania. With POP3, wherever your mail is kept on the Internet, you can retrieve it without changing your mail client's configuration.

The one downside of this is that someone else could pick up your mail in exactly the same way, so it is important to keep your password secure.

The address – and returned mail

Internet addresses should appear along the lines of: `user@host` The `user` refers to the sender's identity and `host` identifies the server where they collect their mail.

If you submit an illegally constructed address, or an address which doesn't exist, your message will be **bounced back** to you with an error message telling you what went wrong.

This usually happens within a matter of minutes. Sometimes, however, your mail will be bounced back after a few days. This usually indicates a physical problem in delivering the mail rather than an addressing error. When this occurs, just send it again. If it's your end that has caused the problem, you'll probably have a whole batch of mail to re-send.

Sending mail to Commercial Services

To make life a little harder, not all mailing addresses you encounter are going to be in the standard `user@host` format.

To send to **CompuServe** subscribers, for example, you have to use the host name `compuserve.com` and replace the comma in the user name with a period. Thus to send mail to CompuServe member `12345,678` you would have to change it to `12345.678@compuserve.com`

Other Online Services maintain a regular Internet form in their addresses. For example to send to Brian McClair at **America Online**, you would probably address it to `brianmc@aol.com` while Ryan Giggs at **Prodigy** might be `giggsy@prodigy.com` These Online Service subscribers get to choose their "nickname" address, just as regular Internet users do.

It is worth keeping in mind, in addition, that several of the Online Services – CompuServe, notably – levy a **charge for mail** received from the wider Internet (ie, any mail sent by non-CompuServe members). So if your recipient doesn't choose to pay for your message, they won't receive it. They will, however, have seen it arrive, and turned down the privilege of accepting delivery!

Finding an email address

The simplest way to find out someone's email address is to call and ask them or someone who works with them. There is no international email directory – and with good reason. Email addresses are confidential, and the last thing you want is to have to spend money downloading junk mail.

There are, nonetheless, several tools you can use **through the World Wide Web** to sleuth for information. Most of the handiest tools are available through Netscape's "Directory" menu option; these include such services as the Internet White Pages, Netfind, Knowbot, and Whois. Infoseek's Usenet database (for more on which, see p.96 and p.170) is also useful, and there is a regularly updated FAQ compiled by Jonathan Kamens called "How to find people's email addresses." It's often posted to such newsgroups as `comp.answers`,

```
comp.mail.misc, news.newusers.questions and
soc.net.people, and is stored on FTP sites such as
ftp.sunet.se/pub/usenet/comp.
answers/finding-addresses
```

Staying anonymous

Occasionally when sending mail or posting to a newsgroup, you may wish to conceal your identity – to save
embarrassment on health discussions, for example.
There are two main ways to send mail anonymously.

The first is a little unethical. You can just **change
your configuration** so that it looks like the mail is
coming from somebody else, either real or fictitious.
However, if anyone tries to reply, it will attempt to go
to the alias, and not you. You'll probably get a few
laughs out of discovering this, as many people are
unaware you can do it. But, be warned, they can trace
the header details back to your server, if they are
really keen. Your local law enforcement agency is
that keen.

The other way is to register with a server dedicated
to **redirecting anonymous mail**. These generally work
by acting as go-betweens. When someone receives such
mail, it is obvious that it has been masked, as it comes
from an obviously coded email address. When they
reply, the anonymous server handles the redirection.
That's as good as it gets, but if you break the law in the
process, they can still find you by demanding your
details from the server's administrator. For more information, mail a blank message to help@anon.penet.fi

The Net by email

If your Internet access is restricted to email only, you
can enjoy many of the Internet's star attractions via
```
```

automatically responding mail-servers (see the section following). No-one would suggest it's on a par with full access, but you're not shut out altogether. For example, if you can't use FTP, you could try using an FTP mailserver to supervise the transfer. It's even possible to retrieve Web page text. There's more about these alternatives in the following chapters.

You have no new mail.

OK

Mailing lists

If you want to receive a lot of email, the surest way is to join a mailing list. There are thousands available via the Net, all intended to disseminate information or encourage discussion on a specific topic. This is the Internet's easiest way to keep up with special interest news and discussion, as all you have to do is collect your mail.

Joining is easy. In most cases, you simply "subscribe" by sending a single email message. Once aboard, you'll receive all the messages sent to the list's address, just as everyone else on the list will receive what you send. Unsubscribing is equally simple. Luckily so, as you may get a fright at the amount of mail some lists generate.

Mailing list basics

Each mailing list has two addresses. The **mailing address** is used to contact others on the list and the **administrative address** to send commands to the server or the maintainer of the list. Don't get them mixed up or everyone else on the list will see you're a bozo.

Most lists are unmoderated, so they rebroadcast messages immediately. Messages on moderated lists must first be approved by human intervention. Moderation can be used as a form of censorship, but more often it's a welcome bonus, improving the quality of discussion and keeping it on topic by pruning out irrelevant or repetitive messages. It all depends on the quality of the moderator, who is rarely paid for the service.

Certain other lists are moderated because they only carry messages from one source, such as the US Embassy Travel Warnings. Such lists often have a parallel list for discussion.

If you'd rather receive your mail in large batches than have it trickle through, request a **digest** if you have the option. These are normally sent daily, depending on the traffic. Most lists are maintained by computer programs these days, but some are still manual. For those, the administrative address is the same as the list's address with `-request` appended. For example, the administrative address of the list `dragster-bikes@sissybar.net` would be `dragster-bikes-request@sissybar.net` To subscribe or unsubscribe to such a list, just send a one-line message to the administrator.

LISTSERV

The most popular automated list system, **LISTSERV**, is now widely available on the Net. Its lists use `listserv` as the administrative address, so to join the list `muck@rake.com` you would send a subscription message to `listserv@rake.com`

Requests are interpreted by a program which usually reads only the message body. Messages may contain several requests as long as they're on separate lines, but you shouldn't include your signature as it will confuse the program. Since all LISTSERV systems are hooked together, you can send your request to any LISTSERV host and your request will be redirected. If you're not sure which host to use, send your request to `listserv@bitnic.bit.net` (in North America) or `listserv.net` (in Europe).

To join a LISTSERV list, send the following message:

```
SUB listname your name
```

To take yourself off send:

```
SIGNOFF listname
```

To find out what options are available send:

```
HELP
```

To find the lists on a LISTSERV system, send:

```
LIST
```

To find lists throughout all LISTSERV systems, send:

```
LIST GLOBAL
```

This will result in a list file being sent to you of around 500Kb, so be prepared!

To be notified of new lists as soon as they appear, join: `new-list` at `listserv@vml.nodak.edu`

Note that many LISTSERV lists are mirrored in Usenet newsgroups (see p.73). To view them, look under the `bit.listserv` hierarchy.

MajorDomo

MajorDomo is another list manager similar to LIST-SERV. It uses the address `majordomo@host`

To join a MajorDomo list, send:

```
subscribe listname address
```

To be removed, send:

```
unsubscribe listname address
```

In both cases adding your email address is optional but useful if you want to subscribe someone else.

To find out which lists you've subscribed to at any MajorDomo host, send: `which`

As MajorDomo hosts are independent, you can't request an overall list – you have to request it from each host individually. To receive the list, send: `LIST`

List compilations

List compilations are available in various places on the Net. The best is Stephanie da Silva's **Publicly Accessible Mailing Lists** or **PAML**. This is often posted in Usenet (try the newsgroup news.lists) and stored on FTP sites, though it's easiest viewed on the World Wide Web at http://www.neosoft.com/internet/paml (see p.85 for details on how to access the Web). This version is handy because it's quick, you don't have to download a monstrous file, it's updated regularly, and you can go straight to your interests.

Another good reference is the **SRI List of Lists**, which sells in hard copy or can be downloaded free. For a free copy, FTP to ftp.nisc.sri.com and look in the path: /netinfo/ or email: send netinfo/interest-groups to mail-server@nisc.sri.com and brace yourself for a hefty file in return.

Starting your own list

To find out how to start your own list, mail: listserv @bitnic.educom.edu and listserv@uottawa.bitnet

Vacation alert!

If you're going on vacation or are not going to able to pick up your mail for a while, consider unsubscribing or turning off your mailings temporarily. It's amazing how long it takes to download a few weeks' mailings.

File Transfer

Before you can crack open the Internet's treasure chest, you'll probably need to stock up on software. Even if you have purchased a kit such as *Chameleon* or *Internet in a Box*, or been supplied with a package by your access provider, it won't be long before you'll want to try out alternative components or add the latest multimedia whistles and bells.

The good news is that almost all the Internet software you'll ever need is available to download for free on the Net itself. And, surprisingly, some of these freely distributed software programs are actually superior to those bundled into commercial packages. In fact, they're almost always better. Don't be afraid to turf components out of commercial packages that you have acquired in a starter kit. As Internet software usually complies with TCP/IP specifications, units should be seamlessly replaceable.

If your kit's TCP/IP socket causes problems, consider replacing it with something reliable like Trumpet

```
┌─────────────────────────────────────────────┐
│ ■           overview.html                    │
├─────────────────────────────────────────────┤
│ Host:  ee.utah.edu                           │
│ Status: Getting                              │
│ State:  Finished                             │
│ Transferred: 2753    Bytes/Sec: 550   Time Left:      le │
│ 226 Transfer complete.                       │
├─────────────────────────────────────────────┤
│ □ overview.html  5k 17/8/94  2  ftp.uni-mainz.de          /pub/security/CERT/nist/fips/fipslist/overview.html │
│ □ overview.html  6k 3/8/95   2  pascal.zedat.fu-berlin.de  /atari/stonx/Doc/overview.html │
│ □ overview.html  3k 1/8/94   2  concert.cert.dfn.de        /pub/osir/nist/fips/fipslist/overview.html │
│ □ overview.html  3k 1/8/94   2  server00.zrz.tu-berlin.de  /pub/security/csir/nist/fips/fipslist/overview.html │
│ □ overview.html  3k 18/5/95  3  ee.utah.edu                /WWW/web/docs/cgi/overview.html │
│ □ overview.html  8k 17/3/95  3  ftp.ugos.caltech.edu       /pub/gema/html/overview.html │
│ □ overview.html  2k 23/6/94  3  ernst.mach.os.cmu.edu      /www/overview.html │
│ □ overview.html  3k 1/1/4    3  ee.utah.edu                /WWW/httpd/httpd_1.3/docs/cgi/overview.html │
│ □ overview.html  3k 11/4/95  5  nic.uakom.sk               /pub/hypertext/docs/cgi/overview.html │
└─────────────────────────────────────────────┘
```

Winsock. Any bundle that won't let you mix and match components isn't worth keeping. The only drawback is that if you install new components you might have to launch them by clicking on their icons and not from the menu in your all-in-one package. But that's no problem.

To download software files, you will want to make use of an FTP (File Transfer Protocol) program. You can use a stand-alone dedicated program or do it all from your **World Wide Web browser**. Browsers such as Netscape are continually improving as FTP clients, but dedicated programs are less demanding on system resources so will work better in the background if you're short on memory.

We have dedicated a whole chapter of this book to a **roundup of software** available on the Net (see p.247–260), giving the FTP addresses to contact. You'll want to refer to it in conjunction with this section.

Free software programs on the Net

The Internet is a real clearing house of freely available software, but it's not all genuinely free. There are three types of programs you're allowed to use without paying. They are called freeware, shareware, and beta programs.

Freeware

Freeware is software donated by its author(s) without any expectation of payment. It could be a complete program, a demonstration sample with crippled features, a patch to enhance another program or an interim upgrade. In some cases, a donation is appreciated.

Shareware

Shareware usually has certain conditions attached, which you accept when you install or run the program.

One common condition is that if you want to use the program after the initial free trial period, you pay the publisher. Another condition may be that you pay if you intend to use it commercially. Sometimes the shareware version, while adequate, is a shortform of a more reliable or heavily featured registered version. When you pay your registration fees, the author or software distributor will mail you the upgrade or give you access to an FTP site so you can download it.

Beta Programs

Betas are distributed as part of the testing process in commercial software development. You shouldn't pay for betas as they're not finished products. They are often good enough for the task, and sometimes, for example the hugely popular **Netscape** browser for the Worldwide Web, at the cutting edge of technology.

With all beta programs, you should expect to encounter bugs and quirks now and again, and don't be too upset by having to restart the program or reboot occasionally – it's all part of the development process. Report recurring faults to the developers, that's why they're letting you have it free. If you notice a pattern, email the distributors and ask for a fix. If it's too buggy, get an alternative.

How to use FTP

Of the several techniques for transferring files across the Internet, by far the most popular is **FTP (File Transfer Protocol)**. Obtaining files by FTP is straightforward, but unless you have a passion for UNIX commands, you need to first get yourself an FTP client with a graphical interface. There are not a lot of differences between programs – anything will do to get started. If you don't like something about your program, you can always download another using FTP.

Unless you've been granted special permission to log into a server and transfer files, you'll have to use what's known as **"anonymous FTP."** These sites follow a standard log-in procedure. Once you are in, you can look through the contents of a limited number of directories and transfer files to your computer.

Many Net servers have areas set aside for anonymous FTP. Some even carry massive specialist file archives. It's becoming common for software companies to provide updates, patches and interim releases on their own anonymous FTP sites. No single server will have everything you need, but you'll soon find favorites for each type of file. Even your access provider will have an FTP area, where you can transfer files for updating Web pages, download access software, and exchange files with colleagues.

FTP sites' addresses are often prefixed by *ftp.* but that's not a rule. When you're supplied a file location it could be in the form `ftp.fish.com/pub/dir/jane.zip` That tells you that the file `jane.zip` is located in the directory `pub/dir` on the `ftp.fish.com` server.

Logging in and downloading a file

Before you can download anything, you'll first need to log on to the server. FTP programs use different terminologies, so it won't hurt to read your help file or the readme file that comes with the FTP program you are starting out with. It will help you figure out what to key in and where. Basically, though, the procedure is fairly routine and goes like this:

To retrieve `ftp.fish.com/pub/dir/jane.zip`, enter the server's address `ftp.fish.com` as **host name**, anonymous as **user name** and your Internet email address (in the form user@host) as a **password**.

Next, enter the **directory** you want to start looking in, in this case, /pub/dir Make sure that the path and file details are entered in the correct case. If you enter Dir instead of dir, on a UNIX host, it will return an error because UNIX is case sensitive. If you have the full location of the file you're seeking, try entering that as the initial directory. Don't be surprised if it isn't where it's supposed to be – system managers are forever reorganizing directories. It's not necessary to get the location exactly right. Once you're in, you can browse around until you find it.

Now, **log in**. If the site gets a lot of traffic, you may not be admitted the first time. Don't let that discourage you. If you can't get in within ten attempts, try again later, perhaps outside the local peak hours. If you're accessing an American site from Europe or vice versa, try when that continent is asleep. You might even get a better transfer rate once you're through.

Once you're accepted, depending on your client, you'll see a listing of the **initial directory's contents**. Every directory should have a file called *readme* or *index*. They're often worth reading as they will tell you about the files in each directory.

Most graphical interface programs work in a similar way to Windows' file manager or the Macintosh folder system. That means when you click, something happens. Look at the top of the directory contents. Clicking on ".." will send you back a directory level. Clicking on "." will take you back to the root. Directories should be distinguishable from files by having a different color, typeface, having a folder icon, or at least not having extensions. Clicking on a directory will open it, clicking on a file will **start the download**.

It's a good idea to read any accompanying text files before commencing the download. You can usually do that by either clicking on them or selecting "view" from the menu. Make sure you select **"binary transfer"** before downloading any files other than unformated text. If you're unsure of the file type, choose binary. It can be used to transfer text files as well, although it will be slower. If you download a graphic, sound, or program as text it will be useless. Everyone makes that mistake at least once.

Your FTP program should give you a transfer progress report to tell you how long it's going to take. You can either sit and watch the bits zip into your hard drive or relegate it to the background while you do something else, like surf the Web. Unfortunately, if the transfer fails or you cancel it, you can't pick up where you left off. You'll have to start again from scratch.

Uploading files

FTP isn't just for downloading files, you can upload as well. It may be practical to submit stories, documents, graphics, and applications this way, rather than burden the mail system with bulky attachments.

For example, suppose you have to submit artwork to a magazine. You could FTP the scans to an area set aside for downloads, (which is often in a directory called incoming), and then notify the editor by email. The editor could then instruct staff to upload some of the graphics for approval. If they're approved they could then be moved to an outgoing directory where a printer could access them.

In some cases an area is set up where files can be uploaded and downloaded to the same directory. This could prove useful if you want to transfer files to a colleague who's having problems with handling mailed attachments (it happens!). It can be quite annoying to have to wait for several megabytes of mail attachments to download and decode before you can read your mail. Especially if it has to be re-sent.

FTP through the World Wide Web

It's approaching the point where you can do almost everything on the Internet from the helm of your **Web browser** (see p.89 for more on these). You can certainly use FTP, and you'll find it very useful as home pages often have links to FTP addresses. In fact, this may be where you'll encounter most of your archive leads.

To **follow an FTP link on a Web page**, just click on it and patiently wait for the log-in to be negotiated (it will take longer than loading a Web page). Depending on the link, you'll either get a page of the directory's contents, or the file you've selected will be on its way to your hard drive. As with any FTP transfer, if the file has moved, you'll either be defaulted back to a higher directory or get an error message. If the file isn't where it should be, or you want to enter a unlinked location, just enter it as a Web address. Instead of `http:` use `ftp:` in the first part of the address. So, to look for a file at: `ftp.hen.com` in the path: `/pub`, enter: `ftp://ftp.hen.com/pub` Once connected, just click on what you want in the usual fashion.

Although you can, in theory, do all your file transfers with a Web browser, a dedicated FTP program will give you more features and greater power.

Files Service Protocol (FSP)

FSP (File Service Protocol), is a more robust method of file transfer. It hasn't caught on in the mainstream yet, but it's commonly used by the digital underground. Although it fulfils exactly the same purpose as FTP, it has several advantages, and uses entirely different protocols. It's main advantage from a user's perspective is that if the server goes down or you break connection, you can pick up where you left off. With FTP, you have to start all over again. There is a small trade-off in speed, however.

To find out more, download the FAQ at `ftp.germany.eu.net/pub/network/inet/fsp` or follow the newsgroup: `alt.comp.fsp` or join the mailing list `fsp-discussion@germany.eu.net`

Making files smaller

There are two reasons why archived binary files are usually compressed. One is to decrease the amount of storage space they consume and the other is to reduce transfer times. Once you've downloaded compressed files, you'll have to **decompress** them before you can use them. Before you can decompress them you'll have to know how they've been compressed and have the right program to do the job.

Luckily it's usually easy to tell what technique has been used just by looking at the file name or where it's located. Unless the site is specifically targeted at one platform, you're usually offered a directory choice between DOS, PC or Windows, Mac, and UNIX. Once you've taken that choice everything contained in that directory and its subdirectories will be for that platform only. If not, you can usually tell by the file extensions. The following table shows common file extensions and the programs needed to process them.

Extension	File Type	Program to decompress or view
.arc	PC Compressed archive	PKARC, ARC, ArcMac
.arj	PC Compressed archive	UNARJ
.bin	MacBinary	MacBinary, usually automatic in Macs
.cpt	Mac Compact Pro archive	Compact Pro
.doc	Word processor document	Any word processor
.exe	PC executable	Self executing from DOS prompt
.gif	Graphic interchange format	Graphics viewer
.gz	UNIX Compressed archive	GNU ZIP
.hqx	Mac BinHex	BinHex
.jpg	Compressed graphic	Graphics viewer
.lha, .lzh	Compressed archive	LHA
.mpg	Compressed video	Video viewer and hardware
.pict	Mac picture	Graphic viewer
.pit	Mac PackIt	PackIt
.ps	PostScript	PostScript printer or GhostScript
.sea	Mac Self-extracting archive	Click on icon to extract
.sit	Mac Stuffit compressed archive	Stuffit
.tif	Tagged image format	Graphic viewer
.txt	Plain ASCII text	Notepad, text editor, word processor
.uu, .uue	UNIX UUencoded	UUDECODE
.z	UNIX Gnu GZIP archive	GZIP
.Z	UNIX compressed archive	UNCOMPRESS
.zip	PC PKZIP compressed archive	PKZIP or WINZIP
.zoo	Compressed archive	ZOO

PC archives will usually end in .exe, .zip, .lzh, or .arj. The .exe files are usually self-extracting archives, which means that they contain a program to decompress themselves. All you have to do is execute them. Just transfer them to a temporary directory and run them from file manager or DOS. If you're running Windows, get the latest copy of **WINZIP** which lodges itself within File Manager. The great thing about WINZIP is that it will handle just about everything. It's easy to configure it to automatically extract archived files just by double-clicking on them in File Manager.

Compressed **Macintosh files** usually end in .cpt, .sit, or .sea. The .cpt files require **Compact Pro**, the .sit use **Stuffit**, and .sea are self-extracting. Files with a .hqx extension have been converted from a binary file to a text file using Binhex. Both Compact Pro and Stuffit can look after the reconversion of those. See the Software roundup (p.247–260) for details of how to obtain these programs.

Finding files with Archie

The biggest problem you're likely to face with files on the Internet is in finding them. Thankfully, there are several tools which can make the job easier – and again, it's possible to locate files through your **Web browser**. To learn how to do this, skip this page and read on.

The best known file search program, however, and until recent months an essential of Net use, is **Archie**, a name probably derived from archive rather than the comic strip character, although it inspired the names Veronica and Jughead for two other Net-tools. As this is in such common use, it merits explaining – though you may decide it's more trouble than it's worth.

Archie creates an **FTP index** by periodically logging in to FTP servers and copying their directory listings. The easiest way to search these databases is through a program with a graphic interface such as **WS Archie** or **Anarchie**. These programs come preconfigured with Archie server addresses. All you have to do is enter a search key for the file you're looking for, choose an Archie host, and sit back and wait.

Sounds simple doesn't it? It is, but it's not always fruitful. **First,** you need to know the file's exact name, not the just the application's name. You might know you're looking for the latest beta of Netdriller, but will you know it's called nqd11b7.zip?

Second, files move. Archie databases, as with all robotically built indexes, can only return the results of their most recent trawl, which may have been a few months ago. If you find that a file isn't where Archie says it should be, remove the file name from the path and search elsewhere in the directory, or in another path. The file may have been superseded by an upgrade or moved into a new directory. If it's a Macintosh file look for a directory called Mac, and for PCs, try Win, Windows, PC, or DOS. Don't forget to check the index file in each directory for clues.

Third, not all FTP sites will be indexed. Archie databases usually give a good coverage of the university sites but rarely search the commercial sites where many programs originate. That's when the World Wide Web comes in handy.

Finally, if your searches are too broad, you'll have to sift through a lot of chaff, if they're too specific you may not get any response. It's wise to give a little leeway, in case the file is stored under an alternative name.

Finding files through the World Wide Web

Archie might be the most common way to search for files you want to download, but there are smarter ways with higher chances of success. The simplest is to fire up your World Wide Web browser and point it toward one of the Web's **search databases** – such as **Infoseek**, **Lycos**, **Harvest**, the **World Wide Web Virtual Library**, or **Yahoo**. As most Web browsers also support FTP, you don't even have to switch applications to download.

Infoseek, the most powerful and comprehensive of these databases, is far more versatile than Archie. You can search through a database of 300,000 Web pages, or the last month's worth of Usenet. As FTP locations are often disclosed in newsgroups, try the Usenet database first. Just enter whatever terms you think will assist the search. For example, if you're looking for the best chess game software, you can just type in: *chess game software best*, and then scan through the results. If you score a direct hit on all terms it will appear on the top of the list.

Virtual libraries such as **Yahoo** have extensive software sections. They're always a good source of specialist pages with links to FTP sites. In the process of searching for a particular file, you may even uncover a whole variety of superior alternatives along with reviews. Even if you can't find the file's location you might have enough to feed into an Archie search.

You can find the **addresses of these databases** in the Internet Search Tools section of this guide (see p.168–172). Several of them are free. Infoseek charges but allows you a free trial period to get hooked.

FTP and Archie software

Most FTP programs are satisfactory, but the outstanding shareware packages are **Fetch**, for the Macintosh, and **WS FTP** for PCs. **Anarchie** is a particularly good Macintosh Archie client, as you can just click on the results to start a transfer. WS Archie works similarly but launches a separate application for download.

Again, see the Software Roundup on p.247–260 for details on how to obtain these programs.

FTP and Archie by email

If you only have email access to the Internet, you can still download software and conduct searches.

Several services offer **FTP by email**. They sometimes take a few days, but should still get the job done. The most widely available are BITFTP and FTPMAIL. To find out more send: *HOWTOFTP* to: `bitftp@pucc.princeton.edu`

Since **Archie searches** are often slow, you might actually find it more convenient to do them via email. To find out how, just send: `help` to `archie@archie.internic.net` or `archie@archie.sura.net` or `archie@archie.doc.ic.ac.uk`

Usenet
Newsgroups

The Internet may be the best place to catch up on the latest bulletins, health warnings, celebrity gossip, sporting results, TV listings, film reviews, and all the other chat commonly known in the popular media as news. It can even be delivered by email, like a virtual newspaper run. But, don't be confused, that's not what's called "news" on the Internet.

News in Net-speak refers to the collection of articles carried in **Usenet**. These articles, or postings, are messages sent as contributions to public discussions. They're similar to email messages but are transmitted in a separate system. Articles are grouped by topic into **newsgroups**. Each newsgroup has a single theme and there's hardly a subject imaginable that's left uncovered. Whether you're interested in baseball, be-bop, Buddhism, or brewing beer, there'll be a newsgroup deliberating over the issues closest to your heart.

With a growing total of over 15,000 newsgroups accessible to more than 30 million users, you can speak directly to – and pose questions for – the world's experts in every field. You want to know who played drums in the original Genesis line-up, or what to do about a strange weed taking over your garden, or how to run your computer on solar power? Fine, just find the right newsgroup to post your bulletin, and wait for the results. It's the Net as Virtual Community in action: fun, heartwarming, and unpredictable – and, after email, the Internet's most valuable resource.

Later in this book – see p.221–246 – we devote a whole chapter to **listings** of some of the most interesting newsgroups. What's covered below are the basics of how to access them and join the discussions.

Access requirements

Usenet is a very flexible medium which can be accessed in various ways. The most convenient is through an account with **full Internet access**: that way you can read and post articles online, switching between newsgroups as you please. If you just have a BBS (Bulletin Board) or "shell" account, you have to subscribe to groups and then wait for articles to arrive. With full access you can read any article in any group at any time, as long as it remains on the news provider's system.

However, even small **bulletin boards** can supply access to at least a limited number of groups for a very small price. And you can get read-only access through some **satellite companies**, too, which provide a decoder which sits between your computer and satellite dish. The entire Usenet database is then transmitted via satellite during the night. You just subscribe to what you want, and when you wake up in the morning, you can search through them at your leisure. As it's a one-way feed, you still have to post conventionally.

Note that even a full Internet connection does not guarantee **access to every group**. Sometimes certain groups are cut, due to logistics or because of a policy to exclude certain types. Although many newsgroups are genuinely educational, businesslike, or informative, there are just as many with pornographic, incendiary, provocative, or just plain moronic material. It's not surprising that many government, educative, corporate, and conservative bodies want to filter them.

How it works

Your Usenet provider keeps a **database of articles** which it updates in periodic exchanges with its neighbors. It receives articles anywhere from once a day to every few minutes, and returns locally created articles as well as the articles it receives from other neighbors. Due to this pass-the-ball procedure, articles may appear immediately on your screen as you post them, but will propagate around the world at the mercy of whoever is in between. Exactly how much you get, and what you see, depends on your provider's neighbors and how often they update their articles.

No provider can keep articles forever as it needs the space for new ones, so it expires them after a certain holding period. It's usual to delete articles more than about four days old and even less for large groups and binaries. Each provider has a different policy. Some newsgroups are "moderated." which means that postings are screened before they appear. This screening can happen anywhere between you and the person who posted the article.

Full Groups
,036 groups

bsu.programming
bsu.religion
bsu.talk
).arnet
).general
b.jobs
ib.politics
adass.archiving
adass.fits.oirfits

New Groups
318 groups

adass.archiving
adass.fits.oirfits
alt.activism.children
alt.animals.horses.icelandic
alt.art.colleges
alt.aviation.bill-mulcahy.screech.babble.dr
alt.binaries.gothic
alt.binaries.pictures.erotica.bears
alt.binaries.pictures.erotica.butts
alt.binaries.pictures.erotica.fetish.faet
alt.binaries.pictures.erotica.oral
alt.binaries.pictures.erotica.zig.and.zag
alt.binaries.pictures.tools

75

This Usenet feed usually comes from your access provider, however it's possible to receive it from anywhere on the Net, as long as you're granted access. There are several **public newsfeeds** available, which provide a way to access groups omitted by your provider. Check the newsgroup news.answers for more on this.

Address hierarchies

Every newsgroup has a simple **address** which will often tell you what it's about at first sight. The first part of the address is the broad category it falls under. Newsgroups are divided according to their specific areas of interest. As the groups form a branch-like structure, these areas are referred to as **hierarchies**. These are some of the top-level and most popular hierarchies.

Hierarchy	Content
alt.	Alternative, anarchic, and free-wheeling discussion*
aus.	Topics of interest to Australians
ba.	Discussion within the San Francisco Bay Area
bionet.	Biological topics
bit.	Topics from Bitnet LISTSERV mailing lists*
biz.	Accepted place for commercial postings
clari.	ClariNet subscription news service
comp.	Computing discussion*
ddn.	The Defense Data Network
ge.	German groups
k12.	Education from kindergarten through grade 12
misc.	Miscellaneous discussions that don't fit anywhere else*
news.	Discussions on Usenet itself*
rec.	Hobbies and recreational activities*
sci.	All strands of science*
soc.	Social, cultural, and religious groups*

| talk. | Discussion of controversial issues* |
| uk. | Topics relating to Britain |

* You'll find most of the activity within these groups.

As you move down each tree, it becomes more specific and each part of the address will distinguish its **focus**. For example `rec.sport.cricket.info` would contain information on the strange recreational sport of cricket.

Although several groups may discuss similar subjects, each will have its own angle. For example, while `alt.games.sausages` might be light and anarchic, `biz.marketing.sausages` would get down to business. To find which newsgroups discuss your area of interest, think laterally and use your newsreader's filtering capabilities to search its newsgroup list for key words.

Your newsfeed may not carry every hierarchy, nor every group within that hierarchy. Many local interest categories, for example, will only be available within their particular locality.

Frequently Asked Questions

Every newsgroup has at least one **FAQ (Frequently Asked Questions)** document. It describes the newsgroup's charter, gives guidelines for posting, and compiles common answers to questions. Many newsgroups carry several FAQs on various topics. They should always be your first source of information. FAQs are periodically posted, usually every couple of weeks.

A comprehensive list of FAQs can be found on the World Wide Web at:

`http://www.cis.ohio-state.edu/hypertext/faq/usenet/FAQ-List.html` or by FTP to: `rtfm.mit.edu` in the path: `/pub/usenet/news.answers`

Newsgroup netiquette

Apart from your provider's contract, the Net itself is largely devoid of formal rules. Instead, there are certain established, or developing, codes of conduct known as **netiquette** (Net-etiquette).

If you breach netiquette, you'll either be ignored, flamed, or lectured by a self-appointed netcop. A **flame** is an abusive posting. You don't have to breach netiquette to get flamed – just expressing a contrary or naive opinion will sometimes do the trick. When it degenerates into name calling, it's called a flame war. There's not much you can do to avoid compulsive flame merchants, but if you follow these tips, you should be welcome to stand your ground in any group.

Read and locate

Most importantly, before posting to any newsgroup, read a range of its **existing postings** first. If it's a big group you might be able to get a good enough idea of what's going on within one session, but more likely you'll need at least a few. Download all the relevant FAQs first, to make sure your article isn't old hat. Some newsgroup users are not very tolerant of repeats.

Next, make an effort to post in the most **relevant group**. If you ask for advice on fertilizing roses in `rec.gardening`, you'll probably be politely directed to `rec.gardening.roses`, but if you want to tell everyone in `talk.serious.socialism` about your theories on Madonna, don't expect such a warm response.

Type and language

Less obviously, **never post in upper case**, unless you're shouting (emphasizing a point in a big way). It is regarded as a sign of rudeness and ignorance. And keep your **signature file** short and subtle. Some people think that massive three page dinosaurs and skyscrapers sculpted from ASCII characters tacked to every Usenet posting gives them credibility. That's unlikely.

In similar fashion, express yourself in **plain English** (or the language of the group) and not in acronyms and abbreviations, except where they simplify technical jargon. Avoid over-using smileys and other **emoticons** (see p.271 for an explanation of emoticons). Some might think they're cute, but to others they're the online equivalent of fuzzy dice hanging from a rear view mirror.

In addition, don't post email you've received from someone else without their consent.

Join in! Be positive!

These warnings aside – and they are pretty obvious – don't hold back. If you can forward the discussion in any way, **contribute**: that's what it's all about. But don't belittle anyone or use inappropriate language. Post positively and invite discussion rather than make abrasive remarks. For example, if you write "Programmers are conceited," you might get personally flamed. But if you try: "Does anyone know any humble programmers?", you'll have a better chance of starting a debate, or at least side-stepping the line of fire.

Overall it's a matter of courtesy and knowing when to contribute. In Usenet, no-one knows anything about you until you post. They'll get to know you through your words, and how well you construct your arguments. If you want to make a good impression, think before you post, and don't be a loudmouth.

Posting and replying to messages

When you subscribe to a newsgroup, you're automatically kept up to date with new articles. When an article
raises a new topic, it's called starting a **thread**. Follow-
ups to the initial article add to that thread. Your Usenet
reader can bundle threads together to follow the
progress of a discussion.

Posting

Posting is like sending email – and extremely simple.
Your newsreader software will offer you the option (at
the end of each posting, or list of postings) of starting a
new thread, following up an existing one, and/or
responding privately by email.

How you go about it depends on your newsreader software. It should automatically insert the newsgroup you
are reading in the *Newsgroups:* line. If you want to
crosspost (post to more than one group), just add those
groups after the first group, separated by a comma, and
then a space. Replies to crosspostings are displayed in
all the crossposted groups. If you want replies to go to a
different group insert it after Follow up - To:

So, for example, if you want to stir up trouble in
alt.shenanigans and rec.humor and have the result
go to alt.flame, the header would look like this:

Newsgroups: alt.shenanigans, rec.humor
Followup – To: alt.flame

When **starting a thread**, pick a subject to summarize
your query or statement. That way people scanning
through the postings will know whether it's of interest.
It will also be included throughout the thread.

Responding

Responding is even easier than posting. Most newsreaders give you the option of following up and/or replying when you read each message. This means you can send your contribution to the relevant newsgroups and/or email the poster directly.

It's usually good practice to **email as well as post**, because the original poster will get it instantly. It's also more personal and it will save them having to scan through the group for replies. It's quite acceptable to continue communicating outside Usenet so long as it serves a purpose. You'll soon find yourself corresponding with a circle of virtual friends.

You also have the option of including part or all of the **original message**. This can be quite a tricky choice. If you cut too much, the context could be lost when the original post is deleted. If everyone includes everything, it creates a lot of text to scan. Just try to leave the main points intact.

Posting commercial messages

Having such a massive captive audience pre-qualified by interests is beyond the dreams of many marketeers. Consequently you will occasionally come across flagrant product advertisements and endorsements within Usenet. There have even been cases where large batches and even the entirety of Usenet was crossposted with advertisements.

This process, known as **"spamming,"** is a guaranteed way to incur the wrath of a high percentage of Usenet users. It usually incites mass mailbombing (loads of unsolicited email) and heavy flaming, not to mention bad publicity.

Use the hierarchy .biz for **commercial announcements**, or tread very subtly if you must publicize your new book, CD, or whatever, in a regular newsgroup.

Sending a test post

As soon as anyone gets Usenet access, they're always itching to see if it works. With that in mind, there are a few newsgroups dedicated to just that purpose. Post whatever you like to alt.test, gnu.gnusenet.test or misc.test You'll get several automatically (and maybe even humanly) generated replies appearing in your mailbox within a few days, just to let you know you're in good hands.

Kill files

If you don't like a certain person on Usenet, you can kill their mail. All you need do is add their email address to your newsreaders **"kill" file**. Then you'll never have to download articles they've posted again. The same applies to any subject or topic: you can just include the recurring string in your kill file. But don't make it too broad or you'll filter out material you might just want to read.

Starting your own group

With 14,000 or so newsgroups in existence, you will need to have fairly specialized tastes to get the urge to start your own group – and you'll also need a fair bit of technical knowhow plus a lot of patience. It's one of the more convoluted and arcane procedures of the Net.

Before you can **create a new newsgroup**, you need to drum up support. It's a good idea to start a mailing list first. You can then build numbers, discuss the proposal in the newsgroups related to your topic and then announce your mailing list.

Once you have a case, and support, you have to put it before the pedantic news.groups for a savaging, unless you want to start an "alt" group in which case you put it to the less ruthless alt.config. Then you have to go through a long process that culminates in an **election** where the number of "yes" votes must be at least 100 more than, and twice the number of "no" votes.

For full details, read "How to Create a Newsgroup," "So You Want to Create an Alt Newsgroup," and "Newsgroup Creation Companion," which are periodically posted to news.answers, and follow them to the letter.

Image and sound files – and decoding

As with email, Usenet can carry more than just text. Consequently there are entire groups dedicated to the posting of binary files such as images, sounds, patches, and even full working programs. Such groups usually have **.binaries** in their address.

Again like email, binary files must be processed, most commonly in UUencoding, before they can be posted or read. You can use a separate program to handle this but it's more convenient to leave it up to your newsreader, which will do the job for you automatically.

To **post a binary**, just attach it as you would in email, and your newsreader will look after the rest.

Searching Usenet

Searching through Usenet can take a lot of time which racks up online charges. One alternative to raking through the groups looking for answers is to use the Web instead. **Infoseek**, for example, allows you to search through the current month's Usenet for key words. This way you can search for all the posts on a topic, and then either retrieve existing messages on that topic or find what groups discuss the topic and subscribe to them. You can also compile a digest of all your postings and replies by using your name or email address as a search term. A trawl through Infoseek is also a great way to catch up when you get back from a break.

For details on accessing Infoseek, see p.96 and p.170.

Newsreaders – and using Netscape

There are several excellent shareware **newsreaders** for every computing platform. Your access provider should supply one in your sign-up kit, and that should do to start with. Once you gain confidence on the Net, you might like to try a few alternatives.

Some **mailreaders** and **Web browsers** can also do the job of newsreader. **Netscape**, for example, is useful in that you can seamlessly zip from the Web to newsgroups and back. This saves memory by not having to open a second application and enables you to follow news links built into Web pages. However, at this stage in Netscape's development, it doesn't support automatic decoding, so it's not much use for binary groups.

The PC news program that stands head and shoulders above the rest is **Agent** from Forte. So far it's the only one that allows you to "queue" multiple articles for download. It has two versions: Free Agent, which is free; and Agent, the registered full-featured edition.

For a full list of newsreaders, refer to the Software round-up on p.252 (PC) or p.258 (Mac).

World Wide Web

If you've ever seen something that looks like `http://www.woof.com/~bow/Wow/Wow.html` tacked on to the bottom of an advertisement, referred to in the newspapers, printed on someone's business card, or flashed across your TV screen, you've been invited to the World Wide Web (WWW). That cryptic address is nowhere near as daunting as it first looks. It's beckoning you into the most exciting and fastest growing medium in the world today, and equipped with a graphical browser it is unbelievably simple to find your way around – if not always to find quite what you thought you were looking for.

The Web's popularity is deserved, because it has made navigating the Internet as simple as pointing and clicking. However, you do need a little help to get started. That's why most of the second half of this guide is devoted to Web site reviews. This chapter covers the basics of how to go "surfing" (as Web browsing is often called) without getting wiped out, and how to find what you want without losing your mind.

What to expect

The Web is the glossy, glamorous, user-friendly face of the Internet: a media-rich potpourri of virtual shopping malls, music samples, online magazines, art galleries, libraries, museums, games, job agencies, movie previews, and plenty more. Once you're online, for the most part, it's all free. Its coverage includes over 30,000 companies, everything from Disneyland to Wall Street, and everywhere from Iceland to Johannesburg, all from the keyboard of your computer. If it's not happening on the World Wide Web, it's not happening anywhere.

Requirements

Make no mistakes. The Web is one hungry beast. It will lap up every bit of computer power, technology, and connection speed you throw at it, and still want more. While you can get away with yesterday's computers in the rest of the Net, the World Wide Web is far more demanding.

That means you'll need a **computer** with at least a 486 DX 33 PC with 8 MB of RAM or a Macintosh 68030 with 8MB of RAM or the equivalent Atari or Amiga machine. It will need to be hooked to the Net at a **modem speed** of at least 14.4 kbps, preferably 28.8 kbps, or better still via an ISDN link. Sure, you can get away with less, but it will groan. You will too as you wait for graphic intensive pages to load.

Home pages

In the World Wide Web, **home page** has two meanings. One definition refers to the document that appears when you start up your browser and acts as a home base for exploring the Web. Whenever you get lost or want to return to somewhere familiar, just click on the "home" button. The other definition refers to any entity's representative Web document.

For instance, Rough Guides' own home page – to be found by keying http://Roughguides.com/ – is the top page in its set of Web documents. Its Web site includes this home page, as well as numerous interconnected

Document : Done.

pages, published as a set. Each page can be accessed simply by keying its unique Web address into your browser or by following a link from another page. Web addresses are formally known as **URLs** (Uniform Resource Locators).

Using URL addresses

You've almost certainly been exposed to a few **Web addresses**. You might not have taken much notice at the time, but you'll need to in future because those addresses will help you find what you want on the World Wide Web. To visit an address, you simply key it in to the **"URL," "Go To,"** or **"Open Location"** box on your Web browser. If all works well, your browser will retrieve the page and display it on your screen.

Remember, path names in UNIX are **case sensitive**. Key URLs carefully, taking note of capitals.

Web (http) addresses

If URLs look alien at first glance, they soon make
sense. Consider an address as having three parts.
Reading from left to right they are: the **protocol** such
as http://, ftp://, news:, or gopher://; the **host
name** (everything before the first single forward slash);
and the **file path** (everything after and including the
first single forward slash).

Let's look at the following address:

http://wwwcs.uit.no/~paalde/Revenge/index.html

The *http://* tells us it's a **hypertext file** located on
the World Wide Web, the **domain** wwwcs.uit.no tells us
it's in Norway, and the **file path** indicates that the file
index.html is located in the **directory**
/~papaalde/Revenge/

Although the majority of URLs include the file's path,
the trend is moving toward shorter addresses,
especially for the home page. For example, if you key
in: http://www.apple.com you'll reach Apple's home
page, but key in: http://www.apple.com/documents/
aboutapple.html and you'll find another document
deeper within Apple's site.

If you're using **Netscape**, the most popular browser
right now, you needn't key *http://* as it's an
automatic default. It's likely that other browsers will
follow suit in later releases.

FTP, Gopher, Telnet, and Usenet addresses

As discussed in earlier chapters, you can access **FTP**,
Gopher, **Telnet**, and **Usenet** from the wheel of your
Web browser.

To use **FTP**, just add *ftp://* to the file's location. So, to retrieve *duck.txt* located in the directory */yellow/fluffy* from the anonymous FTP site ftp.quack.com, enter:

ftp://ftp.quack.com/yellow/fluffy/duck.txt

Gopher and **Telnet** work in exactly the same way, but **Usenet** omits the // Thus, to access the newsgroup *alt.ducks* key: news: *alt.ducks*

Hypertext

Web documents are written in a language called **HTML (hypertext markup language)**, which enables you to embed links to other documents within the text, thus creating a third dimension. You'll be familiar with this concept if you've ever used Windows Help or Macintosh Hypercard.

Depending on how you've configured your browser, text which contains links to other documents (or even to another part of the same document) is usually **highlighted or underlined**. To pursue the link, you simply **click on the highlighted text or object**. When the new document appears, it will be entirely independent of the previous one. The old document is now history. Since the new document needs no connection with the old one, there might not be a reciprocal link. However, there is an easier way to return, as you'll soon see.

Browser Basics

Web browsers are a new and meteorically developing technology. It's likely that between writing and the time you read this, they will have moved forward by several generations. During the first half of 1995, it seemed as if only a couple of weeks would pass between new

Netscape and **Mosaic** releases, with each new release introducing radical features.

Despite the various enhancements which distinguish browsers they achieve the same end through similar means. The following intrinsic functions are described for Netscape and Mosaic – the two most popular browsers – but will be common to all latest generation browsers:

A dialog box in which to enter URLs

This box runs horizontally above the browser window. In **Netscape**, when it's blank, it says "Go to:" beside it, and when it retrieves the URL the wording changes to "Location:". Irrespective of what it says, just key the URL in there, or choose "Open Location" from the File menu, and enter it in there. In **Mosaic** the box is called "Document URL:", and "Open URL" in the File menu.

Whatever it's called the effect will be the same. After you've typed in the URL, click on "Enter," or type the "Return" key, and wait. It rarely takes more than a minute or two to locate and load Web pages, and if you've got a fast modem and good connection it can be a matter of seconds.

Navigation buttons to take you back, forward, and home

The navigation buttons are also located above the browser window. Displaying them is usually optional, but it's hard to live without them. To refer to a previous page that you've viewed, just click the "back" button until you reach it. To return, keep pressing "forward." The extent of how far you can go depends on the amount of cache allocated or the "number of documents stored" chosen in the configuration preferences. "Home" returns to the document chosen as your start-up page.

A history file, which shows you where you've been and allows you to return

Rather than repetitively clicking the "forward" and "back" buttons, you can open up the history file or choose the previous page from a menu. It's under the "Go" menu in Netscape and the "Navigate" menu in Mosaic. In Netscape however, when you return to a previous page and pursue a link, it loses all the backtracked pages.

A button to stop transfers in progress

To cancel a transfer, because it's taking too long, or you've made a mistake, just hit the "stop" button. In the middle of a transfer, you might have to hit "stop" before "back" will work.

The option of not loading images

The drawback of the Web's graphic richness is the time it takes to download images. To speed things up, consider choosing the option of not loading images. To view the images after the page is loaded, either click on them individually, choose "load images" from the menu, or hit the "images" button.

The option of choosing your initial home page

Browsers usually come preconfigured with a default home page – their own, which will include information about their new products and a range of search options. If you'd prefer an alternative home page, you can just specify it in the configuration preferences.

It's handy to have a page which links to your favorite search tools or perhaps one that gives regular sports or news updates. Hitting "home" will load the page. Be sure, however, to choose one that's quick to load or it will delay the start of each session. In fact, you may prefer to select the option to load a blank page at start-up and then specify your favorite search tool as the home page. That way, you're ready to go immediately, and can just hit "home" to conduct a search.

A hotlist, or bookmark file to store useful URLs

Whenever you find a page that's worth another visit, file its location. To do that, just "add" it to the option labeled "hotlist" or "bookmarks." These files are transportable, so you can edit them, or send a friend your favorite sites, just by attaching the file to email. They can then open it as a local hypertext file or even specify it as their home page.

The ability to send mail and read Usenet newsgroups

Browsers generally run "straight out of the pack," without any configuration. However, there are several boxes hidden away in the configuration preferences that will need to be completed to get the most out of your session. Before you can **send email** and **post to newsgroups** directly from a browser, you'll have to complete your email and news-server details. Your provider will supply this information. If you're not sure what to put, give them a call.

Web pages often give various **email opportunities**. You'll often see a contact name inviting email. When you click on it, a dialog box should appear. Just type in your message and send it. Replies arrive through the normal email channels.

To see a **list of all the available newsgroups** type: news:* , or hit the "newsgroups" button if available. The first time could take several minutes. If the browser builds a local index file, later attempts will be almost instantaneous. Once the newsgroups are listed, just click on them to retrieve articles and post in the same way as any newsreader.

Browsers are good for accessing newsgroup references from Web pages and vice versa but lack many of the advanced features of dedicated newsreaders. So, if you're planning a serious Usenet session, fire up a newsreader instead.

Autolaunching Telnet and other external applications

Every browser has a daunting looking configuration section where you nominate the external applications to handle various file types and events. As yet, no browsers handle **Telnet** internally, so you'll have to source and specify a client, to have it launched automatically.

It is, however, becoming increasingly common for browsers to throw in an external application or two, such as **graphics viewers** and **sound players**. When they do, they also preconfigure those applications to be launched automatically. If you get one that does, such as Netscape, that's at least one less thing to worry about. Otherwise get a **sound player**, an **image viewer**, and a **quicktime movie player** from the Net, and choose them to be launched by their respective file types. That way, when you download a sound or movie file it will be played instantly. Although browsers can adequately display images for most purposes, they'll need an external viewer to be enlarged or manipulated.

Copying and pasting

Text can be copied from Web pages just like any other document. Just highlight the section, choose **"copy"** from the Edit menu (or use the shortcut keys) and paste it to a word processor, text editor, or mail program.

Saving pages as local files

If a page is saved as a **bookmark**, you must go online to access it. If it's not likely to be changed, it's best to save it to disk. Choose **"Save as"** from the File menu. It will give the option to save it as text or HTML – choose HTML. To view it on your browser, choose **"Open local file"** from the File menu. It can then be saved as a text file to remove the hypertext tags. At this stage in browser evolution, images must be saved separately.

Retrieving images

Most Web pages display reduced images. Such images contain an active link. Just click on them to display the full image. To **save an image**, either open it by clicking on it, and choose **"Save as"** from the File menu, choose **"Save this link as,"** and click on the link to the full image, or in Netscape, hold the mouse button down and choose **"Save this image as."** The actual menu wording changes between platforms and releases, but the results will be the same.

Mouse menus

Netscape enables or activates the most useful commands from your **mouse button** (the right button on PCs). Just hold it down and try them out. "Save this link as," for example, can come in handy when you're having difficulty loading a large page.

Identifying links

Links can be customized using underlining and/or a special color. Most people choose to underline them in blue. Followed links can be made a different color, for example red. That way you can see where you've been.

These customized links also have an optional expiry period, after which they revert to the normal color. If you choose "never", they will always show which sites you've visited. This works by storing the URLs in a history file independent of the page where you first encountered the link. That means that all followed links will be red, even if they're on a page you've never visited. It's not wise to let this history file get too big as it's likely to slow things down.

Viewing the document source

To see a page's raw HTML coding, just choose **"Source"** from the View menu. This is a good way to learn how to design Web pages.

Power browsing

The good news is that surfing the Web is very easy. It's just a matter of keying in the odd address and then clicking on whatever looks interesting. It couldn't get much simpler than that. The bad news is it's massive, so if you're looking for something specific, you're going to need directions.

Since the Web isn't organized by any particular body and doesn't have any formal directory, you'll have to rely on the ingenuity of the various search engines and virtual libraries.

Search engines

When you're looking for a specific topic or combination of topics, especially if it's obscure, use a **search engine** such as **Infoseek**, **Lycos**, or **Harvest**. These work by

accumulating a database of URLs and document samples, by periodically trawling the Web.

These automated surfers are known as robots, worms, crawlers, spiders, and various other unsavory names. The amount of intelligence and resultant quality varies. Most of these services are free, so they can be very difficult to get on to at times. If you don't mind paying a small amount use **Infoseek**. It's the quickest, easiest to access, and gives the best results. Lycos comes second, but you have to deal with a lot of duplicates and its popularity can sometimes make it impossible to access.

Virtual libraries

To get an idea of the Web's diversity, check out one of the virtual libraries such as **Yahoo**, the **World Wide Web Virtual Library**, **GNN** (Global Network Navigator), and the **Subject Orientated Clearinghouse**. These categorize URLs by subject, include a brief description of the contents, and allow searches by key words.

Such databases are organized into subject trees, like Gophers. Simply keep clicking on what interests you most, to narrow the field. Eventually you'll be presented with a list of site links. This is often the best way to find specialist pages. Although the number of URLs represented is much lower than with search engines, the quality may be higher and you might have a better idea of what to expect when you get there.

Specialist pages

Whatever your specialist interest is, you can bet your favorite finger that it will have a dedicated Web page. It's even more likely that several people have devoted all or parts of pages to the area and that someone else has catalogued their efforts by compiling a **list of links** to them. If not, maybe you should. These mini-catalogs are a boon for keeping track of new pages. If you have similar interests, email the pagemaster and introduce yourself. That's what the Web is all about.

Lists

The Web is littered with hundreds of sites proclaiming what's hot, what's cool, what's new, and what's on. You'll always find something of interest there, and in many cases it's the best place to find brand new sites long before the crawlers get there. Some great lists are Netscape's **"What's Cool"** and **"Today's Cool Site,"** NCSA's "Hot List," *Internet* magazine's **"What's On,"** and **"Mirsky's Worst."** See our Web directory chapter for their locations.

Magazines

Both paper and electronic publications can be ideal sources of URLs. Dedicated Internet magazines pay staff to scavenge the Net, looking for the best sites. It's worth subscribing to at least one to keep track of new software, events, and unmissable URLs. The UK magazine

Internet, stands out by lengths in this regard, publishing reviews to around 600 sites each month. The US magazines *Internet World*, *Net Guide*, and the ever-cool *Wired* are also useful, but more for news than sites.

The best online publications are Wired's *HotWired* offshoot (free – though you will be asked to fill out subscription details) and the *Netsurfer Digest* (which is also available free by email. Again, see our World Wide Web directory chapter for addresses of these and other online digests of reviews.

Problems

Sometimes even after you've resorted to the dreaded manual, things still won't work. You've entered the address three times, but it still won't connect. Don't worry. It happens all the time.

Connection errors

There are two basic causes of **connection errors**: incorrect addressing and system failure. To identify the source of the problem, you'll first need to get familiar with your browser's error codes. When something goes wrong and you receive an error number and message, those instructions are coming from your browser, not the Net.

Each browser will return different error messages, but they'll indicate the same things. To get to know your browser, learn to identify the following errors:

Incorrect host name
When the address points to a non-existent host, your browser will return an error saying "Host not found." Test this by keying: http://www.rufgide.com

Illegal domain name

If you specify a host name or protocol that the browser recognizes is illegal, it will tell you.

Try this out by keying `http://wwwrufguide` and then `http:/www.ibm.com` noting the single slash.

File not found

If the file has moved, changed name, or you've neglected the capitalization, your browser will tell you the file doesn't exist on the host. Test this by keying a familiar URL and slightly changing the path.

Busy host or Host refuses entry

Occasionally you won't gain access because the host is either overloaded with traffic, or it's temporarily or permanently off-limits. This sometimes happens with busy FTP servers, like Netscape's. It's a bit hard to test this one, but you could try visiting Netscape's "Cool Site of the Day." It's always busy. You might also make a habit of accessing foreign sites when locals are sleeping – it's usually quicker.

More troubleshooting

Now that you're on speaking terms with your browser, you're set to troubleshoot that problem URL. The first thing to verify is that you really have a connection. Try another site. If it works, you know the problem's with that URL.

When no URLs work

If you can't connect to anything, **close your browser and re-open it**. It could be a bug. If that doesn't fix it, you'll have to check your connection to your provider and its connection to the Net.

First, **check your mail**. If that looks dodgy, log off and then back on again. Check it again. If something is still fishy, ring your provider. If the line's engaged, chances are someone else is having the same problem. Your provider should be able to get to the bottom of it.

If your **mail reader connects** and reports your mail status normally, you know that the connection between you and your provider is OK. Now, you'll need to test its connection with the Net. Try **Pinging** (see p.122) a known host, say www.ibm.com or logging in to an FTP site. If this fails, either your provider's connection to the Net is down, or there's a problem with your Domain Name Server. Get on the phone to them.

If you've verified that all connections are open but your browser won't find any URLs, the problem lies with the **browser**. Check its configurations and re-install it if necessary. If you're using Windows 3.1, make sure that the winsock.dll and browser directories are both included in the autoexec.bat path statement. And finally, check that you have the right browser for your operating system. Netscape, for example, has a 32 bit version for Windows 95.

When one URL doesn't work

If you can't connect to one URL, you know that either the address is wrong or the host at the other end has problems. Since you've familiarized yourself with the error messages you can now deduce the error source. Now you have to fix that address so it works.

Web addresses disappear and change all the time, there's nothing you can do about it. It's often because the address has been simplified, for example from http://www.netflux.co.uk/~test/New_Book/Com-Plex.html/ to http://roughguide.com/ If you're lucky, the site will have had the sense to leave a pointer, but sometimes even that pointer gets out of date. Since the Web is in a constant state of construction, just about everything is a test site in transit to something bigger.

Consequently, when a site gets serious, it might relocate to an entirely new host and forget the old address. Who said the life of a professional surfer was easy?

Finding that elusive URL

The most obvious clues in tracking elusive URLs are to use what you've deduced from the error messages. If the problem comes from the host name, try adding or removing the www section, or adding or removing a slash at the end of the address. For example, with http://roughguide.com,

try `http://www.roughguide.com` or `http://roughguide.com/` (the correct address).

Other than that you can only guess. Host names are case-insensitive, so changing that won't help. If the host is busy, refusing entry, or not connecting, try again later.

When you succeed in connecting to the host, but the file isn't there, there are a few further tricks to try. Check **capitalization**. Try removing the file name and then each subsequent directory up the path until finally just the host name. In each case, if you succeed in connecting, try to locate your page from the links presented or by browsing through directories and hotlists.

If you haven't succeeded yet there's still hope. Try using the main **key words** from the URL's address or title in one of the search tools such as Infoseek, Lycos, or Yahoo. Failing that, try searching on related subjects.

By now, even if you haven't found your URL, you've probably discovered half a dozen similar if not more interesting pages.

Choosing a browser

The browser market is exploding across every platform, and each new release leapfrogs its rivals in features. Most are shareware and available on the Net. At the time of writing there doesn't seem much point in using anything other than **Netscape**'s continually improving **Navigator** (or whatever its current release may have been renamed). It is becoming the accepted standard, to an extent that many sites use "Netscape enhancements" – HTML extensions used only by Navigator. Such sites look quite odd viewed from any other browser.

It wouldn't hurt to try a few other browsers, but watch Netscape's home page for news. As soon as there's a new release, get it. Web technology is moving so quickly that it's hard to predict with any certainty which package will be leading the fray by the time you read this. The best advice is to download the latest copy of Navigator from Netscape's FTP site (see our Software Round-up in Part Four for details on this), try a few others such as Mosaic, and settle with the one that suits you best. At this stage though, the smart money wouldn't have anything but Netscape.

See the Software Roundup on p.252 (PC) or p.259 (Mac) for details of FTP sites where you can **download Netscape** and other browsers.

Publishing your own Web pages

Before long you'll want to publish your own efforts on the Web. This used to require writing raw HTML code, but simple applications are emerging to automate the process. If you intend to publish you'll still need to understand the basic language, but it's possible to compose simple pages using add-ons to your word processor. Microsoft offers a freeware extension to Word 6.0 for Windows called **Internet Assistant**. Quarterdeck's **Web Author** is very similar. Macintosh users should investigate the recently released Adobe Page Mill which promises WYSIWYG (what you see is what you get) creation of HTML pages. It costs $99 and claims to be just like using a desktop publishing package. See!: *http://www.adobe.com./Apps/PageMill/* for more information.

Before you can put anything on the Web, someone has to supply you with space on their hard disk. Speak to your access provider, many of whom offer a small amount of space for free with your connection. If not, you shouldn't have to pay more than a few dollars per megabyte per month.

Once you've published your page and transferred it to your provider's site, you just have to get people to visit it. That's the hard part.

Internet Relay Chat

There is a facet of the Internet that is often described as the online equivalent of CB radio. A feature that enables you to hold live keyboard conversations with people all over the world. That mechanism is called Internet Relay Chat, or IRC, and it's beginning to gain popular acceptance as a cheap alternative to long distance telephone calls.

Since its development in Finland in 1988, IRC has played a worthy part in transmitting the latest eye-witness accounts of every major world event – including the Gulf war, the Californian disasters, the Kobe earthquake, and the Oklahoma bombing. During the Gulf war, for example, IRC channels formed to dissect the latest news as it came in from the wire services. But, as you'll soon discover, politics and crises are not the only things discussed.

Unlike Usenet, on IRC your **conversations are live**. What you key into your computer is instantly broadcast to everybody else on your channel, even if they're logged into a server on the other side of the world. Some channels are obviously dedicated to particular topics, for example, #cricket, #doom, and #worldcup, but most are just informal chat lines. Who knows, your perfect match could be waiting for you in an online chat channel like

#hottub. You might think that's unlikely, but IRC has brought many couples together and some have even held their wedding ceremonies online. If you ever get to attend one, be sure to throw some rice, like this: """"""""""". If you want to enter the more geekish domains of the Internet, read on.

Requirements

When you enter something into an IRC channel, everyone else on that channel, wherever they are, will see it almost immediately. The only way that can happen is through full Internet access. However, you don't need a particularly fast connection nor a powerful computer. Ideally, you don't want to be paying timed online charges either, because it's another medium where once you're hooked, you'll want to spend hours online.

Many users have free direct connections through university or work, so they can afford to leave their line open all day. That's one of the reasons why you'll often find channels with people on them, but nobody talking. When you enter the channel and "beep" the person in it, if they're in the vicinity of the terminal, they'll answer your call. It's also possible that they're chatting in other channels.

A caution

Of all the Internet's features, IRC is the one most likely to trip up newcomers. What makes it so different is that you can't hide your presence. For example, on Usenet, unless you add to a newsgroup by posting a message, no-one will know you've looked at it. However, the second you arrive in an IRC channel you will be announced to all and your nickname will remain in the names list for as long as you stay.

Sleuthful chatsters can quickly find out who you are behind your nickname and probably tell whether you're a newbie from your settings. There are even a few devious people who might try to mislead you to enter commands, which could give them control of your computer. Never enter an unfamiliar command at the request of another user. If someone is bothering you, change channels. If they persist, get them kicked out by an operator.

Getting started

Net software bundles don't always include an **IRC client** or program. If that's the case with yours, fire up FTP and get the latest **GUI client** (again, see our Software Roundup on p.250/p.256). Once it's installed, read its configuration instructions as well as all its tutorials and assorted text files.

It might sound a bit boring to have to read the instructions first but in this case it's necessary. GUI IRC clients have an array of cryptic buttons and windows that are less intuitive than most Internet applications. Before you start randomly clicking on things to see what they do, remember that people are watching.

Additionally, before you can get started, you'll need to **configure** your client to connect to a specific IRC server's address, as well as entering your nickname, real name, and email address. If you're worried about embarrassing yourself, you can try using false details. Some servers, however, refuse entry if their reverse lookups detect discrepancies.

The servers

To ease the strain on network traffic, try to use a nearby host. There are hundreds of open **IRC hosts** worldwide. The best place to get a list, or indeed any information about IRC, is from the `alt.irc` newsgroup. Failing that, you can get one by FTP at `h.ece.uiuc.edu/irc/` in a file called `servers.txt`.

For starters, try one of the following, using port 6667:

US
irc.colorado.edu
irc.ucdavis.edu
sanjose.ca.us.undernet.org
chiron.cs.uregina.ca

Canada
montreal.qu.ca.undernet.org
io.org
clique.cdf.utoronto.ca

Europe
uxbridge.uk.eu.undernet.org
irc.funet.fi
oslo.no.eu.undernet.org
caen.fr.eu.undernet.org

Australia
jello.qabc.uq.oz.au
yoyo.cc.monash.edu.au
wollongong.nsw.au.undernet.org

IRC commands

The IRC language has over 100 **commands**. Unless you're very keen, you'll only need to know a few. However the more you learn, the more you can fine-tune your position. If you're using a GUI client, you can almost get away without learning any commands at all, but it won't hurt to know the script behind the buttons, and you may even prefer to use the commands. Your client won't automate everything, so each time you're online try out a few more. Its Help file should contain a full list. If not, download the IRC Primer FAQ by FTP at

cs.bu.edu in the directory /irc/support.

To find out more about IRC in general try:
http://www.singnet.com.sg:80/public/IRC/
index.html

There are far too many commands to list here, but those below will get you started. The server interprets anything following a forward slash as a command. If you leave it off, it will be transmitted to your active channel as a message.

Commands are not case sensitive

Command	Description
/AWAY <message>	Leave a message saying you're not available
/BYE	Exits your IRC session
/HELP	Returns a list of available commands
/HELP <command>	Returns help on the specified command
/IGNORE <nickname><*><all>	Ignores output from specified nickname
/IGNORE <*><email address><all>	Ignores output from specified email address
/IGNORE <*><*><none>	Deletes ignorance list
/JOIN <#channel>	Join specified channel
/KICK <nickname>	Boot specified nickname off channel
/LEAVE <#channel>	Exit specified channel
/LIST <-MIN n>	Lists channels with a minimum of n users
/MOP	Promotes all to operator status
/MSG <nickname><message>	Sends a private message to specified nickname
/NICK <nickname>	Changes your nickname
/OP <nickname>	Promotes specified nickname to operator status
/QUERY <nickname>	Starts a private conversation with specified nickname

Command	Description
/TOPIC <new topic>	Changes the topic of the channel
/WHO*	Gives a list of users in the current channel
/WHOIS <nickname>	Displays identity of nickname
/WHOWAS <nickname>	Displays identity of nickname who has left

Step by step through your first session

By now, you've configured your client, given yourself a nickname that you'll never use again, and are raring to go. The aim of your first session will be to connect to a server, have a look around, get a list of channels, join one, see who's on, say something public, say something private, leave the channel, start a new channel, make yourself operator, change the topic, and then exit IRC. The whole process should take no more than around ten minutes. Let's go.

✦ Log on to one of the listed servers and wait to be accepted. If you're not, keep trying others until you succeed. Once aboard, you'll be greeted with the MOTD (message of the day) in the server window. Read the message and see if it tells you anything interesting.

✦ You should have two windows available. One is for input and the other to display output from the server. Generally, the two windows form part of a larger window, with the input box below the output box. Even though your client's point and click interface will replace most of the basic commands, since you probably haven't read the manual yet, you won't know how to use it. Let's use the commands instead.

✦ To find out what channels are available, type: /LIST You'll have to wait a few moments and then a window will pop up, or fill up, with hundreds of channels, their topics, and the number of users on them. To narrow the list down to those channels with six or more users, type: /LIST -MIN 6 Now you will find the busiest channels.

✚ Pick a channel at random and join it. Channel names are always preceded by #, so to join the *mustard* channel, type: `/JOIN #mustard` and then wait for the channel window to appear. Once the channel window opens, you should get a list of all the people present in the channel probably appearing in yet another window. If not, type: `/WHO*` to get a full list including nicknames and email addresses.

✚ Now say something clever, type: `Hi everyone, it's great to be back!` This should appear not only on the screen in your channel window, but on the screen in every other person's channel window. Wait for replies and answer any questions as you see fit.

✚ Now it's time to send something personal. Choose someone in the channel and find out what you can about them first, by typing: `/WHO` followed by `their nickname`. Your client might let you do this by just double clicking on their nickname in the names window. Let's say their nickname is Hank. To send a private message, just type: `/MSG Hey Hank, I'm a newbie, let me know if you get this so I won't feel so stupid.` If Hank doesn't reply, keep trying until someone does. Once you're satisfied that you know how that works, leave the channel by typing: `/LEAVE` Don't worry, next time you go into a channel, you'll feel more comfortable.

✚ Now to start your own channel. You can pick any name that doesn't already exist. As soon as you leave, it will disappear. To start a channel called *shambles*, just type: `/JOIN #shambles` Once the window pops up, you'll find that you're the only person on it. Now promote yourself to operator, type: `/OP` followed by `your nickname` Others will be able to tell that you have channel operator status because your nickname will appear with a @ in front of it. Now that you are an operator, you have the power to kick people off the channel, change the topic, and all sorts of other things that you can find out by

reading the manual as recommended. To change the topic,
type:/TOPIC followed by whatever you want to change the
topic to. Wait for it to change on the top of your window and
then type: /BYE to exit IRC.

That's it really, a whirlwind tour but enough to learn
most things you'll need. But, before you can communicate with the people in IRC, you'll need to speak their
language.

The language of IRC

Just as CB radio has its own dialect, so too has IRC.
Chat is a snappy medium, messages are short and
responses are fast. If messages are too long they can be
hard to follow within the client's channel window.

Unlike CB, people don't ask your "20" to find out
where you're from, or type "breaker" when they enter a
discussion, but they do use **short-forms**, **acronyms**, and
smileys (:-). Acronyms are mixed in with normal speech
– and range from the innocuous (BTW = by the way) to a
whole panoply of swearwords. Don't be too shocked. It's
not meant to be taken seriously. And don't be ashamed
to use ordinary English language, either. You will probably have a better chance of being understood than the
out-and-out geeks.

For a sample of some of the abbreviations and
acronyms you might encounter, see p.269.

IRC netiquette

IRC attracts a diverse group of people for a variety of
reasons. You're just as likely to encounter a channel full
of Indians following a ball-by-ball cricket commentary as
a couple of lovers chatting intimately. Provided no-one

rocks the boat too much, everyone can co-exist. There's bound to be a little mischief now and then, but that usually just adds to the fun of the whole event.

However, some actions are generally frowned upon and may get you kicked from channels, or even banned from IRC. These include dumping large files or amounts of text to a channel, harassing others, using inappropriate language, beeping channels constantly to get attention, and inviting people into inappropriate channels. Finally, if you make a big enough nuisance of yourself, some vindictive person might track you down and make you regret it.

IRC games

Many IRC channels are dedicated to games. You sometimes play against other people, but programs called **"bots"** are more common opponents. Such programs are written to respond to requests in a particular way, and even learn from the experience.

To find out more about IRC games,

send: info irc-games to listserv@netcom.com:

see: http://www.cris.com/trieger/irc games.html

or look in the newsgroup alt.irc.games

IRC picture gallery

Once you've used IRC a few times, you'll recognize many regulars, and they'll recognize you. If you'd like to put a face to their names, check out the **IRC picture gallery** on the World Wide Web at:

http://www.powertech.no/IRCGallery

You're welcome to add your own, and if your online friends haven't already done so, suggest it.

Rolling in the MUD

Before Space Invaders – apart from the ubiquitous paddle game Pong – the only computer games to speak of were of the adventure variety. The ones where you'd stumble around imaginary kingdoms looking for hidden objects, uttering magic words and fighting monsters. They were pretty tame compared to the likes of today's DOOM and Descent. But the funny thing is, these adventure games are still going strong in the UNIX world of the Internet.

Admittedly, they've come a long way, and have blended with the whole Dungeons and Dragons caper perfectly, but they're still mostly text-based. That's "mostly," because a few are starting to appear with graphical interfaces. What sets them apart from conventional arcade games is the community that evolves from them. Within each game, participants develop complex alter egos enabling them to live out their fantasies and have them accepted within the group. But, it can also become an obsession where the distinction between the alter ego and the self becomes blurred, and players retreat into the reassurance of the game. If they're dialing in from a home account, it can also become an expensive one.

On the Internet, such games are known as **MUDs (Multi User Dimensions or Dungeons)**. If they have a graphic component, they're called **GUI MUDs** (gooey muds). They can be classified further into combat, role play, and social MUDs. Combat MUDs are the original medieval adventure games, role-play MUDs have more flexible modern themes, while social MUDs involve more interplayer activities. A social MUD can also called be called a MOO (MUD Object Oriented), MUSE (Multi User Shared Dimension), or MUSH (Multi User Shared Hallucination). Got that?

Connecting to MUDs

You usually connect to MUDs via **Telnet** (see p.121), although initially you might find the link in a **Gopher** (see p.118), or on a **Web page**, where they are fast migrating. As every MUD is different, be prepared to have to learn a set of complex commands before you can play. However, don't let that intimidate you as newbies are always welcome, and other players will help point you in the right direction.

For more about MUDs, see:

http:www.cis.upenn.edu/~lwl/mudinfo.html
http://www.ccs.neu.edu/home/lpb/muddex.html
and the newsgroup hierarchies *alt.mud* and
rec.games.mud

And to find out about a new GUI MUD called Terradome that's set to take the MUD world by storm, see: *http://terrradome.ds~data.dk*

Other Internet Programs

If you've read this far you know all you need – and more – to get connected to the Internet and find your way around it. But there is still an almost infinite number of Net accessories and software, navigation tools, and troubleshooting programs to explore. Most you'll never need, but the odd one will come in handy. Some were once major players in the network's development, but have now been engulfed by the powers of the World Wide Web and its user-friendly browsers. Others, by contrast, are cutting edge Net programs, allowing you to hear Real Time sound and download video – developments worth keeping up with on an almost daily basis – and even to use the Internet as a cheap alternative to making international phone calls.

To go through all these programs in depth is well beyond the scope of this guide, but these pages should prove a jumping-off point for the curious or committed. It is hard to overstate how quickly things are changing, so do check out the addresses here for new software, keep an eye on busy home pages such as Netscape's, and consider subscribing to one of the Internet magazines. The cutting edge right now is in **real time sound**, and if you're a music fan you will certainly want to keep an ear open for developments.

For the **addresses** of where to download these various tools, see our **software roundup** starting on p.247. In addition, you might check out two excellent general sites on the Web detailing what tools are on offer:

John December's Internet Tools summary at: `http://www.rpi.edu/Internet/Guides/decemj/itoo ls/internet-tools.html` This covers most of the established popular tools.

Stroud's Comsummate Winsock Applications Page at: `http://cwsapps.texas.net/` This site covers the latest PC Internet software. It's updated daily and worth checking at least weekly for new releases.

AT THE CUTTING EDGE

These are a few programs that are on the verge of happening in a very big way. Be there at the beginning!

The Internet Phone

When Mosaic was first released as a way to navigate the World Wide Web, it was hailed as the "killer application of the nineties." It's possible that the same accolades could now apply to the Internet telephone. This little invention means that – if you and your friends around the world are online and have the same software – you can use your computer as a phone, dialing around the world at local charge rates. Neat, huh?

The mechanics are really quite obvious. Just as text can be instantly transmitted internationally on the net, so too can voice. Hardware-wise, you'll need a sound-card, speakers, and microphone – all routine features on modern multimedia computers. If your soundcard permits **duplex transmission**, you can hold a normal conversation just like on a regular telephone, otherwise it's more like a walkie-talkie where you have to take turns to speak.

The most popular **Internet audio chat** product so far is Vocaltech's Internet Phone software which enables you to transmit voice over IRC. To find out more about this and other aspects of the Internet Phone, email: info@vocaltech.com

Maven

Maven was the first Macintosh audio-conferencing tool. Its feeble compression algorithms make it tough on Internet bandwidth; it needs a minimum of 16 kbps throughput to achieve real-time audio transmission; and the ebbs and surges of network traffic can cause choppy fidelity.

However, it's a sign of things to come, and you can try it out on the radio station **WXYC**
(http://sunsite.unc.edu/wxyc/)
to sample the future of broadcasting technology.
More about Maven can be found at:
http://pipkin.lut.ac.uk/WWWdocs/LUTCHI/misc/maven.html

Real Audio

Another audio application which looks set to launch Web pages into a new dimension is Progressive Networks' **Real Audio**. It works for both PCs and Macs and promises to deliver real time sound reproduction as soon as you commence download. It also allows instructions to be simultaneously encoded to launch events. This is achieved through a compression rate of up to 14:1.

See http://www.realaudio.com for more details.

CUSeeMe

CUSeeMe is a video-conferencing client for UNIX, PC, and Macintosh. Unfortunately the audio channel doesn't yet function on PCs but they're working on it.

Don't get your hopes too high on this one. Even with a fast connection and snazzy graphics hardware, it's not exactly what you'd call real-time video. For more information see: *http://www.indstate.edu/CU-SeeMe/index.html*

OLD BUT VALUABLE TOOLS

A round-up of some useful tools – and a few old Internet standards that still do their work as well as anything.

Time synchronizer

If your computer's clock is always wrong let it talk to the atomic clock at: *time-a.timefreq.bldrdoc.gov* or any Internet server using a time synchronizer. Some programs can automatically change it. Others just report the difference.

Gopher

Before the World Wide Web's explosion, **Gopher** provided the friendliest and most efficient way to search the Internet's vast archives. As the name suggests, Gopher is used to "go for" information. Although it stores data in an entirely different architecture, it looks and acts similar to the World Wide Web. In many ways, the Web is its natural successor. However, it's still a useful archiving technique, and a gateway to a large percentage of the Net's wealth.

When you link out of the Web and into a Gopher site, you may not recognize the change. It looks much the same at first with its clickable menus sending you around the world to vast libraries of information, but you'll soon notice that Gopher burrows are dead-ended. You can surf from page to page following links all day on the Web, but with Gophers, once you find your file, you have to tunnel back out again. It's best to think of Gopherspace as being a separate entity to the Web. Even though it forms a subset of it in practice, once you cross the border, the laws change.

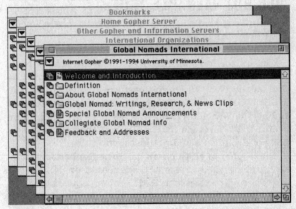

There's no real reason to get a dedicated Gopher program as you can do it all from your Web browser. To access a Gopher from the World Wide Web, key in *gopher://* before the address. For example to access the "Mother of all Gophers" at Minnesota University key: *gopher://gopher.umn.edu/1* as your URL. You'll find all you need to know about Gophers at this site, including how to search by subject or geographic region.

Finding your way around Gopherspace is even easier than the Web, once you know how. Individual Gophers are internally searchable – just look for the menu entry. It's also possible to keyword search the menu titles in "all Gopherspace" using **Veronica**, which is to Gopher what Archie is to FTP. Veronica's database is compiled by trawling Gopherspace every couple of weeks, and retrieving the menu titles. All Veronicas should contain the same information although some might be slightly more up to date. Veronica searches produce a menu of Gopher items, which point to gopher data sources.

Veronica is available from the "Other Gophers" menu on Minnesota's gopher server, or at:

gopher://futique.scs.unr.edu/11/veronica

You'll also find that many of the Web's search tools and libraries, such as **Lycos** and **Yahoo**, cover Gopher as well as the Web. When you perform a keyword search using Lycos, you'll find Gopher addresses interspersed among the Web addresses. Web searches are often more useful than Veronica, particularly if they retrieve sections of documents and not just menu titles.

The Gopher of all Gophers has to be Gopher Jewels at: *http://galaxy.net/GJ/index.html* or
*gopher://cwis.usc.edu/11/other_gophers_
information_resources/gophers_by_subject/
gopher_jewels*

This provides a catalog of Gopher resources and contains over 2000 pointers by category.

Telnet

Telnet is a powerful tool that enables you to log in to a remote computer via the Internet to run programs or access local data. Although its technology is definitely useful, you're probably not going to have much call for it as services move on to the Web and more tasks become automated. Many online games, however, such as the previously discussed MUDs, require you to Telnet to a host before you can play.

Web browsers must be configured to launch a separate Telnet client, in order for Telnet Web links to work. To log on to a remote server, you need only enter the server's address, and then follow the prompts. It may require a login and password, which you should have. If you don't, try hitting return instead. If that doesn't work, you'll either have to go back to where you got the address and get the login details, or learn to hack. The bad news about Telnet is that although you can run it from a GUI client, you can't point and click. That means learning a few UNIX commands.

Ping

If you're having trouble accessing another computer on the Internet, it's useful to check the connection between the two machines. The problem could be that your access provider or server's connection is down, the other machine is offline or busy, or a fault in between.

Ping acts like an Internet Sonar by sending a series of ICMP ECHO_REQUEST packets to the other machine. Packets are numbered to identify dropouts and determine the connection's quality. If the other machine is online, the TCP/IP protocol requires it to respond. If Ping can't get through, nothing will. If no hosts respond, chances are the fault is at your end. If you do get response, by comparing the round trip times, you can tell how well your connection is coping with traffic.

Finger

Finger can be used over the Internet to find information from email addresses. Some mail programs, for example Eudora, come with it built in, but there are also dedicated programs. Not all servers will allow Finger access as it's regarded as a minor security risk. Most systems that support Finger also give users some control over what is said about them. If you'd like to add your own Finger information, speak to your provider or system manager and ask to change your UNIX "plan."

For an example of just what it can do, Finger: *yanoff@alpha2.csd.uwm.edu* for information on how to get the latest Yanoff special Internet connections.

Twinsock/TIA/SLIPknot

If you don't have a full Internet connection, the programs **TIA** (The Internet Adapter), **Twinsock**, and **SLIPknot** work by emulating TCP/IP connections through cheap UNIX shell accounts. They don't provide a genuine IP connection, so you won't be able to do everything, but you will be able to surf the Web at least in a limited fashion with a text-based browser such as Lynx. All these programs do however require that your provider has the host software at its end.

TIA is a commercial product for both Mac and PC, while Twinsock is PC freeware. You can find out more about **Slip** emulation in the newsgroup: *alt.doc.slip-emulators* and more about **TIA** by mailing: *tia-info@marketplace.com*.

Twinsock can be downloaded at: *ftp://oak. oakland.edu/simtel/win3/winsock/twnsck14.zip*

For more about **SLIPknot**, email: *slipknot@micromind.com*

PART TWO

The Guide

World Wide Web
Usenet Newsgroups
Software Roundup

WEB SITES DIRECTORY

Most human (and extra-terrestrial) life has found its place on the World Wide Web, so it doesn't exactly lend itself to categorization. The headings below are those we've adopted to make these listings easier to navigate. Obviously, they blur into each other at the slightest opportunity. So, if you're interested in politics, you'll want to look under "Politics," "Community Groups," "Government," and "News, Newspapers, and Magazines." If you're on for fun, check under "Comedy," "Entertainment," and "Weird," and so on. To search by subject or keyword on the Web, try the tools in our "Internet Search Tools and Directories" section.

A Guide to World Wide Web sites

It's impossible to say exactly how many addresses are accessible from the World Wide Web, but it must be in the millions. That's because the Web is an ever-evolving beast with tentacles reaching into Usenet, Gopher, FTP, and Telnet. It's the most popular part of the Internet and, with its graphic capabilities, the most exciting. In fact, it is a bit like having your own library, including newspapers, magazines, academic journals, and fanzines from just about every obsessive, enthusiast and wacko out there.

Technically, Web site addresses start with the prefix *http:* – anything else, although accessible from the Web, really belongs to another system. What sets the Web apart is its **hypertextual navigation**. Any Web page can link to any other Web page, whether it's on the same system or on the other side of the world, and almost all Web sites contain links to other similar sites as well as to some of general interest.

For example, at the Virtual Pub, you'll find original content as well as links to other beer-related sites. Take one of those links, and you'll probably arrive at another site with links to even more related sites, which might include the one you've just come from. So even though there are only about 500 sites reviewed in the following pages, once you get the swing of it, you'll have access to hundreds of thousands.

Finding what you want

The keys to finding your way around the Web are the Internet search tools and guides. The **search tools** are either indexes compiled by setting robots out on to the Web to retrieve addresses, titles, and document samples, or major digests of links sorted by subject. The **guides** are less extensive but more focused and packed with useful links or advice on specific subjects.

Understand the search tools and accumulate useful guides, and you'll master the Web.

How to get there

To reach a site, taking note of capitalization, carefully enter its address into your browser's **URL** (or "Location") window. You don't need to type the *http://* part if you're using Netscape or other state-of-the-art browsers. First the browser will verify that it's in the right format, then it will go to a name server to be converted to an IP number, the host will be contacted, let you in, and then the page will appear on your browser.

If you don't have the patience to wait for images, choose not to load them. However, you might have to turn them on occasionally to navigate through sites which exclusively use clickable image maps. You'll know when you strike one – it'll have image icons, but no links.

How Web sites work

Web pages contain **links** which stand out from the normal text. Click on them, and something will happen. Most of the time it's like hitting hyperspace on a computer game – they will take you somewhere else. It could be elsewhere on the same page, another page on the site, another site, a newsgroup, an FTP site, a Gopher, or it could open up a Telnet session. Equally, it could initiate the downloading of a file, a sound clip, an image, an animation, or even start up a Real Audio transmission of live music. The possibilities are endless.

How to find it again

When you see something you like, save it to your **bookmarks** or **hotlist**. That way you can access it from your browser's menu at a later date. Alternatively you can save the page to disk. But remember, you have to save the images separately.

When it's not there

Some of these sites will have disappeared, but don't let that deter you. Refer to p.101 for advice on how to find them. The easiest way is to enter the title, and/or related subjects, as keywords into one of the search engines such as InfoSeek, Lycos, or Yahoo (see p.168 for URL addresses of these). Once you've mastered them, you'll be able to find anything.

So, wax up and get out there!

For more on the practicalities of using the World Wide Web, see the section beginning on p.85.

ART, COMICS, AND GRAPHICS

@art gallery

http://gertrude.art.uiuc.edu/@art/gallery.html

This digital art gallery has a new exhibition every six weeks, but don't worry, all the old ones are archived.

17th Digital Picture Archive

http://olt.et.tudelft.nl/fun/pictures/oldpictures.html

A massive digital picture archive of art and graphic downloads, categorized in directories such as art, paintings, comics, computer-generated, faces, nature, technology, space, etc. The pornography section recently closed down due to over demand.

Acid Junkie's Anime

http://www.cyberspace.com/~dixie/

This hard core anime may disturb more than just those whose bedtimes are set by others.

ArtAIDS Link

http://artaids.dcs.qmw.ac.uk:8001/

An Internet equivalent to the AIDS patchwork quilt.
Participation is encouraged: upload your own tribute to this
ever-growing mosaic of love, loss, and memory.

Art on the Net

http://www.art.net/

This gallery provides a well-structured environment to post
your own art or view the creations of others. It's not just
pictures though, there's even a gallery for hackers.

Comics'n'Stuff

http://www.phlab.missouri.edu/HOMES/c617145-www/comix.html

A long address for comic strips, but, as *Wired* magazine put it,
this is "the Web mother lode of Western comics info."

Computer Graphics

http://mambo.ucsc.edu/psl/cg.html

Here's a heavy page to load, but if you're into graphics it's well
worth it. It's a collection of links to numerous computer-
generated art resources, using distinct thumbnails as captions.

Core – Industrial Design Resources

http://www.core77.com/

Are you a budding industrial designer, just waiting for a break?
Maybe you'll find some help here. It provides marketing tips,
employment opportunities, discussion forums, recommended
reading lists, and design school addresses. If you're still stuck,
maybe the student projects from Pratt's design program in New
York will provide some inspiration.

The DRC Virtual Gallery

http://dougal.derby.ac.uk/gallery/

An interesting gallery site, active since June 1994, posting
electronic and public art, a show by photocopy artist Peter
Rowe, and more. Visit and leave your comments.

DTP on the Internet

http://www.cs.purdue.edu/homes/gwp/dtop/dtp.html

An excellent jumplist for graphic artists and designers, pointing
your way to all kinds of DTP resources, like fonts to download.

Infinite Grid

http://sunsite.unc.edu/otis-bin/showgrid

Use the infinite grid selector to tailor this psychedelic collage to your favorite of 12,288,000,000 possible configurations.

Kodak

http://www.kodak.com/

Here's where to find out about Kodak's products, services, and latest developments, particularly its PhotoCD technology. There are digital images in both JPEG and ImagePac formats, as well as the necessary viewing software, for download.

Offworld Metaplex

http://offworld.wwa.com/

The suit greeting you at the entrance would have you believe this is yet another Net mall. Perhaps it will be, but at this stage it's a commercial digital art gallery with the most vivid backdrops and Netscape enhancements you're likely to encounter. It also provides a mirror to the superb Consummate Winsock Applications page.

OTIS

http://sunsite.unc.edu/otis/

OTIS (operative term is stimulate) is an extensive, well-planned gallery of photos, drawings, tattoos, raytraces, video stills, record covers, sculpture, and the like.

Ping Datascape

http://www.artcom.de/ping/mapper

If you can decipher what's going on here, you'll find it's a 3D flight through the Web, to which you can add your own creations. It was originally intended to be used as a television test pattern but seems to have come off the rails.

Rayboys

http://www.world.net/~arki/rayboys.html

Apart from showcasing John Hooper's graphic talents, this is the Net's definitive guide to photo-realistic hyper-reality. Most of these works are created with Persistence of Vision, a shareware ray-tracing package which appeals to those who, rather than drawing, prefer to create images as a sum of their mathematical parts. By setting certain constraints such as surface texture, reflection, refraction, and light source positions, objects can be replicated so closely, they make photographs look phoney.

Sandra's Clip Art Server

http://www.cs.yale.edu/homes/sjl/clipart.html

Somewhere down the artistic spectrum beneath Pierrot dolls, velvet prints, muzak, and butt photocopies, lies clip art. For some reason, these soulless images are often used to inject life into documents and overhead transparencies. If you want your next presentation to look thoroughly canned, dig in here.

Strange Interactions

http://amanda.physics.wisc.edu/show.html

Personal art show by John Jacobsen. This was an early art site on the Web and it's an interesting example of how an artist can showcase their work – in this case, a surreal array of etchings, lithographs, woodcuts, and oils.

The Writing on the Wall

http://www.gatech.edu/desoto/graf/Index.Art_Crimes.html

This diverse collection of international graffiti art makes an eloquent case for its art status.

BANKING

→ See also "Business" and "Finance".

Bank of America

http://bankamerica.com

Locate your nearest Bank of America branch or ATM, apply for a job, or read press releases. The big news is its new service to access and self-manage your account online. Now you can balance your books, monitor check clearances, transfer and stop payments, and view your balance, all via your PC.

Barclaycard Netlink

http://www.barclaycard.co.uk

This is as staid as you would expect from the UK's largest credit card company. In the future it promises serious online features such as credit card applications and help desk support, but at this stage it's just the stuff in the leaflet dispensers.

DigiCash

http://digicash.com

DigiCash are one of the frontrunners in the race to develop an acceptable "smart" currency for Net transactions. Right now, it's all experimental but it hopes its ecash will soon become a global standard. You can register, pick up an electronic wallet of ecash, and use it to purchase various intangibles at hundreds of participating stores around the Net. You won't get anything in return except the satisfaction of helping build the future of commerce.

First Virtual

http://www.fv.com/

First Virtual operates a third party clearing house for Net transactions on electronically transferable items such as software, text, and advice. Participating vendors deliver the goods first. If you're satisfied, you instruct First Virtual to pay. Purchases are accrued and charged against your credit card monthly. Since you phone your credit card details upon joining, no sensitive information ever passes over the Net. Its InfoHaus has hundreds of distributors waiting for your money.

MasterCard International

http://www.mastercard.com/

Mastercard's presence in this attractive array of international
fables, technology exhibits, and shopping links is so gentle and
subdued that you could easily forget you're dealing with a major
financial institution.

Network Payments and Digital Cash

http://ganges.cs.tcd.ie/mepeirce/project.html

Some say paper cash is going the same way as pieces of eight,
sea shells, and salt. Judge for yourself how close we are to
obtaining an alternative global currency or, more urgently, an
acceptable method of completing online transactions.

Visa

http://www.visa.com/visa/

Find out about the future of Visa, electronic banking, its
product range, and your nearest ATM. Will Visa succeed in
achieving "One world, One currency – Visa"? Find out here.

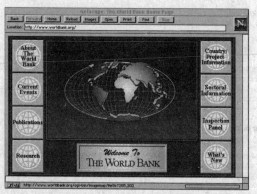

World Bank

http://www.worldbank.org

The World Bank's major role is to help developing countries
reduce poverty and sustain economic growth. These pages

extensively document the bank's projects and aspirations. If you're perplexed by how it can give away so much money and still stay afloat, you might come away a little more enlightened, if not somewhat optimistic for the future.

BOOKS AND BOOKSTORES

Atomic Books

http://www.clark.net/pub/atomicbk/home.html

The bizzaro director of such classics as Pink Flamingos and Hairspray, John Waters, recommends this Baltimore store for its insane books about every kind of extreme. He says it's just like his own library. It's a great place to order such oddities online.

Banned Books

http://www.cs.cmu.edu:8001/Web/People/spok/banned-books.html

This exhibit is presented by Carnegie Mellon University, where the administration recently removed more than 80 sex newsgroups. You can find out which books have been banned or come under attack, and why, by reading the contentious extracts. Many of these titles are now regarded as classics.

Cambridge University Press

http://www.cup.cam.ac.uk

As well as the standard online catalog and publisher's details, there is information about future titles, such as the Cambridge Encyclopedia of the English Language.

Educational Texts

http://www.etext.org/

This archive contains hundreds of thousands of words, ranging from the complete works of Shakespeare to the script of a lost episode of Star Trek. It also has links to similar archives of religious, political, legal, and fanzine text.

Elsevier Science

http://www.elsevier.nl

Elsevier claims to be the world's leading supplier of scientific information. On board is a comprehensive list of journals, publications, and multimedia products, plus reviews and

ordering facilities. Links include an excellent science Gopher
and the WWW 94 conference proceedings at CERN.

Future Fantasy Bookstore

http://futfan.com/home.html

Palo Alto's Future Fantasy Bookstore specializes in fantasy,
horror, science fiction, and mystery books. You can search
through its online library and if anything takes your fancy,
order it by email.

Kegan Paul International

http://www.demon.co.uk/keganpaul/

A neat web site where you can order Kegan Paul's works on and
from the Middle East, Africa, Japan, and Asia. There are also
some fascinating snippets of news from these regions.

Laissez-Faire Books

http://www.xmission.com/~legalize/lf/Laissez-Faire.html

Laissez-Faire has been a source of libertarian books and tapes
for twenty years. It offers titles by the likes of Ayn Rand,
Thomas Jefferson, Ludwig von Mises, P.J. O'Rourke, Milton
Friedman, Thomas Szasz, and, of course, Adam Smith, on topics
like education, drug policy, gun control, objectivism, free
marketeering, economics, and humor. You can email order from
anywhere in the world.

Loompanics

gopher://gopher.well.sf.ca.us/00/Business/catalog.asc

It's best to save this long, single page catalog as a text file, and
read it off line. It's crammed with reviews and ordering details
of subversive, strange, and even downright nasty gems of
anarchic and alternative writing.

Macmillan USA

http://www.mcp.com/

The Macmillan USA Information SuperLibrary goes farther than
most publishers, not only providing a searchable titlebase, new
releases, and discounted email order, but putting searchable
contents pages and full chapter samples for many of its
thousands of books online. What's more, you can download
copies of any software included with their computer titles, here
or from its FTP site.

Online Books

http://www.cs.cmu.edu/Web/books.html

There are complete texts tucked away in obscure archives all over the Net. Here's an index of about a thousand titles as well as links to almost one hundred specialist repositories.

Online Bookshop

http://www.bookshop.co.uk/

This claims to be the biggest online bookstore in the world, with over 750,000 titles available from a myriad of publishers such as Penguin, McGraw Hill, Butterworth, and Oxford University Press. And that's without including all the other bookstores it's linked to, all cross-referenced by subject, with synopses and links to related material. Some are available through its central ordering mechanism and others direct from their publishers.

Outpost: Culture

http://www.outpost.calnet.com/outpost.html

Homepage for the Inland Book Company – a US distributor of over 2000 small presses. It features discussion pages, plus links to many of the presses, and to bookstores which stock the titles. Lots of good stuff.

Penguin Books

http://www.Penguin.com or http://www.Penguin.co.uk

The US and UK Penguin companies have separate Web sites,
each worth exploration. Penguin UK promises to post first
chapters of all its new fiction titles – a fabulous idea if it follows
through. There are also links to publishers distributed by
Penguin, such as, uhh, the very wonderful Rough Guides.

Project Gutenburg

http://jg.cso.uiuc.edu/PG/welcome.html

Fifty years after authors die, their copyrights pass into the
public domain. With this in mind, Project Gutenburg is
dedicated to making as many works available online as possible
in plain vanilla ascii text. Not all the books are old; some, such
as computer texts, have been donated.

Sun Tzu's The Art of War

http://www.cnu.edu/~patrick/taoism/suntzu/suntzu.html

Discover Sun Tzu's *The Art of War*, with or without a guide. At
2400 years old, it's believed to be the world's oldest military
treatise. Like other Chinese wisdoms such as the teachings of
Confucius, much of it still rings true and its adages can be
applied to any conflict. So much so, that it became the Yuppies'
surrogate bible. Oh well, battles do have their casualties.

Ventana

http://www.vmedia.com/

Order online from Ventana's range of popular computer texts, or
download programs from its companion disks. There's also a
useful archive of DTP, Internet, and AutoCAD shareware.

BUSINESS

Africa Commercial

http://www.africa.com/

This is a Cape Town service to encourage business with and
within the newly acceptable South Africa. The facilities are in
place, but at this stage not many have taken up the offer. If you
want to do business in this region, or are curious about
opportunities and protocol, it's a place to put your feelers out.

Barcode Server

http://www.milk.com/barcode/

Not only can you find out how bar codes work, you can even generate your own.

Business Index

http://www.dis.strath.ac.uk/business/index.html

A useful annotated guide to business information sources across the Web, maintained by Scottish university, Strathclyde.

CommerceNet

http://www.commerce.net

CommerceNet is a not-for-profit consortium of companies which have come together to ease the transition on to the Net. If you're planning to set up on the Web, you might find this a useful resource for news, advice, and contacts.

Cyberpreneur's Internet Guide

http://asa.ugl.lib.umich.edu/chdocs/cyberpreneur/Cyber.html

Links to tips for new players in Net commerce.

Direct Marketing World

http://mainsail.com/dmworld.htm

Direct marketing resources such as lists, list-builders, copywriters, consultants, and agencies. There's a growing employment section, literature for sale, and guides to direct marketing on the Internet.

FedEx

http://www.fedex.com/

Federal Express has revolutionized the way companies haul freight, take orders, and service customers. This foray into online parcel tracking marks yet another industry first.

Friends and Partners

http://solar.rtd.utk.edu/friends/home.html

This US–Russian joint venture aims to create a better understanding between the two nations. There is plenty of info on topics such as economics, education, geography, music, weather, and health, plus a literature section which contains the full text of The Brothers Karamazov and Anna Karenina. It's primary focus however is encouraging trade.

Internet Business Resource Directory

http://www.netsurf.com/nsf/v01/02/resource/index.html

ISPs, business directories and publications, advertising
agencies, lawyers, bankers, venture capitalists, and other
commercial resources to help get your outfit flying on the Net.

Sony

http://www.sony.com/

This US site of the Japanese electronic and multimedia giant
features news, service and support, product information and
material from its huge stable of film, music, broadcast,
publishing, video, games, and electronic interests. For instance,
you can get full biographies, discographies, and in some cases
audio clips from its artists, who include the likes of the Boo
Radleys, Trans Global Underground, and St Etienne.

COMEDY

Bonk Industries

http://www.telegate.se/bonk/

In a subtle satire of corporate propaganda, Bonk highlights how
we are conditioned to accept unethical business practices when
they're cloaked in the right language.

Cathouse British Comedy Pages

http://cathouse.org/BritishComedy/

Links to a multitude of British comedy archives and Web sites
such as the Goons, Alan Partridge, Absolutely Fabulous, Fist of
Fun, Blackadder, Stephen Fry, and Private Eye.

LaughWeb

http://www.misty.com/laughweb

You'd have to be pretty miserable if you can't get a smirk here.

Milk Kommunications

http://www.milk.com/

A selection of incredible or shameful but true stories, anecdotes,
and jokes well worth a place on your bookmarks. Don't miss the
original name-change press release from the artist formerly
named after a dog.

Quote Generator

http://www.ugcs.caltech.edu/~werdna/fun.html

Get a random quote from such sources as Dan Quayle, Dr Who, Webster's, Zippy, Arnie, and your mom.

Spatula City

http://www.wam.umd.edu/~twoflowr/index.html

If you're a fan of 3D rendering, you'll probably overlook the inanity of the gags hidden in this collection of pointedly and pointlessly odd pages. Don't push the big button that really doesn't do anything.

Stevec's UUUUUU

http://ftp.std.com/homepages/stevec/index1.html

This set of very original and often funny gags is more sophisticated than most individual home pages.

COMMUNITY GROUPS

Black Information Network

http://www.bin.com

This not-for-profit organization concerned with promoting educational, recreational, social, and supportive communication within the African-American community has produced a very pretty and polished if somewhat staid site.

MIT Arab Student Organization

http://www.mit.edu:8001/activities/arab/homepage.html

If you've been looking for pointers to Arabic pages, this is your lucky day. Here are links to Arabic software suppliers, student groups, cultural organizations, reference works, photo libraries, Middle Eastern servers, and other Arabic pages, sorted by country of origin.

Queer Resources Directory

http://www.qrd.org/qrd/

AIDs, legal news, attitude trends, clubs, publications, broadcasts, images, political action, community groups, etc.

COMPUTER HARDWARE

Apple

http://www.apple.com

A plethora of information and resources – everything from
Apple's press releases through to current product information,
technical support, and developer data, together with links to
other Internet sites that hold Apple-related information.

Compaq

http://www.compaq.com

Product literature, software, and support for Compaq machines.

Dell

http://www.us.dell.com

Dell provides online access to its spare parts, technical support,
BBS files, catalogs, press releases, and international phone list.
The site has all the charm of an accounting firm's year-end
report, but if you use Dell and need help, it's useful enough.

Hewlett-Packard

http://www.hp.com

Product support, literature, tutorials, drivers, and patches for
HP's products.

IBM

http://www.ibm.com   http://www.ibm.net

Key the first address to find out what's going on in IBM's
corporate world – including full info on their OS/2 Warp
operating system for easy Web access. The "net" address
features details of IBM's Global Network, plus a helpful set of
tutorials and links to get you started on the Net.

Silicon Graphics

http://www.sgi.com/

Silicon Graphics' stylish site has all the corporate and product
resources you'd expect plus demonstrations and samples of what
its high-end graphics workstations can do. That makes it quite a
bit more entertaining than the usual hardware manufacturers'
pages. For example, check out Surf Zone, for a taste of what's to
come in virtual reality.

Sun Microsystems

http://www.sun.com/

Sun is the Net's biggest hardware player and a major sponsor in the development and use of new Net technology, including the much-talked-about "Hot Java" – an animation program demonstrated on these pages. Sun's globally scattered sites also provide easy access to public domain software, government information, product support, and hundreds of innovative projects such as the Sunergy broadcasts and Internet radio.

COMPUTER SOFTWARE

Adobe Systems Inc

http://www.adobe.com

Apart from information and support on Adobe's desktop publishing software, this site offers an opportunity to download its free Acrobat reader which will enable you to view the increasingly popular PDF (portable document format) files. It also has links to a multitude of other sites, such as the New York Timesfax, which use the format.

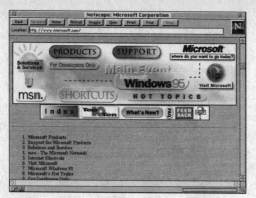

Microsoft

http://www.microsoft.com

Microsoft never goes about its business in half measures. Consequently this site is crammed with documentation, downloadable files, updates, development tools, and reams of Softie news. However you can't help feeling that its own Microsoft Network will become the focal route for support.

Software.net

http://software.net/

The time can't be far off when it's standard practice to distribute commercial software either via a secured Internet connection or by direct dial access. Software.net is close to achieving this here, with several titles for download through a secured link. Most, though, are conventionally boxed for Fedex delivery.

Symantec

http://www.symantec.com

Free software, updates, and support on Symantec/Norton's award-winning virus checking and disk management utilities.

Virtual Shareware Library

http://audrey.fagg.uni-lj.si/cgi-bin/shase/Form

This Slovenian shareware database overcomes one of Archie's shortcomings, by enabling you to search through file descriptions as well as names. It includes many renowned FTP archives such as Microsoft, CICA, Linux, and InfoMac. Once you've found your file, just click to retrieve it.

The Windows Internet Headquarters

http://www.windows95.com/

The transition onto Windows 95 is nowhere near as easy as Microsoft would have you believe. This outstanding site is chocked with online tutorials, tips, advice, and 32-bit software pointers to help ease the pain.

EDUCATION AND KIDS' STUFF

Animal Information Database

http://www.bev.net/education/SeaWorld/homepage.html

This Sea World USA database is an educational service for teachers and children. It includes information, games, teaching guides, and quizzes about animals children love, such as whales, dolphins, dugongs, gorillas, lions, tigers, and walruses. Its interactivity attempts to inject some fun into learning.

The Human Languages Page

http://www.willamette.edu/~tjones/Language-Page.html

The Web is a great place for language learning tools, and there's a lot of activity in the area. This is a good first stop, with links to texts available on the net in different languages, and to language learning pages, from Japanese to Klingon.

Interactive Frog Dissection

http://curry.edschool.virginia.edu/~insttech/frog

This step-by-step frog disembowelment is one of the Web's most popular and talked about sites. It might be because it's educational, interactive, and finely detailed, but more likely because it's so gruesome. All you have to do is set up your frog, grab your scalpel, and follow the pictures.

Kids Web

http://www.npac.syr.edu/textbook/kidsweb/

Choose from a range of 19 main subject categories of educational interest. Don't be put off by the kids emphasis:

there's something here for allcomers. Other links include instructions on how to set up a Web server in your classroom and a collection of other sites set up for children.

Make a Map

http://ellesmere.ccm.emr.ca/wnaismap/naismap.html

Tailor-make your own Canadian map. You can specify all sorts of multiple constraints, layers and relief projections, political boundaries, geological provinces, even the grizzly bear range.

Math Magic Activities

http://www.scri.fsu.edu/~dennisl/topics/math_magic.html

Card, rope, and calculation tricks that require no mirrors, just a basic understanding of mathematical principles.

EMPLOYMENT

America's Job Bank

http://www.ajb.dni.us/

America's Job Bank links over 1,800 US state Employment Service offices and lists over 100,000 vacancies. And because it's a state project it's free for all.

CareerMosaic

http://www.careermosaic.com/

Search for vacancies in a rapidly growing field of heavyweight clients, such as Chemical Bank, Intel and National Semiconductor, or through opportunities posted in Usenet. As with most employment sites, there's plenty of advice on resumes, career trends, and salaries. Each client has its own set of pages with extensive details on its conditions and activities.

Interactive Employment

http://www.espan.com/

There are supposedly thousands of jobs on offer here, but its database has such a clumsy interface it's hard to know.

Jobs at Microsoft

http://www.microsoft.com/Jobs/

Join Big Brother's march across the globe.

Monster Board

http://www.monster.com/

Search for professional employment in the US and abroad.

Price Jamieson

http://www.gold.net/PriceJam/

This international recruitment agency eventually intends to place all its professional job listings online, updating them at least weekly. After you've qualified by sending in your CV, with a bit of luck, they'll call you in.

Reed

http://www.reed.pipex.com/reed/

Post your CV and apply for positions with Reed, the UK's largest employment agent. It caters to a broad spectrum of vocations such as nursing, computing, catering, accounting, driving, charity, insurance, and project management.

Virtual Headroom

http://www.xmission.com/~wintrnx/virtual.html

Post your headshot and resume here and take a shortcut to the stars. It'll cost you to post but not to scout for talent. And then there's the couch to deal with.

ENTERTAINMENT

A Thousand Points of Sites

http://inls.ucsd.edu/y/OhBoy/randomjump1.html

Go blindly where ye have not been before.

Ask Joe

http://fishwrap.mit.edu/News/AskJoe/AskJoe.html

You can ask Joe anything, and, if he feels like it, this MIT chemistry student will answer. You can read past questions and answers in the archives to estimate his competence.

Astrology

http://www.realitycom.com/cybstars/stars.html

Look here for weekly updated astrological predictions,

astrology FAQs, and links to other soothsayers. There's still no forecast for the thirteenth sign.

The Avenger's Handbook

`http://www.cs.uit.no/~paalde/Revenge/index.html`

There'll be no more Mr. Nice Guy once you've paid a visit to this armory of extreme nastiness. Much of it is compiled from the archives of the Usenet group *alt.revenge*, the definitive meeting place for suburban terrorists. It includes vicious programs, things to do before you quit your job, school pranks, and oodles of treacherous anecdotes about getting even. John Steed would never stoop this low.

Bianca's Smut Shack

`http://bianca.com/shack/index.html`

Bianca's shack is an absolute labyrinth of surprises, trap doors, and vulgarities. To explain too much would spoil some of the effect, but be warned the deeper you go, the darker and more revealing it gets.

Build a Card

`http://infopages.com/card/`

Compete for the tackiest virtual Valentine or greeting card, with this ingenious step-by-step online art studio.

Cyberia

`http://www.easynet.co.uk/pages/cafe/`

Cyberia is a very hip London net café, and its home page links to fun spots such as art galleries, astrological forecasts, cool sites, museums, film databases, music pages, UK guides, a virtual nightclub, sports pages, campaigns, and even a dating agency.

Doug and Lisa's Disneyland

`http://www.best.com/~dijon/disney/index.html`

Trip through the parks, comics, films, and works of the Disney empire courtesy of two of its most dedicated fans. You can even find out where all the subliminal Mickeys are hidden around Disneyland. Surely, you must want to know that.

I-Ching

`http://cad.ucla.edu:8001/iching`

If you're not happy with your fortune as told by this interpretation of the Chinese I-Ching, you can always reload and get another one.

Internet Casino

`http://www.casino.org`

This online casino caused quite a legal stir when it announced it would be opening a Bahamian gambling haven to anyone on the Internet. While it doesn't encourage you to break the gambling laws of your state, it does automatically deposit your funds into an offshore account and will even pay for your connection if you're a high enough roller.

Kellner's Fireworks

`http://www.kellfire.com/fireworks.html`

Kellner has been in the fireworks game for almost fifty years and will ship to anywhere in the world. You can order its catalog online, but not its products.

Lego Home Page

`http://legowww.homepages.com/`

It's a bit too good for just the kiddies, Lego. Surfing through these pages of robots, raytraced models, production line updates and other Legophernalia will make you yearn for those bygone days of playing with plastic blocks.

Lockpicking

`http://www.lysator.liu.se/mit-guide/mit-guide.html`

Thanks to the great minds at MIT, an indispensible illustrated lock-picking guide for potential felons. They laughed when I told them I was learning to burgle, but when they came home...

London Club Guide

http://www.spods.dcs.kcl.ac.uk/~henerz/londonclubguide

Stay in touch with where it's at in London's dynamic club scene.

Paddynet

http://www.paddynet.ie/

This Dublin-based online service is a combined effort of over 25 international Web weavers. It's being sponsored by the black brew to provide a place for Irish creatives to air their works. In line with Guinness's general marketing plan, expect obtusity and froth at every turn.

Penn and Teller

http://www.solinas.com/penn-n-teller/

While, regrettably, the Penn and Teller input here is fairly minimal, it has enough links to other magic and entertainment sites, including other Penn and Teller exhibits, to make it worth the visit. Although you can't email the duo directly, it does offer a forwarding service.

The Postcard Store

http://postcards.www.media.mit.edu/Postcards/

This is a novel way to send a groovy e-postcard. You pick a card and the server emails the recipient a Pin number to collect the card from the site's pick-up window.

Practical Jokes

http://www.umd.umich.edu/~nhughes/htmldocs/pracjokes.html

This collection of larks and laughs at the expense of others has been compiled from the Usenet archives of *alt.shenanigans*

Rome Lab Snowball Camera

http://www.rl.af.mil:8001/Odds-n-Ends/sbcam/rlsbcam.html

Step right up and try your luck throwing virtual snowballs at Rome Laboratory's engineers.

Starwave

http://www.starwave.com/

It can't be long before this taste of Starwave's multimedia plans develops into something bigger and more commercial. So far it includes sports, family, showbiz, and outdoors sections, as well as Ticketmaster Online.

Trading Card Dealers

http://www.webshop.com/collectors/cards/dealers/

Find that elusive baseball, football, or phone card, using this US dealer directory.

Tarot Information

http://cad.ucla.edu/repository/useful/tarot.html

Choose from a short three-card tarot reading or the full Keltic cross. Even if you think it's solid nugget it can still leave you feeling quite unsettled.

Underground/Underfed

http://www.bazaar.com/

If you want to pick up the Cool Site of the Day award, look here for inspiration. So far, it's picked up seven awards for its individual exhibits such as Megadeth, Lollapalooza, Rocktropolis, OscarNet, the Beatles, and Crash Site. But there's still more where they came from, mostly with a music bent, and and all rich in multimedia treats.

Voice Synthesizer

http://wwwtios.cs.utwente.nl/say/

Enter your profanity, hit return, and wait for the response to be automatically launched by your sound player for the mirth of all within earshot. If you try spelling words phonetically you may get a greater success rate.

Web Voyeur

http://www.eskimo.com/~irving/web-voyeur.html

Spend a night peeping through the Net's many cameras, then go to bed safe in the knowledge that you've sat with pioneers at the very cutting edge of technology. Now, check that off the list and get on with your life.

Zodiac Forecasts

http://www.metawire.com/stars/

The UK Daily Mail's Jonathan Cainer presents free daily forecasts in text or Real Audio.

EZINES

Ezine-List

`http://www.meer.net/~johnl/e-zine-list/index.html`

While this is widely regarded as the Net's definitive source for
Ezine links and reviews, it's not that well organized. Each
review has its own page, so it'll take you forever to scan through
all 500-odd. It might be more practical to download the entire
text version and read it offline.

FiX Magazine

`http://www.widemedia.com/FiX/docs/`

This UK lifestyle ezine has stories on sex, travel, music, fashion
and health as well as free online counseling, a 48-hour dream
analysis service, and a soap opera about life in the slow lane
called Boozers. It's irreverent, stylish, and claims to be the
"world's widest magazine."

HotWired

`http://www.hotwired.com`

Hotwired's hipness could only be rivaled by its hard copy
brother *Wired* magazine (whose back issues it archives). It
carries consistently clear, well-written articles on the stylish
edge of the techno-recreation age, covering commerce, travel,
new journalism, gossip, music, and the arts. Plus, its Worldbeat

section features a joint venture with Rough Guides, making available our entire USA guide (more to follow), complete with hypertext links across the continent. All this – and it's free.

Phrack Magazine

http://freeside.com/phrack.html

Phrack magazine has printed controversial articles for the hacker community since 1985. You can download or browse back issues and subscribe free to the quarterly.

Psyche Journal

http://psyche.cs.monash.edu.au/

An electronic interdisciplinary journal of consciousness research with articles, commentaries, and book reviews on such subjects as vagueness, semantics, the language of thought, delineating conscious processes, and contrastive analysis. When you've figured that lot out, you can try the links to other philosophical Gophers and resources.

Urban Desires

http://desires.com/

Billing itself as an interactive magazine of metropolitan pleasures, this glossy modern ezine really delivers. It has well-written modern city stories on technology, eating, sex, music, art, performance, style, politics, and more.

FASHION

Fashion Page

http://www.charm.net/~jakec

The Web is not yet ready for traditional fashion mags – they're just too image dependent for low bandwidth users to tolerate. This site favors a more textual approach than your average fashion rag. It's a little like hearing about it on the radio.

Ntouch

http://www.dircon.co.uk/lcf/ntouch.html

This offering from students of the London College of Fashion is arty and cutting edge – and Net-friendly, posting essays illustrated with light graphics. You may well see it first here.

Thread Web

http://www.widemedia.com/threads

Thread Web's clickable map takes you to the UK's top fashion
designers, recognized design courses, upcoming events on the
British catwalk calendar, and other sites to keep you in vogue.

FILM AND TV

BBC

http://www.bbcnc.org.uk/

This general information service on the BBC's broadcasting
schedules and activities is growing at a meteoric rate. It seems
every troupe in the Beeb's massive media circus is scrambling to
find its niche on the Net. There's public access to TV and radio
listings, educational resources, online projects, album charts,
and even Radio 1's playlist and rotation schedules. So far,
unfortunately, no BBC newswires.

Beavis And Butthead

http://calvin.hsc.colorado.edu/

Not only does this rabid fan of the dysfunctional duo have
nothing to do with MTV, he uses this page to vent spleen against
its programmers. Apart from that, there's an entertaining
selection of B&B gossip, extracts, and episode guides.

Buena Vista Pictures

http://bvp.wdp.com/BVPM/

Preview forthcoming Touchstone, Disney, and Hollywood films.
All have short synopses, minute-long sample clips, interviews,
and assorted press releases.

Capt James T Kirk Sing-a-Long

http://www.ama.caltech.edu/~mrm/kirk.html

Audio excerpts from William Shatner's bold vinyl masterpiece
"The Transformed Man." Inspiring stuff!

Channel 4 TV

http://www.cityscape.co.uk/channel4/

Home page of the UK's Channel Four broadcasting – which
includes some of the most adventurous programming around.

FBI X-Files Division

http://www.ssc.com/~roland/x-files/x-files.html

This improbable television drama has stimulated more online discussion than any other non-sexual, non-computing, non-Kurt Cobain-topping-himself topic. Find out whether Scully ever wakes up to the fact that Mulder's always right.

Hong Kong Movies Home Page

http://www.mdstud.chalmers.se/hkmovie/

Get to know the action director's director John Woo's catalog, plans and regular actors such as the genius Chow Yun Fat. If you've seen any of his gems such as "Hard Boiled," or "God of Gamblers," you'll know why he's received such cult notoriety. But it's not all Woo and Fat, there's much more, including a searchable database, movie clips, pictures, FAQs, interviews, news Gophers, and even the Hong Kong Popstars Archive.

Internet Movie Database

http://www.cm.cf.ac.uk/Movies

An exceptional relational database of movie, cast, and review information. Selections can be cross-referenced to find an actor's complete biography by clicking on their name in another cast list. Most films are rated by online voting and you can add your own reviews. Definitely one to check out.

Les Simpsons

http://www.unantes.univ-nantes.fr/~elek/simpson.html

Listen to how the French have to hear Homer, El Barto, et al, and maybe you'll go a bit easier on them in future.

MCA/Universal Cyberwalk

http://www.mca.com

See what the MCA/Universal movie and music stable has in store this season. All sorts of fun promotional gimmicks like being able to interview the stars by email, or download short clips.

Power Rangers

http://kilp.media.mit.edu:8001/power/homepage.html

Save this one for when a certain noisy junior Power Ranger interferes with your hangover. Point their head this way while you go back to bed. Downloading all the heavy graphics, at say 2400bps, should give you ample time for some shut-eye.

Soap Links

http://www.cts.com/~jeffmj/soaps.html

Keep up with who's doing what to whom, who they told, and
who shouldn't find out, in the surreal world of soap fiction.

The Picture Palace

http://www.ids.net/picpal/

Only weird, daring, and truly offbeat films get shelf space in
this online video store. Each film has a short review and some
have images and sound samples. There's some really choice gear
in the Exploitation, RIP, Japanimation, Hong Kong, Horror, and
Film Noir genres. Have your credit card ready.

The Simpsons

http://www.tiac.net/users/jimt/simp/simpage.html

There's no shortage of Simpsons sites – you can get to several
from here. Then you'll be able to listen to Homer drool "Two all-
beef patties, special sauce..." and the like. The stills and
animations are as good as you would expect and the sound files
have a certain cutesiness which true fans will tirelessly enjoy.

TV Net

http://tvnet.com/

This site has as close to everything televisual as is mentally
healthy. That includes places to vent your gripes, email
addresses, and home pages of broadcasting networks, schedules,
job vacancies, and links to fan pages of just about every show
ever made. By the time you get through this lot, you'll be lucky
to have any time left for the neon bucket itself.

What Miles is Watching

http://www.csua.berkeley.edu/~milesm/ontv.html

So what is Miles watching on TV? Tune in to see the current
screen shots. Although, shouldn't you be out making friends?

FINANCE

Current Oil and Gas Quotes

http://baervan.nmt.edu/prices/current.html

Get the latest spot and future prices on oil and gas.

DowVision

http://dowvision.wais.net/

Dowvision is a press clipping service from Dow Jones and WAIS, including the full text of the *Wall Street Journal*, *Dow Jones News*, *Japan Economic Newswire*, *Canada Newswire*, *Business Wire*, *PR Newswire*, *Investext Abstracts*, and *Professional Investor Report*. It's presently in a free beta phase, but it plans eventually to charge.

Experimental Stock Data

http://www.ai.mit.edu/stocks/

Not all the S&P 500 stock prices are available but there's still a generous amount for a free experimental service. You can generate daily price/volume charts or download at least a year's back-data for import into your own analysis package.

PAWWS, Wall Street on the Internet

http://pawws.secapl.com/

Why pay for North American stock quotes when you can get them free at this online portfolio manager? You can make your own technical prophecies, based on its quarter-hourly updated index charts, or try your hand at fund building in the portfolio challenge. The more meaty stuff is in the subscription service, which offers online brokerage, portfolio management, real-time quotes, research, and all the other services you would expect from a stockbroker.

QuoteCom

http://www.quote.com

Unless you're willing to pay, this service will only supply a few free quotes per day. Once you join, however, you can access a vast spectrum of international securities and services. There is a rudimentary charting package but nothing to satisfy fans of Gann, Candlestick, or Elliot theory. As there's plenty of dial-up competition in this market, shop around first, and avoid paying for too much historical data, as you can probably swing some for free if you put your feelers out in Usenet.

Shareholder Action Handbook

http://www.bath.ac.uk/Centres/Ethical/Share/

When you buy shares in a public company, it gives you certain voting rights. By putting the entire text of the Shareholder

Action Handbook online, this site hopes that you'll exercise those rights to the benefit of your community.

Stocks and Commodities

http://www.onr.com/stocks.html

More and more financial data is becoming available on the Web every day. Much of it, though, relates to stocks trading on the NYSE. Here are links to such industry identities as J. P. Morgan, the CME, and Holt's Stock Market Report.

TaxNet

http://www.purple.co.uk/purplet/tax.html

Get free help with filling out your UK tax claim.

Wall Street Direct

http://www.cts.com/~wallst/

Technical analysts contend that market prices reflect fear and greed or supply and demand rather than inherent fundamental value. Extreme wings such as Elliott wavists believe that the indices follow predestined cycles, or mass psychological trends, which unwittingly requires certain spiritual assumptions. It can seem far fetched and complex, but investing without understanding at least a few basic tenets is akin to reckless gambling. This site should help point you in the right direction.

FOOD AND DRINK

Celestial Seasonings

http://usa.net/celestial/

Unless you live in the US, you won't be able to order from Celestial Seasonings' diverse range of exotically flavored teas, tea related gifts and apparel. But you'll know what to look out for at the supermarket.

Chile-Heads

http://www.netimages.com/~chile/

Dip into Chile recipes, chemistry, botanical facts, gardening tips, and some general blurb. You can find out what's the hottest pepper, what makes it hot, how your body reacts, and identify that mystery one in your kebab.

FREE TRIAL OFFER

Internet

The Essential Monthly Guide to the Internet

[**& great subscription savings!**]

Whoever you are, whatever your interest in the Internet, there's only one monthly magazine that's essential reading: **Internet.**

See for yourself with this free sample copy offer.

Fill in your details below and post or fax them to:
Internet Magazine Subscription Offer, FREEPOST KE 7001,
EMAP Computing, Greater London House, Hampstead Road,
London NW1 7BR. Fax no. 0171-388 2620

---

*Please send me a free sample copy of **Internet**, together with details of the special subscription offer for Rough Guide readers.*

Name: _____

Address: _____

_____

_____Postcode: _____

Email address: _____

RUFF   See our subscription offer at **http://www.emap.co.uk**

Internet Magazine
Subscription Offer
FREEPOST KE 7001
EMAP Computing
Greater London House
Hampstead Road
London NW1 7BR

No stamp
required if
posted in
the UK.

Welcome to the NEW Chocolate Lover's Playground!

Godiva Shopping

What's New?

GODIVA
Chocolatier

Summer Delights

Recipes

Chocolatier
A TASTE OF THE GOOD LIFE

Chocolate Resources

Caramel
The consummate candy
Feature

[Godiva] [Shopping] [Chocolatier] [Feature] [Recipes] [Seasonal] [New] [Resources]

Document : Done.

Chocolate Lover's Playground

http://www.godiva.com/

This page almost hurts, with its mouth watering chocolate recipes and meanderings into chocoholism. It delivers, but only within the US.

London Pubs Reviewed

http://www.cs.ucl.ac.uk/misc/uk/london/pubs/index.html

Find out why Londoners practically live in their locals. You can even add your own, if it's not already there.

Over the Coffee

http://www.infonet.net/showcase/coffee/

Enough coffee trivia, mail order firms, reviews, anecdotes, and links to similarly minded sites to keep any addict happy.

Pizza Net

http://www2.ecst.csuchico.edu/~pizza/

What a shame this experimental and example-setting online pizza delivery service only delivers graphic facsimiles and not the real McCoy. Wouldn't it be great to sit down to a piping hot feast of bugs, bolts, kittens, hammers, footballs, goblins, and some of the other paraphernalia on the menu? Nevertheless, it does lay the foundation for a successful fast food scheme.

PizzaNet

http://www.pizzahut.com

This pioneering service is becoming as famous as the Internet itself, even though it can only deliver in California. However, the server is way over in Kansas so there's no reason why this electronic storefront should not come to a Pizza Hut near you. If it turns out to be profitable, that is.

Spencer's Beer

http://guraldi.itn.med.umich.edu/Beer/

Here's the place to find find out how to perfect your brew. It carries several hypertext home-brew recipe books, including the entire Cat's Meow series. Bottle-spotters will be thrilled to find a gallery of 228 labels displayed in 128 shimmering colors.

Tasty Insect Recipes

http://www.public.iastate.edu/~entomology/InsectsAsFood.html

Dig in to such delights as Bug Blox, Banana Worm Bread, and Chocolate Chirpie Chip Cookies (with crickets).

Virtual Pub

http://lager.geo.brown.edu:8080/virtual-pub

Don't expect to read tales such as waking up naked in a strange room with a throbbing head and a hazy recollection of pranging your car. In this virtual pub, beer is treated with dewey-eyed respect, with everything down to the specific gravity.

Wine Net

http://wine.net/index.html

Join in wine forums or link to vineyards, vendors, clubs, and wine fanciers' pages.

GAMES

Carlos' Colouring Book

http://robot0.ge.uiuc.edu/~carlosp/color/

Useless as they are, sites like these can be fun. In this case, you select a segment of a picture, choose a color, and shade it in. You can do one at a time or a batch, and it's destined to inspire a whole new generation of interactivity.

The Chess Server

http://www.willamette.edu/~tjones/chessmain.html

Find and play a live opponent (with any number of spectators)
on this experimental chess server. Its realistic graphical
interface makes a pleasant change from the alphanumeric
displays on BBSs.

Connect 4

http://csclub.uwaterloo.ca/u/kppomaki/c4/

Challenge the computer to connect four, or any number for that
matter. For tips on how to beat the system, read Victor Allis's
master's thesis on expert play.

Doom WWW

http://www.ping.de/~sven/doom/

Billed as the best place to make new enemies, this site acts as a
dating service to meet other Doom addicts, so you can hunt
them down and kill them via your modem. If you don't fancy
killing fellow players, you can always join forces and go into
battle together.

Fractal Explorer

http://www.vis.colostate.edu/~user1209/fractals/mandel.html

A fractal is a complex self-similar and chaotic mathematical
object which reveals more detail as you get closer. You can
explore the most famous example of these, the Mandelbrot set,
by changing the color palette and zooming in by clicking on the
image. Even if you can't understand how this complex iteration
works, you can still generate wild graphics.

The Games Domain

http://wcl-rs.bham.ac.uk/GamesDomain

Whether you're after full games, demos patches, hints, cheats,
reviews, or gamezines, this must be your first stop. It's
crammed.

Graffiti Capital

http://darkwing.uoregon.edu/~econpeer/graffiti/graff.html

Spray your thoughts in HTML for all the Web to enjoy. Like all
graffiti, it'll get wiped off and sprayed over by someone else
sooner or later.

Interactive Web Games

http://www.yahoo.com/Recreation/Games/Internet_Games/

Interactive_Web_Games/

Pit your wits against the computer or remote opponents on a whole variety of games.

Lite-Bright

http://www.galcit.caltech.edu/~ta/lb/lb.html

This is fun. You insert colored pegs into a board, one color at a time, to create a pretty picture. After you've finished, you can title it and then submit it to the gallery for others to admire. Hours of gainful employment.

Mr Edible Starchy Tuber Head

http://winnie.acsu.buffalo.edu/potatoe/

Create your own customized Mr. Potato Head.

Play Battleships

http://manor.york.ac.uk/htdocs/bships.html

A one-way game of battleships against the computer. There is a way to cheat – see if you can work it out.

The Riddler

http://www.riddler.com

The idea of this online scavenging hunt is to rove around the Web, picking up clues to answer a cryptic riddle. First with the answer wins a cash prize. All player, however, get exposed to some advertising.

Sega

http://www.segaoa.com

News, special events, promotions, new releases, hints, product descriptions, screen shots, audio/video clips, and support for Sega computer games.

The Talker

http://www2.infi.net:80/talker/

Choose an icon, alias, and attitude and bluff your way through this virtual party. Bear in mind that whoever else you meet must have little else to do.

GOVERNMENT

CCTA Government Information

http://www.open.gov.uk/

If you're looking for information on any UK government authority, here's where to come. Just go to its colossal directory, scan down the list, make your choice, and before long you'll be nodding off, just as if you were actually there.

CIA Factbook on Intelligence

http://www.odci.gov/cia

Find out about the CIA's role in international affairs, the intelligence cycle, its history, and real estate. But that's not what you're after is it? You've seen it on the movies and read about it in the *Weekly World News*. You want to know about political assassinations, arms deals, Latin American drug trades, spy satellites, conspiracy theories, phone tapping, covert operations, government-sponsored alien sex cults, and the X files. You must have the wrong CIA.

Declassified Satellite Photos

http://edcwww.cr.usgs.gov/dclass/dclass.html

This is what you've been expecting to stumble across on the Net: the first spy pictures taken from satellites and then dropped to earth by parachute. They've just been declassified and there are plenty more to follow. Look closely and see the Soviets knitting socks in preparation for a cold winter.

Her Majesty's Treasury

http://www.hm-treasury.gov.uk

Another gripping UK site. Read press releases, ministerial speeches, minutes, economic forecasts, and the budget, and decide whether your tax pounds are going to worthy causes.

US Census Bureau

http://www.census.gov/

There are more statistics here about the US and its citizens than you'll ever want to know. You can search the main census database, read press releases, view the poster gallery, check the projected population clock, listen to clips from its radio broadcasts, or link to other serious info-head sites.

US Federal Government Servers

`http://www.fie.com/www/us_gov.htm`

Extensive listing and contents of Federal government servers.

Welcome to the Whitehouse

`http://www.whitehouse.gov`

Have you ever heard Bill Clinton cited as an extreme example of the type of person who uses the Internet? Well, here's proof. He might not really be at his PC when you choose to "speak out" through the provided form, but you never know, something just might filter through. It's easy to be cynical about this PR exercise, particularly the moribund guided tour of the White House, but it does show the doors of democracy at least ajar. Plus there's a popular page on Socks, the cat.

HEALTH

Alternative Medicine

`http://www.pitt.edu/~cbw/altm.html`

Part of the Net's ongoing research function is the ability to contact people who've road-tested alternative remedies and can report on their efficacies. Use this page as an index to more specific sites and newsgroups.

Biorythm Generator

`http://cad.ucla.edu:8001/biorhythm`

The Skeptic's Dictionary says biorythms are bunkum. Generate your own and put it to the test.

The Drugs Archive

`http://hyperreal.com/drugs/`

These articles, primarily accumulated from the *alt.drugs* newsgroup, provide first-hand perspectives on the pleasures and dangers of recreational drugs.

First Aid Online

`http://www.symnet.net/Users/afoster/safety`

A useful site to consult about snakebites and the like.

Guide to Women's Health

`http://asa.ugl.lib.umich.edu/chdocs/womenhealth/womens_healt`
`h.html`

Abundant pointers relating to women's emotional, physical, and sexual health, plus a wide range of topics such as partner violence, shyness, bulimia, dating, contraception, etc.

Interactive Patient

`http://medicus.marshall.edu/medicus.htm`

Determine whether you're really cut out for the quackhood with this doctor/patient simulation. You get to fire a lot of questions, make an examination, x-ray, diagnose, and finally prescribe a remedy. It's just a shame you can't send a hefty bill and then take the afternoon off to get blotto at the golf course.

Medscape

`http://www.scp.com`

While this medical forum is primarily aimed at health professionals and medicine students, it's of equal interest to anyone who's concerned with their general wellbeing.

Online Allergy Center

`http://www.sig.net/~allergy/welcome.html`

Online advice, news, and diagnosis for allergy sufferers.

Poisons Information Database

`http://biomed.nus.sg/PID/PID.html`

Swallowed the wrong bottle? Been bitten or stung? You can find out what lies in store, and how to avert it, here.

Smart Drugs and Nootropics

`http://www.damicon.fi/sd/`

If nootropics really make you smarter, how can we not afford to take them? Both sides of the argument are presented here, as well as mail order catalogs, government regulations, case studies, and information on smart drugs.

The Virtual Hospital

`http://indy.radiology.uiowa.edu/VirtualHospital.html`

The Virtual Hospital is a continuously updated medical multimedia database intended to provide patient care support and distance learning to practicing physicians. It has links to many online health books, medical journals, newsletters, surgical simulations, and multimedia textbooks.

The Visible Human Project

`http://www.nlm.nih.gov/extramural_research.dir/`

`visible_human.html`

This project generated a lot of publicity on launch, not just for itself but for the Internet's use as a visual teaching aid. What really caused the stir, and what isn't mentioned here, is that the 1,878 CT scans are from the frozen body of an executed serial killer. The image database is intended to be used for teaching applications such as identifying anatomic structures.

INTERNET BROADCASTING

Monitor Radio

`http://town.hall.org/radio/Monitor/index.html`

Home page of the *Christian Science Monitor*, which many regard as the USA's most unbiased news, reporting, and cultural analysis service. Program schedules and background are available, as well as past highlights in audio files. The big news is that a 24-hour Internet audio channel is planned.

Radio Station WXYC

`http://sunsite.unc.edu/wxyc/`

WXYC is the first real-time radio station on the Internet. This page explains how to connect, what software you will need, and what you'll hear. It works through Maven or CU-SeeMe, although unfortunately only on Macs and Unix for the time being. All software can be downloaded from here. Reception quality depends on a number of factors, particularly system demand and connection speed. If the signal is bad, try again later, preferably outside US peak hours.

Real Time in Real Audio

`http://www.cbcstereo.com/RealTime/soundz/realaudio/ra_menu.html`

A remarkable demonstration of the powers of Real Audio. As long as you have a soundcard you can listen to this Net radio's broadcasts on your PC or Mac. It's not quite live – you choose what you want to listen to from a menu of pre-recorded specials.

Shortwave Radio Catalogue

http://itre.uncecs.edu/radio/

If it's not on the Net, maybe it's crackling over the airwaves.
Find out what's on and where to find it through this superb
transmission schedule database as well as logs, station ID clips,
maps, news, satellite information, propagation, sunspot activity,
spy stations, and all sorts of data, including updates on
experimental Internet transmissions.

INTERNET GUIDES

Best of the Web Awards

http://wings.buffalo.edu/contest

Once a year, a panel of judges at the WWW conference pick their
top Web sites in a range of categories.

Internet Magazine's What's On Guide

http://www.emap.co.uk/comp/whatson/

The UK's *Internet* magazine publishes the World's largest set of
Web reviews monthly. You'll find many of these reviews there,
since, well, this author is reviews editor.

Justin's Underground Links

http://www.links.net/

Almost every link from this popular and well-maintained site is
worth a look. There's a particular focus on the clandestine, the
visual, and the bizarre as well as ample advice on how to publish
your own page. In addition, if you're looking to explore the most
twisted sites on the Net, Justin's choices will get you well on
your way.

Liptonice Awards

http://www.liptonice.com/cubes

Nominate your favorite sites in 8 categories for the October
Liptonice awards, or try out the weekly updated cool picks.

Mirsky's Worst

http://turnpike.net/mirsky/Worst.html

If your page turned up here, you might think you'd have to be
doing something very wrong. Well, not necessarily. While some

of Mirsky's choices are genuine shockers, others are actually quite entertaining in their ineptitude.

Netscape

`http://home.mcom.com/home/welcome.html`

You won't have any trouble finding this site if you're using Netscape – it's accessible from several buttons and menus on the browser, and it's Netscape's default start-up home page. Drop in regularly to see if there's a new release and to catch with the latest sites in the What's New, What's Cool, and Galleria, and find references to search tools, tutorials, and Net guides.

Netsurfer Digest

`http://www.netsurf.com/nsd/index.html`

One of the best ways to keep up to date with what's happening on the Web is to subscribe to the Netsurfer Digest. If you subscribe to the HTML edition, you can save it as a text file, open it up with your browser and take advantage of the hyperlinks. Back issues are also available here.

The Revolving Door

`http://www.galcit.caltech.edu/~ta/cgi-bin/revdoor-ta`

You can add your favorite URL, delete a URL, or visit one already on the menu. This makes it an ever-changing and quasi-democratic hot list maintained entirely by visitors.

INTERNET RESOURCES

A Beginners guide to HTML

`http://www.ncsa.uiuc.edu/demoweb/html-primer.html`

A very long primer on HTML and an excellent one at that. It doesn't just explain the code, it gives style hints, troubleshooting advice, and provision for avoiding errors.

Blacklist of Internet Advertisers

`http://math-www.uni-paderborn.de/~axel/BL/`

Find out how to deal with electronic junk mail and pesky advertisers buzzing your favorite newsgroups. There's also a list of crafty Net abusers, which aims to discourage you from joining their ranks.

Browser Checkup

http://www.city.net/checkup.cgi

Want to see something spooky? Not only does it know what browser you're using, it can tell if it's time for you to upgrade. Think about that for a while.

CERN

http://www.cern.ch

Apart from being the prime spot to freshen up on a bit of nuclear physics, CERN (the European Laboratory for Particle Physics) in Geneva is the definitive source for information on the Web's development. The fact that it basically invented the Web may be the reason for that.

Cryptography

http://draco.centerline.com:8080/~franl/crypto/

System security is undoubtably flavor of the year and a justifiable concern. Many see the key to tighter security in devising clever codes to encrypt transfers so that intervening parties cannot decipher them. This site contains links to FAQs, publications, papers, utilities, and government policies on this subject, as well as alternative payment systems.

Digital Planet

http://www.digiplanet.com/

Digital Planet is the creative team behind several of the Web's super-multimedia sites such as Tank Girl, MCA, Universal, MGM, and AT&T. Keep an eye on this site for new ventures – they're almost always ground breaking.

HomePage Publisher

http://www-bprc.mps.ohio-state.edu/HomePage/

Here's a chance for you to try your hand at page publishing. This free service lets you create your own page using a forms-based HTML editor. You can even add pictures by referencing another URL.

The Internet Society

http://info.isoc.org

This organization, with both corporate and private members, coordinates the development of standards and codes of conduct for the Internet. There's detailed information about its activities and an encyclopedic collection of information on the Internet's development. However, it's starting to look quite dated.

Internet Underground

http://www.engin.umich.edu/~jgotts/underground.html

Although this site compiles detailed information on phone tampering, encryption, hacking, and the hacker subculture, it claims that it's only a guide of what not to do. Even if you have no intention of trying out any of these schemes, it can provide an illuminating insight into the mindset of hackers.

Publishing on the Web

http://www.webcom.com/~webcom/html/

This guide to preparing your own pages isn't bad, especially if you are compelled to do it all from first principles. It goes into great detail explaining the code, its uses, and its limitations. Fortunately there are increasing numbers of compilers, forms, and software extensions becoming available, which can automate a lot of the hard work.

UK Internet Lists

http://www.limitless.co.uk/inetuk/

This is the best set of UK Internet resources available. It has lists of access providers, Internet consultants, training courses, publications, and a hotlist chock full of links to useful information, guides, tools, and services.

Your Own Domain Name

http://www.links.net/webpub/domains.html

Find out how to register your own domain name, using both official and subversive means.

INTERNET SEARCH TOOLS AND DIRECTORIES

ArchiePlex

http://web.doc.ic.ac.uk/archieplexform.html/

Archie is a popular way to search anonymous FTP sites for specific files. This site provides a Web front end to the Archie routine. It doesn't however overcome any of its shortcomings such as having to know at least part of the file's name.

Commercial Sites on the Net

http://www.directory.net/

Like the Internet Yellow Pages, this directory indexes
commercial sites. It's essential if you're looking for something in
particular and you want to compare the market. If you search
on, say, vitamins it returns all the sites which mention vitamins
in their announcements. Or, you can scan subject hierarchies.

DejaNews

http://www.dejanews.com/

DejaNews' searchable Usenet database is on the right track. It
has several advantages over InfoSeek such as being able to
collate threads and profile posters. However it falls far short in
practice. Although it stores up to a year's archives for some
groups it omits the alt.*, soc.*, talk.* and *.binaries groups, and
that's where most of the action is. It is free though.

Global Network Navigator

http://www.gnn.com/gnn/gnn.html

The admirable and pioneering GNN has a number of corners to
help you find your way around the Web. Its Whole Internet
Catalogue splits sites by subject and carries quite detailed
reviews. It also carries NCSA's What's New as well as sections on
shopping, finance, travel, books, sports, and education. Another
essential hotlist/bookmark entry.

Harvest

http://harvest.cs.colorado.edu/

Harvest has a number of searchable indexes which can retrieve
Web addresses, software sites, AT&T 800 numbers, Securities
and Exchange Commission documents, and computer science
technical reports. It's another one that's well worth throwing
into the tool box.

Infoseek

http://www.infoseek.com

InfoSeek is, without question, the Web's premier search tool and
arguably its most valuable site. It indexes Web pages, the most
recent month's Usenet news, and continuous newswires, as well
as various business, computer, health, and entertainment
publications. It charges around 10¢ per search which is easily
offset by the time it saves. Try it free for a month and then see if
you can live without it.

Lycos Database

http://lycos.cs.cmu.edu/

Lycos is a massive database of document titles, URLs, headings,
and page excerpts periodically gathered by a Web crawler. You
can search it to find links to Web pages and Gophers. Although
its bigger than InfoSeek, and can return more hits, it's slower,
less discriminatory, and you'll often have to weed out a lot of
rubbish. But it's free.

Publicly Accessible Mailing Lists

http://www.NeoSoft.com/internet/paml/

Stephanie da Silva's massive Publicly Accessible Mailing Lists
directory is available here in hypertext. This is far more
convenient than the text version as you can click on the email
contacts, cut and paste the subscription request, and mail it
directly from your browser. There are thousands of specialist
lists organized by name or subject, with ample details on their
traffic, content, and joining instructions.

Search Engine Links

http://www.earthlink.net/free/bigbee/webdocs/links.html

Open this page, go to your browser menu, and save it to your
bookmarks or hotlist. Now you have all the Net's best search
tools under one roof.

Subject-Orientated Clearinghouse

`http://www.lib.umich.edu/chhome.html`

This guide is maintained by a whole tribe of editors, each with their own style and approach to indexing. You can browse by subject and its reviews will save you chasing the wrong links.

Today's Cool Site

`http://www.infi.net/cool.html`

This site is so popular that some cool sites have received enough traffic to bring down their servers.

World Wide Yellow Pages

`http://www.yellow.com/`

Yes, yes, yes. This is what we've been waiting for – a centralized business registry. It means you only have to look in one place, instead of scouring every corner of the Net. Setting out to be the "Yellow pages for the next 100 years" might be a tad ambitious, but it's looking good so far. Let's hope it can handle the traffic.

WWW Virtual Library

`http://info.cern.ch/hypertext/DataSources/bySubject/`
`Overview.html`

Unlike most Internet search tools, the massive WWW Virtual Library is not confined to one server. Its tentacles reach out to sites all over the world, each with its own subject specialty. Most are diligently maintained, with partial reviews and sub-directories, and many are the definitive digests in their genre.

WWW Worm

`http://www.cs.colorado.edu/home/mcbryan/WWWW.html`

The Worm is another search engine in Lycos vein, which allows you to search a database accumulated from trawling the Web. It's well worth a look when all else fails.

Yahoo

`http://www.yahoo.com`

Yahoo is by far the Net's best arranged and most thorough hierarchical index. Its deep subject-based menus can hyperlink you to Web sites, Gophers, newsgroups, and FTP sites. When you want to see the range of offerings within a specific field or just poke about and see what's on the Net, Yahoo should be your first choice.

Yanoff's List

`http://www.uwm.edu/Mirror/inet.services.html`

Like Yahoo, this exceptional list breaks down Web sites and
other Internet resources into categories. However it's not quite
as well organized. Instead of making each category a separate
page, it breaks the list in three. It's useful, but a bit of a pain to
scan through.

INTERNET SOFTWARE

CU-SeeMe

`http://www.indstate.edu/CU-SeeMe/index.html`

CU-SeeMe is a public domain video-conferencing client for
Windows, Macintosh, and Unix. It eats a lot of bandwidth so if
you're running at 14.4 kbps, don't bother. Even at 64 kbps it's
still more of a succession of stills than real time video. And, as
yet, it still doesn't have an audio channel for Windows.

HTML Converters

`http://union.ncsa.uiuc.edu/HyperNews/get/www/html/`

`converters.html`

Trying to convert something into HTML format to put it on the
Web? Here's where to find help.

Real Audio

`http://www.realaudio.com`

Real Audio offers real time sound over the Net. Unlike standard
audio files, it plays sound as it arrives. This has opened up a
whole range of new broadcasting opportunities. It's starting to
become somewhat of a new audio standard, but don't expect high
fidelity. Sign up here to download a free copy, browse through
its directory of participating sites, and try it out.

SATAN

`http://gatekeeper.dec.com:80/pub/net/SATAN/`

This is the place to find out about, and retrieve, the security hole
sniffing software that all the fuss was about. It only runs on
UNIX but will find imperfections in any system. If you're a
network manager, test your system before someone else does.

Stroud's Consummate Winsock Applications

http://cwsapps.texas.net/

Like everyone else on the Net, you're looking for the latest
release shareware and alternatives to your present set-up. Here's
the place to find just that, for PCs anyway, along with reviews,
ratings, and FTP links. It's updated daily, so check in regularly
to make sure you're surfing with the newest and best. This is
about as essential as Web sites get.

INTERNET STATISTICS

GVU's WWW User Survey

http://www.cc.gatech.edu/gvu/user_surveys/

The GVU Center is the biggest and oldest periodic Web user
survey. Its latest results show a marked change in profiles
reflecting the Net's convergence with the mainstream.

Hermes Study

http://www.umich.edu/~sgupta/hermes/

The Hermes Study analyzes the demographic profiles of Web
users from a commercial perspective. If you intend to market on
the Net, read the lastest results here to size up your quarry.

Values and Lifestyles

http://future.sri.com/

The VALS program is digging deeper into the psychographic
profiles of Net users with each new questionnaire. If you
complete the survey you'll discover whether you're regarded as
an Actualizer, Fullfilled, Achiever, Experiencer, Believer, Striver,
Maker, or Struggler. Marketeers, like astrologers and royals,
need to class people to help justify their existence.

LAW

Advertising Law

http://www.webcom.com/~lewrose/home.html

Advertising law at first sight seems very basic. If you're honest,
you might think, you shouldn't have any problems. However, it

is getting decidedly more tricky with hot issues such as privacy, semantics, product safety, testimonials, environmental issues, baiting, and refunds. With the meteoric speed of the Internet's acceptance as an advertising medium, it's very hard for even the legal profession to keep up. This site acts as a clearing house for articles, cases, regulations, and discussion.

Bentham Archive of British law

http://www-server.bcc.ac.uk/~uctlxjh/Bentham.html

If you're interested in British law, this independent site isn't a bad starting point. It provides a rundown on criminal, Roman, European, and property law, as well as a repository of UK legal threads and essential lawyer jokes. The criminal law section even gives advice on how to get away with it once you're caught.

Internet User Detained

http://raptor.sccs.swarthmore.edu/jahall/dox/freakout.html

There's a lesson for pranksters in this first-hand account of police surveillance of Internet postings. The joker who maintains this page requested advice on suicide drugs and wound up in the lock-up for two days.

West's US Legal Directory

http://www.westpub.com/WLDInfo/WLD.htm

Are you being accused of grand theft, arson, or murder one? Then whip through this database of over half a million US lawyers who'd rather see you go free than go without their fee.

WWW Virtual Law Library

http://www.law.indiana.edu/law/lawindex.html

You'll never be short of legal advice with this cornucopia of law resource links at your disposal.

LIBRARIES

Cabot Science Library

http://fas-www.harvard.edu:80/libraries/cabot/cabot.html

Harvard University library's is an ideal place to start any scientific research. Apart from information about the library's catalog and policies, it has links to the Harvard Computing

Review, Elektra, and other online student publications as well as
to other campuses and external databases.

Vatican Library

http://www.ncsa.uiuc.edu/SDG/Experimental/vatican.exhibit/
Vatican.exhibit.html

Stroll though several virtual rooms in the Vatican which
specialize in literature, music, nature, archeology, humanism,
biology, and mathematics.

MUSEUMS AND GALLERIES

A-Bomb WWW Museum, Hiroshima

http://www.csi.ad.jp/ABOMB/index.html

Fiftieth anniversary commemoration project detailing the
Hiroshima and Nagasaki bombs, interviews with survivors, and
exhibits from the Hiroshima Peace Park and Museum.

Conservatoire National

http://www.cnam.fr

The Paris Conservatoire's catalog allows a virtual tour of the
Museum of Arts and Crafts, and a nifty picture browser which
takes files from newsgroups (such as *alt.binaries.pictures.misc*)
and compiles them into online contact sheets.

The Exploratorium

http://www.exploratorium.edu

Museums generally haven't translated to the Web too
successfully, but this showing from San Francisco's
Exploratorium is a notable exception. Some of its 650-odd
interactive exhibits have adapted quite well, making it an
engaging and educative experience, especially for children.

Expo Ticket Office

http://sunsite.unc.edu/expo/ticket_office.html

Jump aboard a virtual bus to tour exhibits of the Vatican, Soviet
archives, European exploration of the Americas, Dead Sea
Scrolls, Museum of Paleontology, and the City of Spalato. After
all that, you're dropped off at the Expo Restaurant for a feed of
French cuisine.

Field Museum of Natural History

`http://www.bvis.uic.edu/museum`

This Chicago museum has placed a multimedia tour of its DNA to Dinosaurs exhibit. You can page through the eras, downloading movies and sound bites. There are also displays of Javanese masks, bats, and more to come. It's one for the kids.

Le Louvre

`http://mistral.enst.fr/~pioch/louvre/`

Before you can take this superb tour of Paris's Louvre museum, you'll need to choose your closest mirror in the Webmuseum network. Once there, you'll find exhibitions of famous pictures, a medieval art display, and a gallery of classical music. Paintings are classified by artist and, although not every work in the museum is included, there is an excellent selection of the most famous. Expect it to grow and include more links to similar presences.

The Natural History Museum

`http://www.nhm.ac.uk/`

The is the first major UK museum to enter the Internet age. It has details about the Museum's activities, events, and timetables as well as a selection of image galleries. There are also links to other sources about the earth, life sciences, and the Walter Rothschild Zoological Museum.

UCMP Time Machine

http://ucmp1.berkeley.edu/timeform.html

Jump on the University of California's Museum of Paleontology's time machine for a rocky ride through the geological eras.

Andy Warhol Museum

http://www.warhol.org/warhol

Pittsburgh's Andy Warhol Museum hasn't put all the pop auteur's works online, but you can virtually tour its physical gallery for a contents listing. You can even order the book, postcard set, and t-shirt to prove you've visited.

MUSIC

Note: Rock bands home pages are proliferating apace. For the fullest listings, consult the "Ultimate Band List" and other music page directories listed below.

Bad Taste Records

http://www.siberia.is/badtaste/badhome.htm

The Sugarcubes, whose lead singer Bjork recently rocketed to iconic mainstream acceptance, have made a valiant attempt to bring Iceland's underground talent to the world's attention through their Bad Taste label. Despite their efforts, this may be your only chance to hear it.

Classical Music on the Net

http://www.einet.net/galaxy/Leisure-and-Recreation/Music/

douglas-bell/Index.html

Got that address right? If so, you're in for a hefty, text-only site providing links to pretty much every Classical music Net site.

Cybersight Hot URL Music List

http://cybersight.com/cgi-bin/cs/nnnn/Music

Hyperlink to a music page and then return and rate it with either a thumbs-up or a thumbs-down. The most popular sites gravitate towards the top of the list, which will give you an idea of what's worth a look.

Dead Can Dance

http://www.nets.com/dcd

If you haven't heard the hauntingly beautiful music of the UK gothic group Dead Can Dance, here's your chance. There is a 15-second cut from every song in the band's eight-album history, as well as the usual biographies and tour details.

Dirty Linen

http://www.kiwi.futuris.net/linen/

Online excerpts from the US folk, roots, and world music magazine. Features excellent forthcoming gig guide, plus a host of links to related areas on the Net.

ECM

http://www.ecmrecords.com

Sound samples and online ordering from the German-based jazz and contemporary Classical label, home to the likes of Keith Jarrett, Jan Garbarek, Pat Metheny, and Arvo Pärt.

Folk Roots

http://www.cityscape.co.uk/froots/

The UK's equivalent to *Dirty Linen* (see above) delivers on British and American folk-roots and Celtic music, and has a sublime ear for the best in global sounds. Well worth a monthly scan and, again, includes many related pointers.

Global Electronic Music Market

http://gemm.com

This is a commercial compilation of various music dealers' catalogs as well as a second music trading post. Once you've found what you want, you can contact the vendor directly.

The Grateful Dead

http://www.cs.cmu.edu/~mleone/dead.html

The mother of all Dead pages, with lyrics and concerts sets from throughout history, guides to tape trading, and links to just about every other Dead page on the Net. Thanks, Jerry – RIP.

Helpful Online Music Recommendation

http://jeeves.media.mit.edu/ringo/

Rate and slate a hundred or so artists and have your tastebuds diagnosed. Once it has your ratings, it can then recommend a

selection of music you're likely to enjoy and despise. You'll be
astonished by its accuracy.

HiFi on the Web

http://www.unik.no/~robert/hifi/hifi.html

If the news, reviews, and trade show reports housed on this site
aren't enough to convince you that your hi-fi's crap, link to
another site and find out that no matter how much you've spent,
you're still insulting your ears.

Hyperreal

http://hyperreal.com/

Hyperreal is the one-stop shop for all your raving needs. You
can find out what's hip, where it's at, and what to swallow.

Independent Underground Music Archive

http://www.iuma.com/

IUMA can put you in touch with hundreds of unsigned
underground musicians. All bands provide samples,
biographies, and contact details. You'll need to rummage around
through loads of unfamilar names, but it's worth it.

Japanese Independent Music

http://www.atom.co.jp

The exploding, yet unfamiliar Asian pop scene may not be the
next big thing, but it may just be the next big thing after that.

John Peel's Playlists

http://www.bbcnc.org.uk/bbctv/radio1/j_peel/

See them here two years before they chart in the UK and fifteen
years before *Rolling Stone* catches on.

Juan Luis Guerra

http://www.math.fu-berlin.de/~stolting/JLG/jlg.html

Home page for the Latin superstar, featuring almost complete
lyrics in English and Spanish, plus lots of interviews, and links
to other Merengue and Dominican Republic music pages.

Kraftwerk Infobahr

http://www.cs.umu.se/tsdf/kraftwerk

Demos, live out-takes, interviews, lyrics, and the discography of
the German techno-pioneers, Kraftwerk.

Megadeth, Arizona

http://bazaar.com/Megadeth/megadeth.html

You don't have to be a fan of Megadeth to appreciate this sublime
Web handiwork. But there's plenty for those who are, including
a terrific set of animated screensavers, horoscopes, archives, and
merchandise. It's also home to Troma Films, makers of such
classics as *Chopper Chicks From Zombie Town*.

Motown Records

http://www.elmail.co.uk/music/motown

The home page of Detroit's finest features clips and news from a
selection of new, former, and faithful artists.

Music Resources on the Internet

http://www.music.indiana.edu/misc/music_resources.html

This monolithic single list of music links is split into academic,
non-academic, user-maintained, geographically local sites, and
artist-specific sites. It comes the closest to the impossible task of
completely indexing the Net's vast music content.

MusicBase

http://www.elmail.co.uk/music/

MusicBase is the home to such British labels as WEA,
Parlophone, Creation, UK MCA, William Orbit, and Perfecto

records. Artists featured include the Pet Shop Boys, Supergrass, Blur, Swervedriver, and Black Grape.

Nettwerk Productions

http://www.wimsey.com/nettwerk/

Home to such progressive fringe artists as Single Gun Theory, Severed Heads, MC 900 ft Jesus, Sarah Mclachlan, Consolidated, and the Falling Joys. Keep an ear on this site as Nettwerk often discovers sounds several years before the mainstream.

Polyester Records

http://www.polyester.com.au/PolyEster/index.html

This Melbourne music shop offers a large indie selection for email order. It will ship internationally, but Australia is possibly the world's most expensive place to buy CDs.

The Raft

http://www.vmg.co.uk

You'd never know it unless you were told, but this is Virgin Records' home page. As such you will find multimedia tidbits from several featured artists, such as Verve, Massive, Boy George, and Whale, as well as new talents on the Hut label. It broke ground in several ways with its product – rather than brand – focused marketing, borderless images, multi-storyboarded unsignposted trips, colored text, and musical screen savers. It's a site for sore eyes.

The Residents

http://www.csd.uwo.ca/~tzoq/Residents/

Finding online information about the world's finest and weirdest neo-classical group is almost as hard as figuring out its members. The Residents have performed anonymously, masked by their giant eyeball heads, since the early 70s, so efficient at concealing their identities that even their most avid fans remain in the dark. This site is maintained by one such devotee and although it is the most dedicated tribute to the Residents on the Web to date, there are no actual sound samples, no movie clips and, of course, no pictures of their faces.

Resonance Records

http://www.netcreations.com/resonance/

Check into the listening booth and see what's hot in the jungle, trance, and ambient scenes. It'll ship anywhere in the world.

Rolling Stones

http://www.stones.com

Set up to promote the Stones' "Voodoo Lounge" album, this site has tour dates and video footage as well as loads of sound files, interviews, and pictures. It also hosted the 1994 live Internet concert broadcast which, although not a critical success, was a pioneering foray into what may one day be routine.

The Rough Guide to Music

http://www.roughguides.com/

The Rough Guides site is heavy on its music coverage, and is launching an interactive Net project – the *Rough Guide to Rock*. This includes listings of over 1000 bands, and over the coming months all will have hot links to biographical entries, discographies, and Internet links. Readers are invited to contribute entries, the idea being that the book will be written by fans rather than hacks. You can also access excerpts from the Rough Guides to Classical Music, World Music, and Jazz.

Sound Wire

http://soundwire.com/

Like most indie music shops, this one has lots of stuff similar to, but not necessarily exactly, what you're looking for. Relatively few albums have samples and cover shots, and none have track listings. All the same, it's well worth visiting the listening room – you're sure to discover some obscure gems.

Stereolab

http://www.maths.monash.edu.au/people/rjh/stereolab

Discography, samples, interviews, pictures, and tour dates from the UK's finest "groop to play space-age batchelor music."

Sub Pop Records

http://www.subpop.com

Mail order and archives from the Seattle home of Mudhoney, the sadly defunct Nirvana, the Supersuckers, and their ilk.

Surf the Internet Music Resources

http://www.ozonline.com.au/TotalNode/AIMC/surf.html

Here's another huge collection of music links. Apart from a massive list of international alternative music sites, it previews Australia's emerging music scene and off-beat radio stations.

The Ultimate Band List

http://american.recordings.com/wwwofmusic/ubl/ubl.shtml

Search for, or add, all your favorite pop combo's Internet presences. It's massive and ever-growing.

Vivarin Lyrics Server

http://vivarin.pc.cc.cmu.edu/lyrics.html

Read song lyrics from just about every pop group ever, from Abba to 999. The range is astonishing.

Yothu Yindi

http://www.yothuyindi.com/

Yothu Yindi's blend of tribal techno brought Aboriginal music to the world's attention, and won Mandawuy Yunupingu the "Australian of the Yea" award. Their site has Real Audio tracks, an art gallery, and tales of passion for a sunburned country.

NATURE AND THE ENVIRONMENT

Australian Botanical Gardens

http://155.187.10.12/anbg/anbg.html

Australia's Botanical Gardens, located in Canberra, has put an enormous wealth of information online on its projects, gardens, flora, and fauna. There are tourist guides, flowering calendars, biodiversity studies, mission statements, bird and frog call sound files, fire procedures, and much more. It's like stumbling into a government office and finding reams of magazines and papers strewn across the floor in unrelated piles.

British Trees

http://www.u-net.com/trees/home.htm

Apparently there are only 33 native British trees. You can find all about them here, but they would be easier to recognize if it included some pictures.

Canine Web Links

http://www.life.uiuc.edu/physiology/kathy/links.html

Link to sites devoted to breeds, products, canine organizations, scientific experiments, and all things poochish.

The Electronic Zoo

http://netvet.wustl.edu/ezoodesc.htm

This directory of fauna information can lead you all over cyberspace before you find what you're looking for. Despite its name, it's not a virtual zoo with animal animations and sounds. However, when one arrives, you'll be sure to find it here.

The EnviroWeb

http://envirolink.org

The EnviroWeb claims to be the largest online environmental information service on the planet. This includes environmental links, forums, libraries, databases, and a green-friendly cybermall.

NetVet Veterinary Resources

http://netvet.wustl.edu/

This server is the Net's main hub for veterinary information and includes the NetVet Gopher and the Veterinary Medicine page of the WWW Virtual Library.

Socks

http://www.whitehouse.gov/White_House/Family/images/raw/sock

s-sitting-on-grass.gif

When you're President of the United States, your cat is allowed its own publicly funded home page. And why not?

The Virtual Garden

http://www.timeinc.com/vg/Welcome/welcome.html

These splendid horticultural resources are being constructed by
Time Life, which intends the site to be the most comprehensive
guide to gardening online. It's already that and it's still under
construction. There are links to plant society magazines, special
interest newsletters, and gardening monthlies, all with
interactive capabilities for editorial feedback and shopping.
Parts of the new series "The Complete Gardener" are on show,
including a searchable database which will recommend plants
suited to your soil, zone, climate, and preferences.

NEWS, NEWSPAPERS, AND MAGAZINES

Clarinet News

http://www.clarinet.com/

Clarinet is a high quality subscription news service providing
newsgroup access to such big guns as Reuters, Associated
Press, and Newsbytes. A single user subscription costs about
$40 per month, or cheaper if shared across a site.

Electronic Journals

http://info.cern.ch:80/hypertext/DataSources/bySubject/Elect
ronic_Journals.html

This WWW Virtual Library listing of magazines and periodicals
available via the Internet provides links to either the full text or
details of the publications.

Electronic Newsstand

http://enews.com

Each publication featured on the Electronic Newsstand has a
mission statement, subscription offer, current issue details
including contents, and at least one complete article plus
archives. Despite its reworked graphical interface it'll still throw
you out into Gopherspace when you least expect it.

The Electronic Telegraph

http://www.telegraph.co.uk

London's *Daily Telegraph* is the Net's most complete free
newspaper – ironic, given its conservative politics and

readership. It carries a generous up-to-date dose of the day's news, sports, finance, entertainment, and pictures, and overall makes an acceptable alternative to print. Free at present.

Fortean Times

http://forteana.mic.dundee.ac.uk/ft

Fans of strange, unexplained, and improbable phenomena will relish every entry in this taste of the UK magazine *Fortean Times*. Read about spontaneous combustion, alien sex-beasts, flying saucers, zombies, Uri Geller, and surfing to the stars on warped space. Highlights of the last 20 years include bizarre photographs such as the "magnetic man" and the "kitten with wings." You'll definitely want more.

Free Internet News Sources

http://www.helsinki.fi/~lsaarine/news.html

This guide from the University of Helsinki in Finland offers a veritable smorgasbord of free lunches courtesy of the Internet's news providers. Doubtless, you'll ultimately need to pay to receive the quality, quantity, currency, and convenience you come to expect from news media.

The Gate

http://www.sfgate.com

As you'd expect from the San Francisco-based Chronicle and Examiner, this is an innovative newspaper site, offering Bay Area, national and international coverage, plus bulleting boards and conferences on a whole range of subjects.

Guardian Online

http://www.cityscape.co.uk/online/

At present it's just the Online section and special arts features from by this innovative UK national newspaper.

The Hindu

http://www.webpage.com/hindu/

The online edition of India's national newspaper.

Internet Australasia

http://www.interaus.net/magazine/welcome.html

Australia's first Internet magazine has generously bared many of its articles online.

IGC Headline News

gopher://gopher.igc.apc.org/11/headlines

Ecologically aware news Gopher service from the Institute for
Global Communications. Stories cover issues such as nuclear
testing, refugees, corruption, racism, government policy
changes, Third World crises, and Microsoft's world plan.

MecklerWeb

http://www.mecklerweb.com

As you might expect from the publisher of *Internet World*,
MecklerMedia's online presence is overflowing with Net goodies,
such as shopping links, Net news, employment listings, trade
show notices, and bulletins on the latest Net technologies.

MediaInfo

http://www.nyc.pipeline.com/edpub/

Swithced-on Net publishing news, commentary, and advice from
Editor & Publisher magazine. It also maintains the most
comprehensive and current list of online newspapers.

Multimedia Newsstand

http://mmnewsstand.com

Probably as good a place as any to lodge subscriptions to any of
over 500 popular magazines or email-order videos, though few
magazines give previews, contents, or any details beyond price.

Newsdesk

www.newsdesk.co.uk

Newsdesk's multilingual online news and information service provides journalists, consultants, and industry analysts with updates in the IT and Telecommunication industry.

New York Timesfax

http://nytimesfax.com

An eight-page digest of the *New York Times*, formerly and normally distributed by fax. This electronic edition can be downloaded daily and viewed with Adobe Acrobat (which is also available here for free download).

Pathfinder

http://www.timeinc.com

Time/Warner's pages are among the richest Web publishing ventures with shortform features from *Entertainment Weekly*, *Time Magazine*, *Time Daily*, *The Complete Garden Encyclopedia*, *Money Watch*, and *Vibe*, to name a few.

Popular Mechanics

http://popularmechanics.com/

Popular Mechanics has been showing us "the easy way to do hard things" since the turn of the century. It provides a generous selection of stories, a retrospective, a video archive of America's war machines, Web tools, and much more.

Skeptics Society

http://www.skeptic.com/

The *Skeptics Society*, a private organization of the intellectually curious and the perennially unconvinced, investigates the pseudosciences, paranormal, and claims of fringe groups. At this site, you can subscribe to the magazine, order books, and tapes, read newsletters, and find out what's new in the world of scientific enquiry.

South Polar Times

http://www.deakin.edu.au/edu/MSEE/GENII/NSPT/

NSPThomePage.html

This includes the bi-weekly newsletter of the Amundsen–Scott South Pole Station in the Antarctic as well as links to other gateways to the Antarctic.

The Voice of America

`gopher://ftp.voa.gov/1`

Among other things here, you can download audio clips of the day's news in various languages as well as details of the Voice of America's media activities.

PERSONAL

Lovelink

`http://www.cityscape.co.uk/lovelink/`

Advertise or browse for a potential mate in the UK. To make contact, you must phone a charge call service, enter a pin code, and leave a message.

Queer Resource Directory

`http://www.qrd.org/QRD`

You want sites dealing with gay anbd lesbian dating, parenting, sports, music, even gay Trekkiedom? This superb resource will direct you just wherever you want to get off.

Single Search

`http://nsns.com/single-search/`

There's no need to stay at home alone playing on your computer, now that you know about this commercial online dating service. Just enter your interests such as beer, fast food, computer games, football, engine numbers, and speed metal, and sit back and wait. Before long you'll have to make room for another chair and explain the finer points of Doom's deathmatch mode.

Web Personals

`http://w3.com/date/`

This free cyberdating and friendship service is neatly organized by country and preference. It's slightly moderated and seems generally harmless.

WWW Cemetery

`http://www.io.org/cemetery/`

Erect a memorial, leave flowers, or pay your respects in this non-sectarian virtual cemetery.

POLITICS

Amnesty International

http://www.organic.com/Non.profits/Amnesty/index.html

"If you think virtual reality is interesting, try reality," says Amnesty International, global crusader for human rights. Discover how you can help in its battles against injustice.

Body Shop Campaigns

http://www.bodyshop.co.uk/

The right-on cosmetics merchant plans to showcase its wares on the Net but at present is pursuing the altruistic urges that gave Britain *The Big Issue* magazine for the homeless. Its site directs you to participate in campaigns to locate missing people, save wildlife, petition oppressive governments, and stop violence against women. Good for them, we say.

Bosnia

http://www.cco.caltech.edu/~ayhan/bosnia.html

The information, pictures, and maps provided here give an impression of the conflict, in the former Yugoslavia from a Bosnia-Herzegovinan angle. Unsurprisingly, the list of war criminals and suspects are all Serbian, but if you pursue the provided links elsewhere, you'll get alternative views.

British Labour Party

http://www.poptel.org.uk/labour-party/

"New Labour" shows it's not techno-shy by offering discounted email accounts to its members. While you can't actually join the ranks online (it needs your signature), you can order the necessary form or print one from this page. Keep up with who's who in the party, meetings, and parlimentary proceedings as well as the party's electoral progress.

Noam Chomsky Archive

http://www.contrib.andrew.cmu.edu/usr/tp0x/chomsky.html

Oodles of highly controversial articles on, interviews with, lectures by, quotes from, and literary reviews of Noam Chomsky, Institute Professor of Linguistics at MIT and outspoken critic of US foreign policy. He can change the way you read the world.

DeathNet

http://www.islandnet.com/~deathnet/open.html

A side effect of DeathNet's euthanasia campaign was the media's focus on the Net as a medium for encouraging suicide. Thus a large slab of this "right to die" library is dedicated to examples of the press's propensity to over-dramatize and distort.

Democratic Party

http://www.webcom.com/~digitals/

Democratic homepage linking to a couple of dozen senators, and other party strands. And the Presidential Campaign has begun.

Feminist Activist Resources

http://www.igc.apc.org/women/feminist.html

Hundreds of links to forums, articles, political action groups, legal documents, news items, feminist fun and games, women's organizations, counseling services, etc.

Free Burma

http://sunsite.unc.edu/freeburma/freeburma.html/

A good example of the kind of international campaign that the Net can promulgate. And there are few better causes than this push against Burma's tyrannical military government.

Friends of the Earth

http://www.foe.co.uk/

You can find out about Friends of the Earth's latest campaign, your nearest group, results of environment studies, or how to join forces. There's also plenty of links to other environmental resources and groups.

Gay and Lesbian Alliance Against Defamation

http://www.datalounge.com/glaad/glaad.html

Campaigning against homophobia in the media and beyond. Also links to other gay activist pages.

The Gallup Organization

http://www.gallup.com/

About 20% of visitors to this site fill out the questionnaires and opinion polls. Not a bad response compared to say, visitors to Barclays requesting credit card literature. Gallup promises to provide results of past surveys, which will keep you up to date with trends and ratings such as the fickle swings of Bill Clinton's popularity.

Greenpeace International

http://www.greenpeace.org/

Greenpeace International's Amsterdam-based home page has links to its environmental library in Canada, various campaigns, environmental treaties, a photobook, green Gophers, and other environmentally aware resources.

Location : http://www.greenpeace.org/

 Hot Items: current action campaigns such as nucl

 Continuing **International** campaigns and informa

 Search the Greenpeace International Index

 Greenpeace's North Sea Environment and Action

Intelligence Watch Report

http://sisko.awpi.com/IntelWeb/index.html

Find out what really goes on in the world of espionage through this international intelligence watchdog service. The Intelligence Watch Report gives brief updates on political disturbances, terrorism, and subterfuge across the world. The Secrecy and Government Bulletin, published by the Federation of American Scientists, challenges excessive government secrecy in the US. But then again, maybe it's just a diversion.

Mexico out of balance

http://www.igc.apc.org/nacla/mexico.html

Mexico's Zapatista rebels have received plenty of Nettention recently, with wild rumors of cellular connectivity blending with the reality of EZLN's declaration of war against the government. This is just a sample of what's crossing the Net.

MIT Students for Free Expression

`http://www.mit.edu:8001/activities/safe/home.html`

According to these MIT students, the Internet recognizes censorship as damage and routes around it. Find out what's being done to protect the Net's freedom of speech and link to some controversial sites that certain groups would like to ban.

Newtwatch

`http://www.cais.com:80/newtwatch/`

A full frontal assault on Newt Gingrich. And why not?

Republican Townhall

`http://www.townhall.com`

A meeting place for Newt's own party reptiles.

The Right Side of the Web

`http://www.clark.net/pub/jeffd/index.html`

And more Newt – read and discuss his writings, and those of other right wing luminaries such as Rush Limbaugh and Ronald Reagan. The page is posted by advocates.

Spunk Press

`http://www.cwi.nl/cwi/people/Jack.Jansen/spunk/`
`Spunk_Home.html`

Spunk Press, an electronic publisher of anarchist literature, provides a fulsome index to anarchist resources around the Web. It's a little paradoxical to find anarchists so well organized, but much of the writing here is infantile mischief.

Trinity Atomic Test Site

`http://www.webcom.com/~gwalker/HEW/`

Trinity, the site of the first atomic test back in 1945, has recently celebrated its 50th anniversary by opening its gates to the public. Here's where to find photographs, maps, and details of the action as well as links to other archives of weapon testing including the ongoing French efforts in the South Pacific.

UK Liberal Democrats

`http://www.compulink.co.uk/libdems/`

You'll probably learn more about the UK Liberal Democrat Party from spending a few minutes here than you would from half-

listening to years of hustings' static. You can read its history
and policies and how it intends to reform Britain and its place in
the European Union. Before you sign your life away online, why
not email your core gripes to Paddy Ashdown direct?

United Nations News

`gopher://gopher.undp.org/11/uncurr/DH`

This Gopher provides daily news of the United Nations'
involvement in international affairs.

PROPERTY AND REAL ESTATE

Estate Agent

`http://nysernet.org/cyber/realestate/index.html`

This site is a vehicle for various real estate agents to list their
properties. It makes a convenient way to scout for land as it's
quite detailed and usually includes pictures. However, once you
make an enquiry, you still have to deal with a spieler.

Windermere Real Estate

`http://windermere.com`

Search for properties for sale in Washington, Oregon, Idaho,
and British Columbia, or put your own on the market. There's
also advice on taxes, when to sell, and so on.

World Real Estate Listing Service

`http://interchange.idc.uvic.ca/wrels/index.html`

This service now charges to advertise property for sale in
Australia, North America, and Western Europe. There's ample
room for a detailed description and multiple photographs.

REFERENCE

Acronyms

`http://curia.ucc.ie/cgi-bin/acronym`

Before you follow IBM, TNT, and HMV in initializing your
company's name, make sure it doesn't stand for something rude
by searching through these 12,000 acronyms.

Britannica Online

http://www.eb.com/

It probably makes more sense to reference the massive
Encyclopedia Britannica online rather than fork out for the
whole bulky series only to have it go out of date. This very
impressive service is free while in the beta stage, but the
intention is to launch it commercially before too long.

Computing Dictionary

http://wombat.doc.ic.ac.uk/

In theory you can search here for a definition of any computing
term or acronym. However, as you will find out, the language
evolves all too frequently.

The Devil's Dictionary

http://www.vestnett.no/cgi-bin/devil

No, it's not an occult reference, but a list of cynical definitions
begun as a satirical weekly newspaper in 1881. Time has robbed
most of its venom so that these days it's only likely to offend the
most humorless of the politically correct.

Human Languages

http://www.willamette.edu/~tjones/Language-Page.html

An astoundingly rich digest of links to linguistic resources such
as dictionaries, thesauruses, poetry, publications, and more in
just about any language you can name, including Aboriginal
dialects, Esperanto, Hebrew, Manx Gaelic, and Vietnamese.

Jeffrey's Japanese/English Dictionary Gateway

hhttp://www.wg.omron.co.jp/cgi-bin/j-e

There are plenty of options available in this English/Japanese
dictionary, allowing you to search for translations of words and
expressions either way. You can view text in English and
Japanese characters. You can either use the Japanese character
enhanced version of Netscape or view the text as graphics. It
will take a while to get started, but plenty of help is provided
along the way.

Klingon Language Institute

http://www.kli.org/klihome.html

With multimedia lingual tutorials like this, it's a wonder
Klingon isn't more widely spoken. In fact, if Capt. James T. Kirk

had a better grip on it perhaps the Enterprise would be still in one piece. However, it's a blunt tongue without pleasantries.

Skeptics Dictionary

http://wheel.ucdavis.edu/~btcarrol/skeptic/dictcont.html

You'll be able to blow holes through loads of popularly accepted superstitions and pseudo-sciences armed with this concise, practical, dinner party deflater. Yes, it's really here.

Websters

http://civil.colorado.edu/htbin/dictionary

Enter your mystery word and its definition will be promptly returned. It doesn't help out much with spelling errors, though, and omits most of the words you use when things goes wrong with your computer.

RELIGION

About Witchcraft

http://www.crc.ricoh.com/~rowanf/COG/iabout.html

The Covenant of the Goddess is a league of witch covens throughout North America. It intends to dispel some of the myths behind the persecution of witches over the centuries by creating public access to the rituals of practices of the craft. First you have to take them seriously.

Anglicans Online!

http://infomatch.com/~haibeck/anglican.html

The Anglican and Episcopalian churches seem more willing than most sects to adapt to societal changes since the scriptures were written. This independent site reflects this concern by providing a forum for debate and concerns raised by Anglican youths. It also has links to parishes all over the world.

The Bhagvad Gita

http://www.cc.gatech.edu/gvu/people/Phd/Rakesh.Mullick/gita/gita.html

To view these PostScript Sanskrit pages of the Bhagvad Gita, the most sacred of vedic literature, you'll need a program like GhostScript or a postscript printer. However if your Sanskrit is

not up to scratch you may find the English summary and
translation easier going.

The Bible Gateway

http://www.calvin.edu/cgi-bin/bible

Search the Bible as a database by textual references or by
passage. You can also use it to turn scripture references into
hyperlinks in your own documents by referrring to the gateway
in your HTML code.

Catholic Resources

http://www.cs.cmu.edu:8001/Web/People/spok/catholic.html

Scripture, liturgy, early writings, Vatican documents, papal
encyclicals, pronouncements, and other Catholic interests.

Hell – The Online Guide

http://www.marshall.edu/~allen12/organ.html

Let's face it, this lot have never enjoyed good press. On the rare
occasions they're taken seriously it's only to accuse them of
some heinous crime against humanity, such as backmasking
naughty slogans into heavy metal tracks, inciting suicide as a
fashion statement, or killing the Czar and his ministers.
According to this site, Satanism is a bona fide religion whose
followers do not worship the devil, but follow their Darwinian
urges to disinherit the meek of their earth.

Homosexuals and the Church

http://vector.casti.com/QRD/religion/

This index points to many documents relating to the Church's
attitude to sexuality.

Islamic Resources

http://latif.com/

Gopher links to Islamic FAQs, announcements, conferences and
social events, Qu'ran teachings, Arabic news, and the Cyber
Muslim guide,.

Magick

http://www.nada.kth.se/~nv91-asa/magick.html

Nope, you won't find card tricks, Uri Geller, or sleight of hand
here, this is the corn-thumbed version, spelled with a "k." What
you get instead is an immense stash of links to alternative

spiritualist groups, strange orders, superstitions, soothsayers, and mystical literature. It's all stuff you should know better than to believe in, but it still makes compulsive reading. There are gateways to the Freemasons, Rosicrucians, Temple of the Psychic Youth, and Builders of the Atydium, as well as works on Voodooism, Druidism, divination, astrology, alchemy, and so much more it casts an eerie light on the human condition.

Network for Jewish Youth

http://www.ort.org/anjy/anjy.htm

This network links up to the offices of the All Jewish Youth Organization in order to promote educational and social communication within its community.

Religious and Multifaith Sites

http://www.crc.ricoh.com/~rowanf/religion.html

Whether you're looking for Christian, Islamic, Druid, Pagan, or Voodoo presences, this page will show the way.

SCIENCE AND SPACE

Chicago University Philosophy

http://csmaclabwww.uchicago.edu/philosophyProject/philos.html

This forum was set up to mediate the scholarly discussion of philosophical works. Voice your opinions on such vital subjects as Nelson Goodman's theory of metaphor, the language of thought hypothesis, counterfactuals, and Kripke. Go on, bluff it.

CICA Projects

http://www.cica.indiana.edu/projects/index.html

Details, images, and (in some cases) results of projects undertaken at the Center for Innovative Computer Applications. It features experiments in linguistics, feminism, biology, geometry, fluid flow, 3D, basketball, kinesiology, and more.

Earth Viewer

http://www.fourmilab.ch/earthview/vplanet.html

View the Earth in space and time with this clever simulator. Maps are generated in real time so you can see the current position, lighting, and shadows.

EarthView

http://www.ldeo.columbia.edu/EV/EarthViewHome.html

Find out where it's quaking in the USA or link to other seismological stations around the world.

Entomology Image Gallery

http://www.public.iastate.edu/~entomology/ImageGallery.html

If pictures and movies of lice, ticks, mosquitos, and potato beetles turn you on, you'll leave this area feeling very aroused.

The Kiersey Temperament Sorter

http://sunsite.unc.edu/jembin/mb.pl

This eerily accurate personality test based on the Myers Briggs system will confirm just what a beast you really are.

Known Nuclear Explosions

gopher://wealaka.okgeosurvey1.gov/

Technical details, coordinates, results, and other records of the use and testing of nuclear devices, plus seismic activity.

The Magellan Mission to Venus

http://newproducts.jpl.nasa.gov/magellan/

News releases and historical footage taken from the first
planetary spacecraft launched from a space shuttle. There are
enough images, animations, and technical documents on Venus
and the project itself to satisfy even the most ardent astrophile.
However, don't bother if you're looking for evidence of
extraterrestrial life forms. According to conspiracists, those
photos are kept in a secret vault called the X files.

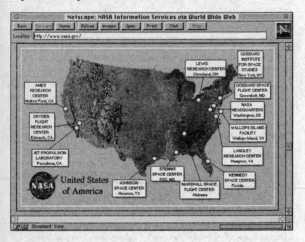

Nasa

http://www.nasa.gov/

This is the top level of NASA's mighty presence on the Web. You
can get to all its projects and databases via the virtual map of
the USA, plus read statements on its policies, missions, and
discoveries. If you lived through the first moon missions in the
late 60s, some of the images are sure to bring back vivid
memories of humankind's greatest step. Check out the Kennedy
Space Center for the latest on the shuttle or visit the HQ in DC
to find out its employees' foreign travel allowance loadings for
an insight into both ends of the space glamor spectrum.

Northern Lights – Aurora Borealis

http://www.uit.no/npt/homepage-npt.en.html

If you're ever lucky enough to see the aurora borealis during a solar storm, you'll never be able to look skyward with the same nonchalance again. It will challenge your paradigm of the visible universe and its relative stasis. This Norwegian planetarium does a commendable job in explaining a polar phenomenon that very few people understand.

Space Calendar

http://newproducts.jpl.nasa.gov/calendar/calendar.html

A guide to upcoming anniversaries, rocket launches, meteor showers, eclipses, asteroid and planet viewings, occultations, and other space happenings in the intergalactic calendar.

Space Environment Laboratory

http://www.sel.bldrdoc.gov

If you've been involved in long distance wireless communication or aviation, you are probably aware of the effects of solar activity. Otherwise, you may be baffled by the significance of the research on these pages. The Space Environment Agency provides current space weather, sunspot levels, solar images, research information, and a brief explanation of its purpose that won't leave outsiders too much wiser.

Stars and Galaxies

http://www.eia.brad.ac.uk/btl/

Take a multimedia tour through the stars. Find out how they behave, how they generate energy, where they come from, and why they burn out.

Volcano World

http://volcano.und.nodak.edu/

Volcanic intelligence, images, and educational material courtesy of NASA. There's no better place on the Web to monitor the latest eruptions, look at photos of every major volcano in the world, virtually tour a Hawaiian smokey, or shop in a Volcano Mall.

Web-Elements

http://www.cchem.berkeley.edu/Table/index.html

An interactive periodic table allows you to click on an element and find out more about its properties. There are also links to a fairly useless element percentage calculator and an entirely useless isotope pattern calculator.

Weird Science

http://www.eskimo.com/~billb/weird.html

Free energy, Tesla, anti-gravity, aura, cold fusion, parapsychology, and other strange scientific projects and theories.

SHOPPING

Barclay Square

http://www.itl.net/barclaysquare/

With Barclay's Bank behind it, and names like Argos, Toys 'R' Us, Sainsbury's, and Eurostar in the aisles, this UK shopping mall might just be able to convince shoppers that the Net is officially open for trading in Britain.

Bargain Finder Agent

http://bf2.cstar.ac.com/bf/

Unlike the usual Internet search tools which scan periodically updated local databases, this prototype music-shopping agent actually trawls live. It's not always too successful in finding the best prices on your CD selection by ferreting through several online music stores, but it does showcase the technology.

Catalog Mart

http://catalog.savvy.com/

Rather than have to hunt through lists of catalogs and contact the firms individually, Catalog Mart contacts them free on your behalf. You just choose the product areas you're interested in, supply your details, and it looks after the rest.

CatalogSite

http://www.catalogsite.com/

This catalog directory does a smart job of listing all the major US mail order houses and providing contact details, but you have to pick up the phone and order them individually.

CDnow! The Internet Music Store

http://cdnow.com/

CDnow! is no half-hearted cybermall. It's an efficiently structured music megastore catering to a diverse range of tastes such as rap, exercise, march, new age, gay, holiday, and more mundane genres like rock, jazz, country, and Classical music. You can browse the associated track listings, biographies, reviews, press clippings, and stories online or even buy the video and t-shirt. It takes international orders, which, in some cases, could work out a fair bit cheaper than buying locally.

Computer Express

http://cexpress.com:2700/

What's great about this directory of over 600 computer suppliers is the way you can search by various parameters to size up the market and make sure you get the best deal. And vendors even agree to match any outside offer. It all adds up to a textbook model for the future of direct sales. To join, you fax your credit card and delivery details in return for a membership number.

Condom Country

http://www.ag.com/Condom/Country

The mail order condoms, sex aids, books, and jokes are pretty harmless, but the mere mention of the penis size ready reckoner may prove disquieting to some.

Downtown Anywhere

http://www.awa.com

Downtown anywhere is a handy directory of online stores, galleries, libraries, museums, sports sites, and more.

Gadgets

http://www.netcreations.com/gadget/index.html

Email order assorted novelty gadgets and useful knick-knacks. While the site's not overly impressive, there are enough links to all sorts of engaging gizmoteers to make it worth the drive-by.

Gifts for Dog Lovers

http://www.onramp.net/imagemaker

Now you've got your Net connection you'll never be short of gift ideas. Imagine your loved one's delight as s/he unwraps a royal corgi-embossed lampshade.

Hall of Malls

http://www.nsns.com/MouseTracks/HallofMalls.html

All cashed up and nowhere to go? Step into any of these
cybermarkets for quick relief.

Highland Trail

http://www.highlandtrail.co.uk/highlandtrail/

Depending on where you live within the UK, Europe, or North
America, you'll be able to enjoy fine Scottish produce such as
malt whiskies, smoked salmon, kippers, oysters, langoustines,
and smoked venison delivered to your doorstep by a range of
merchants. You order via credit card from one secure form.

Khazana

http://www.winternet.com/~khazana/

Collectibles from India and Nepal, purchased direct from the
artisans and artists, with a "fair trade" policy of payment.

Lakeside Products

http://virtumall.com/Lakeside/Lakeside.html

Order the gags and novelties you could never afford when you
really needed them. They're all here, whoopee cushions, xray
specs, itching powder, joke buzzers, and coffin piggy banks,
ripped straight from the pages of your childhood comics. And
it's the still same company flogging them.

London Mall

http://www.micromedia.co.uk/

There's no need to click through the individual pages to this UK
cybermall. Just take the hands-free automatic tour and let
Netscape's server-push technology turn the pages for you.

MarketNet

http://mkn.co.uk

Shop for flowers, insurance, books, shares, travel, legal services,
and more via a secure link to this nonsense-free UK cybermall.

Marrakesh Express

http://uslink.net/ddavis/

Come my friend – I'll show you something special. If you've been
pestered to the end of your tether by Moroccan carpet dealers,
this site will breathe new life into those rugs you tried to avoid.

Susan Davis, a Californian anthropologist, has presented this online souk in such an educative manner, that you're almost tempted to buy a carpet or kilim online.

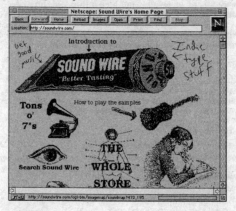

Meckler Mall

http://www.mecklerweb.com

MecklerMedia's shopping mall is one of the best organized on the net, providing links to a superb range of CD/record stores (including Soundwire), and all manner of other products.

Mind Gear

http://www.netcreations.com/mindgear/

There's a theory that if you bombard yourself with certain frequency light and sound, you'll be bludgeoned into a higher state of consciousness. Mind Gear sells various such devices, tapes, and potions to fine-tune and fiddle with your mind.

Online Yacht Brokerage

http://www.aladdin.co.uk/cpy/

Scan through the list of yachts on offer, find something in your price range, and then access a staggeringly detailed description complete with pictures of the craft. When you've narrowed it down to two or three you can email or phone to arrange a viewing. Theoretically, there's delivery anywhere in the world.

Shopping Expressway

http://shopex.com/

Ever wondered where else you can get those revolutionary products advertised on TV, usually late at night when you're most receptive to hypnotic gesturing? Wonder no more, because a large section of this exploding cybermall has been cordoned off for all those money-back guaranteed miracles.

Talking Products

http://www.clickshop.com/speak/

Want a swearing keychain, sneezing salt shaker, rapping Christmas tree, or some other talking novelty? Order it here, or download the sound files for a preview.

UK Internet Florist

http://mkn.co.uk/help/flower/info

If you live in the UK, you can enter your credit card number, apology, and delivery details into the provided form, and be back in the good books before you get home.

Used Software Exchange

http://www.hyperion.com/usx/index.html

This international used software fleamarket is presently a free service. You can search for software by type, price, currency, and platform. When you find something you want, just contact the vendor by email to arrange the trade.

SPORT

Abdominal Training

http://www.dstc.edu.au/RDU/staff/nigel-ward/abfaq/abdominal-training.html

Get "abs like ravioli" with the aid of Queensland University's stomach-shaping research.

Aladdin Sailing Index

http://www.aladdin.co.uk:80/sihe/

This site serves as the main hub for sailing information on the Web. You can check out pages from the likes of the Royal

Yachting Association, Royal Ocean Racing Club, US Coast
Guard, or catch up on racing news and product launches.

Australian Cricket

http://www.physics.su.oz.au/~mar/cricket.html

Don't despair at the domination of American sports on the
Internet. Frolic here and know that there'll always be an
England. Someone's got to defend the bottom of the
international cricket ladder.

ESPN Sportzone

http://espnet.sportzone.com/

Current news, statistics, and commentary on major US sports.

The Female Bodybuilder Page

http://www.ama.caltech.edu/~mrm/body.html

A gallery of proud pictures of the female form pushed to near-
illogical extremes, as well as competition results, videos, fan
mail addresses, workout advice, and links to individual
bodybuilders' pages.

GolfData Web

http://www.golf.com/

When it comes to golf, this one has the lot. That includes
international course maps, pro golf schedules, golf tips, golf
publications, golf merchandise, golf properties, golf travel, golf
weather, and, uhh, more golf.

Internet disc shoppe

http://www.digimark.net/disc/

Why risk your fingernails in a rough sport like rugby or strain
your back over a croquet mallet when you can fling one of these
blighters back and forth? They're totally foolproof and available
where all good ice cream is sold.

Naturists Ahoy

http://www.realtime.net:80/~kr4ah/

If you're struggling to keep up with fashion, why not join the
growing ranks of the nude. All undressed and nowhere to go?
Fret not, here's advice, news, and a round-up of spots to hang
out with other naked fun seekers.

Rugby League

http://www.brad.ac.uk/~cgrussel/

Read how 26 men bash themselves senseless, push each other's faces into the dirt as they're trying to stand up, and then meet for a drink afterwards.

Ski Web

http://www.sierra.net/SkiWeb

Satellite photos, snow reports, ski gear, accommodation, and coming events in resorts across the world.

Soccer Pages

http://www.atm.ch.cam.ac.uk/sports/webs.html

Use this WWW Virtual Library of footie links to make your way to most of the English and European, US, Brazilian, and Japanese clubs. It also links to tables, fixtures, results, news, and all sorts of soccer chat.

Sport Virtual Library

http://www.atm.ch.cam.ac.uk/sports/sports.html

This wing of the WWW Virtual Library has probably the most extensive set of links to sports information on the Internet. And it's not all baseball, grid iron and basketball. Whatever you play, it should be here. If not, start your own page and let them know.

Sportsline

http://www.sportsline.com

US sports news, scores, gossip, and games, including live play-by-play baseball calls.

Stockdog Server

http://dauerdigs.biosci.missouri.edu/stockdog/stockdog.html

Here's a way to keep up with who's who in the stockdog trials. This is where the only two mammals with any mutual affection collaborate to corner a very stupid animal into an enclosure. The ambush is appraised by the dominant species while the subordinates inspect each other's equipment. There are also some sturdy shots of startled sheep, if that's your scene.

The Virtual Flyshop

http://rmii.com/~flyshop/flyshop.html

The fly in the title refers to fly-fishing – the bloodsport least challenged by animal activists. This site is intended to become a meeting point for anglers to talk tips, trips, and tall stories.

WagerNet

http://www.vegas.com/wagernet/

Punt on sports results online via a proprietary secure link to Belize. Even though these offshore ventures can get around local prohibitions, chances are you're still breaking the law.

Weightlifting

http://www.cs.unc.edu/~wilsonk/weights.html

Links to fitness newsgroups, weightlifting FAQs, competitive lifting rules, workout software, dieting advice, routines, and pictures of grimacing men.

SUPPORT GROUPS

Missing Kids Database

http://www.gems.com/kids/ncmec.html

A site that could be an indispensible tool in the search for missing children, though the interface currently limits its usefulness. To identify a missing child, you pick a region, scan through a long list of names, choose a name, and then retrieve the picture. This is fine if you have the real name, not an alias, but if you only have a face it's next to impossible. There's also advice on how to prevent it from happening in your family.

Precious in His Sight

http://www.gems.com/adoption/

Photographs and descriptions of children from all over the world seeking adoption. You will have to make your own mind up whether or not this disturbing site is exploitation.

Psychological Self-Help Resources

http://www.gasou.edu/psychweb/resource/selfhelp.htm

Many psychological disorders can be self-cured. For some, it's the only solution. The answer usually comes through finding others who've overcome the same anxieties or neuroses and taking their advice. The Net is the perfect medium for this sort of interaction as it's easy to make contact and maintain your privacy. This site lists hundreds of resources for such support.

Vietnam Veterans

http://grunt.space.swri.edu/index.htm

Lest we forget.

TELECOMMS

AT&T's 1-800 Information

http://harvest.cs.colorado.edu/brokers/800/query.html

Find those elusive 1-800 numbers and cut your phone bill. That is if your online charges don't negate the savings.

Free Fax Service

http://linux1.balliol.ox.ac.uk/fax/faxsend.html

Theoretically you can use this server to transmit faxes to anywhere in the world via the Internet for the price of your connection. In practice, it only works within limited regions, has long delays, and is rather unreliable. Maybe one day.

Page Mart – Wireless Email

http://www.pic.net/pagemart/pagemart.html

Pagemart's service sends your email messages to your pager, notebook computer, or pocket organizer, anywhere in the USA.

Vocaltec

http://vocaltec.com/

Vocaltech is the force behind the Internet phone, the software package which allows you to use the IRC as a telephone service. It might sound a bit like two cans connected by a piece of string, but it can save you a bundle on international calls.

TIME

28 hour Day

http://www.kaplan.com/etc/bosh/28-hr.html

Living by a 28 hour day, 6 day week regime has a number of
benefits, according to Mike Biamonte. For one, fish finally get
their wish to do away with Fridays.

Cuckoo's Clock

http://www.galcit.caltech.edu/~ta/cgi-bin/cclock-ta

This one gives you the current time in California along with a
suitable sound accompaniment.

Greenwich Mean Time

http://www.cs.yale.edu/cgi-bin/saytime.au

Here's a great service from Yale University. Just enter this
address and within a couple of minutes you'll hear the time
played back to you through your PC speaker.

Time Zone Converter

http://www.cilea.it/MBone/timezones.html

You can link to either of two time zone converters from this
page. One is simple, you just click on a region to find its time.
The other allows you to convert from one time zone to another at
any time and date, not just the present.

Timex World Time

http://www.timeinc.com/vibe/vibeworld/worldmap.html

By clicking on a world map you can find the exact local time,
represented graphically on a Timex watch. A very smart service
and a wonderfully unobtrusive piece of product placement.

TRANSPORT

Aircraft Shopper

http://www.sonic.net/aso/

Troubled by traffic? Rise above it, with something from this
range of new, used, and charter aircraft. Even if you can't fly,
you can sign up for training or a flight simulator.

DealerNet

http://www.dealernet.com

Would you buy a new car off any of these dealers? Unless you're in Washington State, you're not likely to get the chance, but that doesn't stop you from window shopping through the latest range of vehicles on sale there. DealerNet plans to expand to more than 100 cities across the USA, offering online registration, sales, and finance applications.

European Railways Information

http://mercurio.iet.unipi.it/home.html

This site has the usual timetables, news, locomotive pictures, and related links, but what makes it really special are the groovy liveries created by ardent loco locos. Some are faithful reproductions depicting national color schemes while others are fantasy sketches conjuring up futuristic engines.

Goodyear Tires

http://www.goodyear.com

Find where to get the best tires for your buggy, or attend the Tyre School for a Masters in rubber technology. There are also driving tips, troubleshooting lessons, and nuturing pointers for your vulcanized masterpieces.

Paramotor

http://cyberactive-1.com/paramotor/html/para2.html

According to this source, paramotors are among the smallest and safest of all aircraft. They require no license, weigh less than 65 pounds, can be lugged about in a backpack, and can soar to heights of 10,000 feet at up to 500 feet per minute. At only $10,000 dollars, what are you waiting for?

Railroad Internet Resources

http://www-cse.ucsd.edu/users/bowdidge/railroad/rail-home.html

This locophilial banquet includes railroad maps, databases, mailing lists, transit details, and shunts all over the Net.

RailServer

http://rail.rz.uni-karlsruhe.de/rail/english.html

Extensive European rail travel information, with schedules, pictures, prices and discounts, plus hints and links to sites.

TRAVEL

Adventurous Traveler Bookstore

http://www.gorp.com/atbook.htm

No matter how far you're heading off the track, this shop will
have the guide books, maps, and videos to help you on your way.

Air Traveler's Handbook

http://www.cis.ohio-state.edu/hypertext/faq/usenet/travel/
air/handbook/top.html

Now that this FAQ-style travel cookbook has been converted to
hypertext, it's quite easy to find your way through. It aims to
wisen you up to the tricks of the travel trade, help you beat the
system, save you money, and get you home in one piece.

Asia Online

http://silkroute.com/silkroute/

This silk route to Asia promises to open up the digital doors to
Asian travel, shopping, and business information.

British Foreign Office Travel Advice

http://www.fco.gov.uk/reference/travel_advice/advice.html

Use this service in conjuction with the US travel warnings when
planning your next holiday in Afghanistan or Chad. It still
recommends you contact the local consul to get the full story.

CIA World Factbook

http://www.odci.gov/cia/publications/pubs.html

An encyclopedic summary of every country's essential statistics
and details. Disputed zones such as the Gaza Strip and the West
Bank are recognized as distinct political entities. It covers
geographical boundaries, international disputes, climate,
geography, economic indicators, demographics, government,
communications, and defense. It's perfect for a school project , if
not quite enough for a miltary takeover.

City.Net

http://www.city.net/

A regionally sorted digest of links to community, geopolitical,
and tourist information from all around the globe. You can
choose a locality directly or zoom in from a larger region.

Currency Converter

http://bin.gnn.com/cgi-bin/gnn/currency

This nifty program makes currency conversion a doddle. By clicking on one of nearly 60 currencies you can create a new list, with your selection as the basis. Rates are updated weekly.

GNN Travel Resource Center

http://www.gnn.com/gnn/gnn/meta/travel/index.html

GNN has an excellent travel section, with a huge array of links around the Web from its "Travelers' Reading Room." Definitely one for your bookmarks.

Grand Canyon National Park

http://www.kbt.com/gc/

This private guide to the Grand Canyon is a work of great dedication and beauty. There are no half-measures taken in providing trail and locater maps, track descriptions, images, book lists, history, and advice on other local attractions.

Hospex

http://hospex.icm.edu.pl/~hospex/

Home exchanges. Help out foreign tourists by offering them a free place to crash for a few days, and while you're at it, see if someone can put you up on your next vacation.

Hotel Net

http://www.u-net.com/hotelnet/

Find, appraise, and book hotels within the United Kingdom. As yet, though, you can't actually book the rooms online.

Interactive Map of the UK and Ireland

http://www.cs.ucl.ac.uk/misc/uk/intro.html

There's no limitation on the amount of regional data which can or could be retrieved by this site. It includes news, weather, statistics, entertainment listings, transport routes and travel times, interactive rail and city maps, guided tours, and local Web servers. It can only grow from here, maybe with your help.

International Student Travel Confederation

http://www.istc.org

Find out where to get an international student identity card and what it's good for.

Japan – NTT

http://www.ntt.jp/

Tokyo's Nippon Telegraph and Telephone Corporation takes a
back seat in this bundle of Japanese links and tourist aids. It
includes weather, music, customs, clickable maps, travel tips,
audio language lessons, yellow pages, legal matters, sports, and
how to get your browser to read Japanese script.

The Jerusalem Mosaic

http://www1.huji.ac.il/jeru/jerusalem.html

After you've taken this pretty virtual tour through the old city
of Jerusalem, you can discover the rest of Israel by selecting
each region from a contact-sensitive map.

Lonely Planet Guidebooks

http://www.lonelyplanet.com.au

Lonely Planet's revamped site is a useful read, giving a taste of
its multitude of titles (yes, they cover Vanuatu and Lebanon),
and linking these with update reports from readers. There's
enough here to persuade you to discover a world of adventure
away from your monitor. Check out the Postcards from Abroad,
for proof that it's all possible.

Map Browser

http://pubweb.parc.xerox.com/

Xerox PARC (Palo Alto Research Center) brought the world GUIs
(Graphical User Interfaces) and Ethernet. This site provides,
among other things, a nifty map builder through which you can
create maps showing rivers, roads, rail lines, borders, and other
information, by specifying a location on the globe.

MCW International Travelers Clinic

http://www.intmed.mcw.edu/ITC/Health.html

There is token information here on the most prevalent diseases
travelers are likely to encounter, though the list of international
English-speaking doctors could be useful.

Moon city – Amsterdam

http://www.euro.net/5thworld/mooncity/moon.html

This virtual tour of Amsterdam is a veritable labyrinth, not
unlike the tulip capital itself. It's likewise frank, graphic, and
entertaining and can make you yearn for its freedom of

expression. But it's not just marijuana yarns and erotic galleries, there are also guides to the city's food, music, art, history, attractions, cinema, bookstores, and famous coffeeshops. If you can't make it in person, at least visit it here.

Moon Travel Guides

http://www.moon.com:7000/

Moon has been on the Net longer than most, and this well-designed site provides some fine tasters of their guides – which major on US states and Mexico. There's a particularly graphic tour of Big Island of Hawaii. Take a look, too, at Moon's "Travel Matters" newsletter, which has a remarkably open attitude to the subject, is full of interesting snippets from the road, and doesn't just boost its own (fine) line of books.

Outside Online

http://www.starwave.com/outside/

Current and back issues of *Outside* magazine, one of the best sources of information on all kinds of outdoor activities. The site also has links to adventure travel outtfitters, and so on.

Paris

http://www.paris.org/

Feel like a trip to Paris? Here's a virtual tour of popular museums, cafés, monuments, shops, rail systems, educational institutions, and other attraction. It's all in English, though if you want to punish yourself you could browse through the site in a French language version.

PCTravel

http://www.pctravel.com/

Check timetables and book flights with over 500 airlines through the Apollo reservation system. Tickets can be Fedexed anywhere in the world.

Rough Guides

http://roughguides.com/

Okay – we're clearly biased, but this promises to be a site to watch. Rough Guides' home page leads you into an A–Z of titles, with excerpts and (coming soon) updates, including some stirring tales from the *More Women Travel* anthology, and complete menu readers for France and Italy to download. The most exciting feature, however, is a new joint venture with

HotWired, making available the complete 1000-plus pages of the Rough Guide to the USA, complete with hypertext links across the continent to clubs, restaurants, hotels, and every kind of tourist service in the business, where you can browse menus and programs, and make online reservations. Other destinations will follow as 1996 progresses.

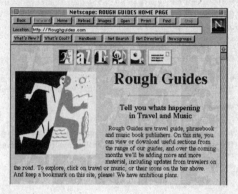

Time Out

http://www.timeout.co.uk

Inside *Time Out*, London's weekly listing guide's Web site, is a bonanza of information on how to pass the time in London, Amsterdam, Berlin, Madrid, New York, Paris, and Prague. It has bi-weekly updated tourist guides to each city, classifieds, postcard stores, city maps, and sample features. Bravo.

Tourism Offices Worldwide

http://www.mb.net.mb.ca/lucas/travel/tourism-offices.html

With a few honorable exceptions (The Netherlands, notably), tourist offices don't have very imaginative presences on the Net. However, if you want to check them out, this is a fine gateway.

Travelmag

http://www.travelmag.co.uk/travelmag/

An enterprising new travel magazine, written and produced entirely by British freelance travel author Jack Barker. Probably the best of its kind, at present, and well worth a browse.

US Travel Warnings

http://www.stolaf.edu/network/travel-advisories.html

This provides essential information if you're planning to visit a potential hot spot, but it's not a definitive guide to safety. It only takes an isolated incident with a foreign tourist to cause panic, while it can take years to settle the fear. Don't ignore these bulletins, but seek other advice before ditching your adventure.

The Virtual Tourist

http://wings.buffalo.edu/world/

Click on the atlas interface to zoom into the region of your choice. Once you're down to country level, you can choose between a resource map, resource list, or general country information. The project aims to link with all Web travel info.

World's Largest Subway Map

http://metro.jussieu.fr:10001/

Pick from a selection of major cities, and choose a starting and finishing destination to estimate the traveling time. It's relatively entertaining but not really practical, due to assumptions such as immediate connections.

WEATHER

Interactive Weather Browser

http://rs560.cl.msu.edu/weather/interactive.html

Interactive temperature map of the USA giving detailed hourly updated weather reports.

National Severe Storms Laboratory

http://www.nssl.uoknor.edu/

If tornadoes, blizzards, flash floods, thunderstorms, hurricanes, cyclones, lightning, and severe storms are just your bag, then step in here. These guys are not put off by a bit of drizzle – they're out whipping up lightning rods on mountain peaks trying to attract the big stuff. If you're a thunder buff, you should read the advice on responsible storm chasing – it may just temper that Pavlovian frenzy for the car keys when the next distant rumble snaps you from your post-prandial stupor.

The Daily Planet

http://www.atmos.uiuc.edu/

Meteorological maps, satellite images, and pointers to sources of climactic data courtesy of the University of Illinois Department of Atmospheric Sciences.

UK Weather

http://www.cs.ucl.ac.uk/misc/weather/weather.html

There are many good reasons to live in the UK. Here's evidence that the weather is not one of them.

Weather Forecasts for the US

Gopher://wx.atmos.uiuc.edu/11/States

This Gopher service gives current weather forecasts and historical statistics on US regions. It's simple to select from the menu, which is broken down by state, city center, and district.

WEIRD

Anders Main Page

http://www.nada.kth.se/~nv91-asa/main.html

Anders Sandberg has put together an immense digest of information about and links to a diverse well of extreme oddity. His primary focus is on the occultish side of spirituality, but there's also plenty on transhumanism, mad science, discordia, illumination, and magick.

Astral Projection

http://www.lava.net/~goodin/astral.html

Don't go out of your mind, go out of your body. Here's how to do it, and land back on your feet.

Blue Dog can Count

http://hp8.ini.cmu.edu:5550/bdf.html

Give the blue dog an equation and hear her bark the answer.

Disaster o' the Day

http://www.ora.com/cgi-bin/crash-cal

Enter your birthdate and discover its effect on the world.

Exploding Heads

http://www.mit.edu:8001/people/mkgray/head-explode.html

Worried that your head may explode? These tips will help you identify early symptoms.

Hyper-Weirdness

http://www.physics.wisc.edu/~shalizi/hyper-weird/

This initial hypertext version of Mitchell Porter's "High Weirdness by Email" marks the highway to some of the Web's most impassioned wells of weirdness. You name it: UFOs, cults, political action groups, extropians, fringe science, fantasy, and drugs. Water always seems to find its own level.

Mrs. Silk's Cross Dressing Magazine

http://www.cityscape.co.uk/users/av73/

Mrs. Silk can furnish you with a variety of products to ensure that when you do step out of the closet, it's with style.

Pee on It

http://www.catalog.com/impulse/info/pee

Make urinal hygeine fun.

Ranjit's Lunch

http://moonmilk.volcano.org/

A fascinating itemization of Ranjit Bhatnager's diet with links to Sho Kuwamoto's, Ben Cox's, and other crucial lunch servers.

Steps in Overcoming Urges

http://vector.casti.com/QRD/religion/mormon-masturbation

Having trouble leaving it alone? You'll find timely advice here.

Strawberry Poptart Flame Thrower

http://cbi.tamucc.edu/~pmichaud/toast/

Insert Poptart, depress lever, aim, fire! This innovative experiment turns an innocent kitchen appliance into a deadly incendiary device. As long as you adhere to strict laboratory procedures, you may not even need to call the fire brigade.

A Guide to Newsgroups

Newsgroups (or Usenet groups) are one of the Net's most enjoyable and useful features: bulletin boards for every conceivable interest, obsession, and hobby. They form an instant feed into like-minded people across the globe, to engage with, share and debate ideas, and pose those perplexing questions that have been bugging you for years. They are totally public domain – yours as much as anyone else's – so don't hold back from participating once you've got the feel of what a group's about (see p.73 for the practical stuff).

The following pages contain about 700 of the most interesting newsgroups on Usenet. That might seem a lot, but it's only around five percent of the total. It's impossible to know the exact number because many groups are only propagated within a local area and new groups are added every day.

Excluded from our listings are the depressingly popular newsgroups devoted to what Internet nerds term "adult interests" – sex, mainly in the form of binary images posted from porno magazines. If that's your bag, just browse the *alt.sex* series, and log in according to taste. Expect to be both bored and offended. If you're seeking romance, a sequence of *alt.personals* caters for most permutations.

NEWSGROUPS DIRECTORY

For ease of reference, we've broken down newsgroups into the following categories:

Arts, Architecture, and Graphics

ART

alt.artcom → Artistic community

rec.arts.fine → Broad brush art discussions

rec.arts.misc → Unclassified arts

alt.binaries.pictures → Contemporary art image files

ARCHITECTURE

alt.architecture → Building design/construction

alt.architecture.alternative → Non-traditional design

GRAPHICS

`alt.3d` → Three-dimensional imaging
`alt.ascii-art` → Pictures in ASCII characters
`alt.binaries.pictures.utilities` → Image software
`alt.cad` → Computer-aided design
`comp.cad.autocad` → High-end graphic modeling
`comp.fonts` → Font speak
`comp.graphics` → Computer-created images
`comp.graphics.animation` → Creating moving images
`comp.graphics.raytracing` → Persistence of visionaries

Authors and Books

REFERENCE

`comp.infosystems.interpedia` → The Internet Encyclopedia
`comp.internet.library` → Electronic libraries

DISCUSSION

`alt.books.reviews` → Join the critics
`alt.books.technical` → Technically speaking
`alt.evil` → Tales from the dark side
`alt.fan.douglas-adams` → Hitch-hiking through the Galaxy
`alt.fan.holmes` → Sherlock and Long John
`alt.fan.james-bond` → On his Majesty's Secret Service
`alt.fan.tolkien` → Middle Earth ramifications
`alt.fan.tom.robbins` → Pynchon's pal has high Net appeal
`alt.fan.wodehouse` → Where exactly is Blandings, then?
`alt.horror` → Be afraid, be very afraid
`bit.listserv.rra-1` → Romance Readers Anonymous
`misc.writing` → Literary engineering
`rec.arts.books` → Book nook
`rec.arts.poems` → Poetry in motion
`rec.arts.sf.reviews` → Science fiction critique
`rec.arts.sf.science` → Science or science fiction?

Business and Finance

```
alt.business → Get rich schemes
alt.business.import-export → International commerce
alt.business.misc → All aspects of commerce
alt.consumers.free-stuff → The candies are on us
biz.comp.services → Commercial services postings
biz.general → Miscellaneous business schemes
biz.misc → Commercial postings
misc.consumers → Shopping advice
misc.consumers.house → House hunting advice
misc.entrepreneurs → Get rich quick plans
```

FINANCE

```
misc.invest → Managing finances
misc.invest.real-estate → Position, position, position
misc.invest.stocks → Stock market tips
misc.invest.technical → Predicting trends
sci.econ → Economic science
uk.finance → UK financial issues
```

Buying and Selling

```
alt.cdworld.marketplace → Trading compact discs
alt.co-ops → Collaborative buying
alt.forsale → Step right up
ba.market.misc → Bay Area trading post
demon.adverts → UK network's classifieds
la.forsale → Los Angeles trading
misc.forsale → Trading hierachy
rec.arts.books.marketplace → Online bookshop
rec.arts.sf.marketplace → Science fiction trading
rec.arts.comics.marketplace → Buy and sell comics
rec.audio.marketplace → Low price hi-fi
rec.autos.marketplace → Trade your auto
```

```
rec.bicycles.marketplace → Buying and selling bikes
rec.music.makers.marketplace → Instrument trading
rec.music.marketplace → Record and CD trading
rec.photo.marketplace → Camera trading
rec.radio.swap → Trading radios
uk.forsale → UK trading post
```

Comedy and Jokes

```
alt.adjective.noun.verb.verb.verb → Usenet wordplay
alt.binaries.pictures.tasteless → Spoil your appetite
alt.comedy.british → Best of British chuckles
alt.comedy.slapstick.3-stooges → Pick three
alt.comedy.standup → Comedy industry gossip
alt.devilbunnies → They're cute, but they want our planet
alt.fan.dan-quayle → Gone but not forgotten
alt.fan.monty-python → Dead parrots and suchlike
alt.flame → Insults and abuse
alt.revenge → Getting even
alt.shenanigans → Practical jokes
alt.stupidity → Let everyone know
alt.tasteless → Check your manners at the door
alt.tasteless.jokes → Humor of an out-of-favor flavor
aus.jokes → Trans-Pacific slanging match
rec.humor → Joke cracking
```

Comics

```
alt.binaries.pictures.anime → Japanese animation
alt.binaries.pictures.cartoons → Cartoon stills
alt.comics.alternative → Counter-cultured cartoons
alt.comics.batman → The caped crusader
alt.comics.superman → Mild mannered reporter
rec.arts.animation → Moving pictures
rec.arts.anime → Japanese cartoonery
```

```
rec.arts.comics.info → Comic news and reviews
rec.arts.comics.misc → Comics miscellany
rec.arts.comics.strips → Strips and their creators
```

Computer games

```
alt.binaries.doom → Patches for the popular game
alt.cardgame.magic → Card sharpery
alt.games.descent → Into the maelstrom
alt.games.doom → Ultra-violent cult PC game
alt.games.mk → Mortal Kombat
alt.games.sf2 → Street Fighter 2
alt.games.ultima.dragons → Medieval challenge
alt.games.whitewolf → Gothic/horror role playing games
alt.magic → Nothing up my sleeve
alt.starfleet.rpg → Starfleet role playing games
comp.sys.ibm.pc.games.adventure → PC adventure games
comp.sys.ibm.pc.games.flight-sim → Taking to the skies
comp.sys.ibm.pc.games.marketplace → Games for sale
comp.sys.ibm.pc.games.misc → Assorted PC games
comp.sys.ibm.pc.games.rpg → Role-playing PC games
comp.sys.ibm.pc.games.strategic → War games
comp.sys.mac.games → Macintosh games
rec.gambling → Beating the odds
rec.games.board → Snakes, ladders, and such
rec.games.frp.dnd → Dungeons and dragons
rec.games.frp.misc → Role-playing games
rec.games.mud.misc → Multi-user dungeon games
rec.games.trading-cards.marketplace → Trading cards
```

Computer technology

MISCELLANEOUS

```
alt.computer.consultants → They don't come free
alt.fan.bill-gates → Lovers of the original micro-softie
```

```
alt.folklore.computers  →  Computer legends
comp.ai  →  Artificial intelligence
comp.ai.fuzzy  →  Fuzzy set theory
comp.compression  →  Data compression
comp.newprod  →  New computing products
```

COMPUTER HARDWARE

```
alt.cd-rom  →  Optical storage media.
alt.comp.hardware.homebuilt  →  DIY computing
biz.comp.hardware  →  Commercial hardware postings
comp.dcom.modems  →  Data communications hardware
comp.periphs.printers  →  Relying on paper
comp.sys.mac.hardware  →  Macintosh computers
comp.sys.powerpc  →  RISC processer driven computers
comp.sys.sgi.misc  →  Silicon Graphics forum
comp.sys.sun.misc  →  Sun Microsystems forum
comp.sys.ibm.pc.hardware.cd-rom  →  CD-ROM toys
comp.sys.ibm.pc.hardware.misc  →  PC hardware concerns
comp.sys.laptops  →  Portable computing
```

COMPUTER SECURITY

```
alt.2600  →  Phreaking havoc
alt.comp.virus  →  Keep your computer healthy
alt.security  →  Keeping hackers out
alt.security.pgp  →  Pretty good privacy encryption
comp.society.privacy  →  Technology and privacy
comp.virus  →  Virus alerts and solutions
sci.crypt  →  Data encryption methods
```

COMPUTER SOFTWARE

```
alt.aldus.pagemaker  →  DTP with Pagemaker
alt.comp.shareware  →  Try before you buy software
biz.comp.software  →  Commercial software postings
comp.binaries.ibm.pc  →  PC software postings
```

comp.binaries.ibm.pc.wanted → Requests for PC programs

comp.binaries.mac → Macintosh programs

comp.binaries.ms-windows → Microsoft Windows programs

comp.binaries.newton → Apple Newton files

comp.binaries.os2 → OS/2 programs

comp.databases → Data management

comp.sys.mac.apps → Macintosh software

comp.os.ms-windows.apps.comm → MS Windows software

comp.os.ms-windows.apps.misc → Windows software

comp.sources.sun → Sun workstation software

comp.sources.wanted → Requests for software and fixes

NETWORKING AND EMAIL

alt.winsock → PC TCP/IP stacks

alt.winsock.trumpet → Getting Trumpet Winsock to work

comp.dcom.lans.misc → Local area networking

comp.mail.misc → General discussions about email

comp.os.ms-windows.networking.windows → For Windows

comp.os.os2.networking.tcp-ip → TCP/IP under OS/2

OPERATING SYSTEMS

comp.os.ms-windows.advocacy → MS Windows debate

comp.os.ms-windows.misc → More MS Windows talk

comp.os.ms-windows.nt.misc → MS Windows NT support

comp.os.os2.advocacy → OS/2 support and flames

comp.sys.mac.advocacy → Macintosh fan club

comp.unix.questions → Unix neophytes

Crafts, Gardening, and Hobbies

CRAFTS

alt.sewing → As it seams

rec.crafts.brewing → The art of making beers and meads

rec.crafts.textiles.needlework → Embroidered truths

rec.crafts.textiles.quilting → Patching togetherness

```
rec.crafts.textiles.sewing → A bunch of sew and sews
rec.crafts.winemaking → Creating your own intoxicants
rec.woodworking → Fret-full advice
```

GARDENING

```
rec.arts.bonsai → Horticultural bondage
rec.gardens → Self growth
rec.gardens.orchids → Orchid growing
rec.gardens.roses → Rose growing
```

HOBBIES

```
alt.collecting.autographs → Celebrity-spotters
alt.home.repair → Handy household hints
rec.antiques → Second-hand news
rec.collecting → Obsessive disorders hierarchy
rec.models.railroad → Model trains
rec.models.rc → Radio-controlled models
rec.models.rockets → Making hobby rockets
rec.photo.advanced → Professional photography tips
rec.photo.help → Photography advice
soc.genealogy.misc → Tracing ancestors
```

Dance and Theater

```
alt.arts.ballet → Keeping on your toes
rec.arts.dance → Miscellaneous dance forum
rec.arts.theatre.misc → Theater news
rec.arts.theatre.plays → Dramaturgy and play discussion
rec.folk.dancing → Cajun to Morris techniques
```

Drugs

```
alt.drugs → Getting into getting out of it
alt.drugs.caffeine → The legal addiction
alt.drugs.chemistry → Pharmacologicalities
```

alt.drugs.culture → Stoned raving

alt.drugs.pot → Grassy tales

alt.hemp → Dope and rope

alt.psychoactives → Better living through chemistry

talk.politics.drugs → The great pot debate

Education

alt.education.alternative → Non-traditional schooling

alt.education.disabled → Dealing with impairments

alt.education.distance → Correspondence schools

misc.education → Challenging the educational system

soc.college.grad → Graduate school information

Employment

ba.jobs.contract → Bay Area short-term work

ba.jobs.offered → Bay Area employment

bionet.jobs → Biological science job opportunities

aus.jobs → Jobs offered and wanted by Australians

biz.jobs.offered → Employment opportunities

misc.jobs.offered → More employment opportunities

uk.jobs.offered → UK employment opportunities

uk.jobs.wanted → Brits after work

Film and TV

alt.asian-movies → Chewing the Chow Yun Fat

alt.barney.dinosaur.die.die.die → Get into a barney

alt.celebrities → Tinseltown tales

alt.cult-movies → Fanatical films

alt.disney → Pros, cons, and news of the Disney empire

alt.fan.actors → Star gazing

alt.fan.letterman → When no one else can compere to U

alt.fan.schwarezenegger → He'll be back

alt.satellite.tv.europe → European satellite television
alt.showbiz.gossip → Who's with whom
alt.startrek.creative → Amateur Star Trek writers
alt.tv.red-dwarf → Smeg-heads
alt.tv.simpsons → Homer's odyssey
alt.tv.x-files → Special agent Scully-duggery
alt.video.laserdisc → Films on 45
aus.tv → Australian vidiots
rec.arts.cinema → Film critique
rec.arts.disney → Disney discussion.
rec.arts.drwho → Help conquer the Daleks
rec.arts.movies → Movies and movie-making hierarchy
rec.arts.movies.reviews → Films reviewed
rec.arts.sf.movies → Science fiction films
rec.arts.sf.tv.babylon5 → Babylon 5 discussion
rec.arts.startrek.current → New Star Trek shows
rec.arts.startrek.fandom → Trek conventions and trinkets
rec.arts.tv → Television talk
rec.arts.tv.soaps → Parallel lives hierarchy
rec.arts.tv.uk → UK television talk
rec.video.production → Making home movies

Food

alt.alcohol → Internal preservatives
alt.beer → Elbow raising
alt.coffee → Damn fine coffee!
alt.drunken.bastards → The right place to bring it up
alt.food.fat-free → Laying off the fries and chocolate
alt.food.wine → Fussy drunks
alt.hangover → Hairy dog stories
rec.food.cooking → Meal preparation
rec.food.drink → Liquid refreshments
rec.food.drink.beer → Lager sagas
rec.food.drink.coffee → Something brewing

rec.food.recipes → Cooking instructions
rec.food.veg → Living without meat
rec.food.veg.cooking → Meatless recipes

Health and Medicine

alt.aromatherapy → Get the essential oil
alt.backrubs → Massage messages
alt.folklore.herbs → Herbal superstitions and uses
alt.med.allergy → Fighting allergies
bionet.virology → Battling viruses
misc.fitness → Staying svelte
misc.health.alternative → Alternative healing
misc.health.diabetes → Coping with diabetes
sci.bio → Life sciences
sci.life-extension → Drinking at the fountain of youth
sci.med → Medicine, drugs, and regulations
sci.med.aids → AIDS news
sci.med.dentistry → Caring for teeth
sci.med.diseases.cancer → Cancer advances
sci.med.immunology → An ounce of prevention
sci.med.nursing → Keeping patients
sci.med.nutrition → Eating well
sci.med.pharmacy → Beyond the labels

History, Archeology, and Anthropology

alt.archaeology → Life in ruins
alt.folklore → Miscellaneous legends
alt.folklore.ghost-stories → Tales of spotted spooks
alt.folklore.science → Tales of invention
alt.folklore.urban → Urban legends and tall tales
alt.history.what-if → What if Adam was gay?
alt.mythology → Folk laureates
alt.revisionism → Rewriting history

```
alt.war.civil.usa → Yankees 1 Confederates 0
rec.org.sca → Rennaisance era period play
sci.anthropology → Studing human evolution
sci.archaeology → Can you dig it?
soc.history → Looking backward
```

International culture

```
alt.chinese.text → Chinese character discussion
alt.culture.saudi → Arabian might
alt.culture.us.asian-indian → Native American culture
soc.culture.african.american → Afro-American affairs
soc.culture.arabic → Islamic societal issues
soc.culture.belgium → Belgian meeting place
soc.culture.bosna-herzgvna → Bosnia-Herzegovina forum
soc.culture.brazil → Brazilian meeting place
soc.culture.british → Talk about Brits
soc.culture.europe → The question of one Europe
soc.culture.french → French culture
soc.culture.hongkong → Hong Kong issues
soc.culture.indian → Indian cultural center
soc.culture.iranian → Iranian forum
soc.culture.israel → Israel, Judaism, and Zionism
soc.culture.italian → Italian meeting place
soc.culture.japan → Japanese cultural center
soc.culture.jewish → Jewish culture and religion
soc.culture.pakistan → Pakistani cultural center
soc.culture.palestine → Palestinian politics
soc.culture.russian → Russian forum
soc.culture.soviet → Former Soviet Union forum
soc.culture.turkish → Turkish discussion
soc.culture.usa → Calling all Americans
soc.culture.vietnamese → Vietnamese meeting place
soc.culture.yugoslavia → All ex-Yugoslav factions
uk.misc → All things British
```

Internet Stuff

BBS LISTINGS

alt.bbs → Bulletin board systems
alt.bbs.internet → BBSs hooked up to the Internet
alt.bbs.lists → Regional BBS listings

CYBERSPACE

alt.cybercafes → New café announcements
alt.cyberpunk → High-tech low-life
alt.cyberpunk.tech → Cyberpunk technology
alt.cyberspace → The final frontier
sci.virtual-worlds → Virtual reality

IRC

alt.irc → Internet Relay Chat material
alt.irc.questions → Solving IRC queries

NEWSGROUPS

alt.config → How to start an alt newsgroup
alt.culture.usenet → Finishing school for Usenetsters
alt.current-events.net-abuse → Usenet spamming
alt.test → Posting practice
bit.general → BitNet/Usenet discussion
bit.admin → Maintenance of bit.* newsgroups
bit.listserv.help-net → Help on BitNet and the Internet
bit.listserv.new-list → New list announcements
news.admin.misc → Usenet administration
news.announce.newgroups → Recently added groups
news.announce.newusers → Usenet introduction
news.answers → Usenet FAQ repository
news.groups → New group proposals and voting
news.groups.questions → Usenet help desk
news.lists → Usenet statistics and lists

```
news.lists.ps-maps → Usenet traffic maps
news.newusers.questions → Newbie day care center
```

SERVICE PROVIDERS

```
alt.aol-sucks → Grievances with America On Line
alt.internet.access.wanted → Locating service providers
alt.internet.services → Net facilities and providers
```

WORLD WIDE WEB

```
alt.culture.www → Web manners
comp.infosystems.www → The Web information system
comp.infosystems.www.authoring.html → Web authoring
comp.infosystems.www.misc → Web techie discussion
comp.infosystems.www.providers → Provider issues
comp.internet.net-happenings → What's new on the Net
```

Law

```
alt.censorship → How freely should you speak?
alt.crime → Take now, pay later
alt.law-enforcement → Fuzzy logic
alt.prisons → State or private?
alt.privacy → Keeping out cybersnoopers
misc.legal → Legalities and the ethics of law
uk.legal → The Westminster system
```

Music

GENERAL MUSIC GROUPS

```
rec.music.info → Music resources on the Net
rec.music.misc → Music to any ears
rec.music.reviews → General music criticism
rec.music.video → Budding Beavis and Buttheads
alt.cd-rom.reviews → Read before you buy
```

ROCK AND POP

`alt.elvis.sighting` → Keep looking

`alt.exotic-music` → Strange moods

`alt.fan.devo` → Devotees only

`alt.fan.frank-zappa` → The late Bohemian cultural minister

`alt.fan.madonna` → If you still want to see more

`alt.gothic` → Dying fashion

`alt.music.bootlegs` → Illicit recordings

`alt.music.brian-eno` → Eno's worldly activities

`alt.music.hardcore` → Head banging

`alt.music.kylie-minogue` → Is she Elvis?

`alt.music.lyrics` → Spreading the words

`alt.music.peter-gabriel` → From Genesis to the Real World

`alt.music.prince` → The artist formerly named after a dog

`alt.music.progressive` → Almost modern music

`alt.music.queen` → Keeping faith with Freddie

`alt.rock-n-roll` → Counterpart to alt.sex and alt.drugs

`alt.rock-n-roll.metal` → Good first base for HM

`alt.rock-n-roll.oldies` → The golden years

`rec.music.dylan` → Stuck inside a modem . . .

`rec.music.gdead` → A hyperactive dead-head site

INDIE AND DANCE SOUNDS

`alt.music.alternative` → Indie talk

`alt.music.alternative.female` → Indie women

`alt.music.canada` → Canadian indie scene

`alt.music.independent` → Alternative pop

`alt.punk` → The attitude and the music

`rec.music.industrial` → Metal machine music

`alt.music.dance` → Water? E? OK, let's go

`alt.music.hardcore` → Serious punks

`alt.music.synthpop` → Is this site hip?

`alt.music.techno` → Faster, faster

`alt.rave` → Late-night loonies

RAP

`alt.rap` → For the committed ...

`alt.rap.sucks` → ... and the doubters

WORLD MUSIC AND FOLK

`alt.music.jewish` → Klezmer developments

`alt.music.world` → Tango to Tuvan throatsinging

`rec.music.afro-latin` → African, Latin, and more

`rec.music.celtic` → Irish music mostly – and transatlantic

`rec.music.folk` → Folk/world music, and singer-songwriters

`rec.music.indian.classical` → Raga sagas

`rec.music.reggae` → Reggae and Rasta debate

COUNTRY

`rec.music.country.western` → Country music, new and old

JAZZ

`rec.music.bluenote` → The key site for jazz and blues

CLASSICAL

`rec.music.classical` → Classical music

`rec.music.early` → Early music

MUSIC MAKING

`alt.guitar` → Axe discussion

`alt.guitar.tab` → Guitar directions

`rec.music.makers.guitar` → Six string along

`rec.music.makers.synth` → Synths and computer music

HI-FI AND RECORDING

`rec.audio.high-end` → Audiophile equipment

`rec.audio.opinion` → Hi-fi reviews

`rec.audio.pro` → Professional sound recording

```
alt.binaries.multimedia   → Sound and vision files
alt.binaries.sounds.midi  → Music making files
alt.binaries.sounds.music → MOD/669 format samples
alt.binaries.sounds.utilities → Sound programs
```

Mysticism and Philosophy

```
alt.astrology              → Soothsaying by starlight
alt.consciousness          → Philosophical discourse
alt.dreams                 → Welcome to my nightmare
alt.hypnosis               → You are getting sleepy
alt.magick                 → Supernatural arts
alt.meditation             → Maintaining concentration
alt.paranet.paranormal     → Psychic phenomena
alt.paranet.ufo            → It came from outer space
alt.paranormal             → Bent-fork talk
alt.paranormal.channeling  → Cosmic contacts
alt.prophecies.nostradamus → Deciphering the predictions
sci.skeptic                → Questioning pseudo-science
talk.bizarre               → Believe it or not
talk.philosophy.misc       → Cyber navel-gazing
```

Pets

```
alt.aquaria        → All things fishy
alt.pets.rabbits   → Bunnies
rec.aquaria        → More fish
rec.birds          → General pets discussion
rec.pets           → Animals in captivity
rec.pets.birds     → Fine feathered friends
rec.pets.cats      → Cat chat
rec.pets.dogs.misc → Canine capers
sci.aquaria        → Fish watching
```

Politics and Media

CURRENT AFFAIRS

`alt.current-events.bosnia` → Bosnia-Herzegovinan strife

`alt.current-events.russia` → The rise and fall of the KGB

`alt.fan.oj-simpson` → Defense of the year

POLITICAL ACTION

`alt.activism` → Agitate, educate, and organize

`alt.activism.death-penalty` → For and against

`alt.fan.rush-limbaugh` → Right-wing rhetoric

`alt.india.progressive` → Indian politics

`alt.individualism` → Hanging on to your ego

`alt.politics.british` → A Major controversy

`alt.politics.datahighway` → Information Super-gridlock

`alt.politics.greens` → Ecological movements

`alt.politics.libertarian` → What it means to be free

`alt.politics.radical-left` → Take your Marx

`alt.politics.reform` → Changing the nation

`alt.politics.white-power` → Apartheid revisited

`alt.rush-limbaugh` → Conservative US talk-radio activist

`alt.society.civil-liberty` → Knowing your rights

`alt.society.conservatism` → Playing it straight

`aus.politics` → Australia's professional delinquents

`talk.politics.animals` → Animal activism

`talk.politics.china` → Action behind the bamboo curtain

`talk.politics.medicine` → Health care ethics

`talk.politics.tibet` → The Tibetan crisis

`uk.politics` → Life after Thatcher

POLITICAL THEORY

`alt.conspiracy` → Paranoia and corruption

`alt.conspiracy.jfk` → The Kennedy/Presley cover-up

`alt.illuminati` → Conspiracy theories and secrecy

```
alt.philosophy.objectivism → Ayn Rand's slant
alt.politics.correct → Minding your isms
alt.politics.economics → Economic reason
alt.politics.elections → Political motivation
alt.politics.org.misc → Look right, left, then right again
alt.politics.usa.constitution → Challenging it, mainly
alt.politics.usa.misc → US political free-for-all
talk.politics.misc → Debate everything
```

SEXUAL POLITICS

```
alt.abortion.inequity → Basic rights
alt.culture.riot-grrrls → Angry femmes
alt.dads-rights → Custody battles
alt.feminazis → Feminist flames
alt.feminism → Multiple directions
alt.politics.homosexuality → Gay power
soc.feminism → Yet more directions
soc.men → New men
soc.women → Women's issues
```

US PARTY POLITICS

```
alt.impeach.clinton → Presidential peeves
alt.politics.clinton → Presidential analyis
alt.politics.democrats.d → Democrat party discussion
alt.politics.usa.republican → Republican party reptiles
alt.politics.usa.congress → US congressional affairs
alt.president.clinton → Another spotlight on Clinton
```

MEDIA

```
alt.fan.noam-chomsky → Media watchdogs
alt.journalism → Hack chat
alt.news-media → Don't believe the hype
alt.quotations → The things people say
bit.listserv.words-l → English language mailing list
```

```
biz.clarinet → ClariNet newsfeed announcements
biz.clarinet.sample → ClariNet news samples
uk.media → UK media issues
```

Psychological support

GENERAL PSYCHOLOGY

```
sci.psychology → The science of it all
alt.psychology.help → Trouble-shooting behavior
alt.psychology.nlp → Neurolinguistic programming
alt.sci.sociology → Human watching
```

SUPPORT AND EXPLORATION

```
alt.adoption → Locating parents and finding children
alt.cuddle → Drop in for a hug
alt.good.morning → Big sister of alt.cuddle
alt.homosexual → Talk to other gays
alt.infertility → Difficulty conceiving
alt.lefthanders → Gaucherie
alt.life.sucks → Pessimism
alt.med.cfs → Chronic fatigue syndrome
alt.med.fibromyalgia → Coping with fibromyalgia
alt.missing-kids → Locating missing children
rec.org.mensa → High IQ club
alt.parenting.solutions → You're not alone
alt.recovery.aa → Sobering up
alt.sexual.abuse.recovery → Support for sexual trauma
alt.support → Dealing with crisis
alt.support.anxiety-panic → Coping with panic attacks
alt.support.arthritis → Easing joint pain
alt.support.asthma → Breathe easier
alt.support.attn-deficit → Attention Deficit Disorder
alt.support.big-folks → Reassurance that big is better
alt.support.cancer → Emotional aid for people with cancer
alt.support.depression → Serious cheering-up
```

```
alt.support.diet → Enlightenment through weight loss
alt.support.eating-disord → Dealing with anorexia
alt.support.stop-smoking → Averting premature death
bit.listserv.autism → Autism mailing list
soc.support.fat-acceptance → Live with it, like it
```

Radio and telecommunications

```
alt.radio.pirate → Lend your buccaneers
alt.radio.scanner → How to snoop on the airwaves
alt.radio.talk → Shock waves
rec.radio.amateur.misc → Ham radio practices
rec.radio.broadcasting → Domestic radio broadcasts
rec.radio.scanner → Airwaves snooping
rec.radio.shortwave → Tuning in to the world
uk.radio.amateur → British hams
```

Religion

```
alt.atheism → Dogma discussed
alt.bible.prophecy → Learn the exact date of the end
alt.buddha.short.fat.guy → Waking up to yourself
alt.child-support → Coping with split families
alt.christnet → Christian jamboree
alt.christnet.bible → Bible discussion and research
alt.christnet.christianlife → Living with Jesus
alt.christnet.dinosaur.barney → Barney for Jesus
alt.christnet.philosophy → He forgives, therefore he is
alt.christnet.second-coming.real-soon-now → The date
alt.christnet.sex → Christian attitudes to procreation
alt.freemasonry → The brotherhood
alt.hindu → The Hindu religion
alt.messianic → Christ and other visionaries
alt.pagan → Ungodly messages
alt.recovery.catholicism → Getting over the guilt
```

```
alt.religion.christian → Followers of Jesus
alt.religion.islam → Islamic concerns
alt.religion.mormon → Joseph Smith's latter day saints
alt.satanism → Drop in for a spell
alt.zen → Inner pieces
soc.religion.christian → Followers of Christ
soc.religion.eastern → Eastern religions
soc.religion.islam → Followers of the Prophet
talk.origins → Evolutionism versus creationism
talk.religion.misc → Religious arguments
```

Science

GENERAL

```
alt.sci.physics.new-theories → Unproved postulations
bionet.announce → Biological news
bionet.biology.tropical → Typically tropical lifeforms
bionet.microbiology → Bug watching
bionet.software → Biological software
sci.chem → Chemistry
sci.math → Mathematically speaking
sci.misc → Short-lived scientic discussions
sci.physics → Physical laws
sci.physics.fusion → Thermonuclear reactions
sci.stat.math → Statistically speaking
```

ELECTRONICS

```
sci.electronics → Electronics forum
sci.electronics.repair → Circuitry fixes
```

ENERGY AND ENVIRONMENT

```
sci.bio.ecology → The balance of nature
alt.energy.renewable → Alternative fuels
sci.energy → Fuel for talk
```

sci.environment → Ecological science
talk.environment → Not paving the earth
uk.environment → British ecological action

ENGINEERING

sci.engr → Engineering science
sci.engr.biomed → Biomedical engineering
sci.engr.chem → Chemical engineering
sci.engr.mech → Mechanical engineering

GEOLOGY

sci.geo.geology → Earth science
sci.geo.meteorology → Weather or not
sci.geo.satellite-nav → Satellite navigation systems

Space and aliens

alt.alien.research → Identifying flying objects
alt.alien.visitors → Here come the machin' martians
sci.astro → Staring into space
sci.space.news → Announcements from the final frontier
sci.space.policy → Ruling the cosmos
sci.space.shuttle → Space research news

Sports

alt.fishing → Advice and tall tales
alt.surfing → Surfboard waxing
aus.sport.rugby-league → The world's roughest sport
bit.listserv.scuba-l → Scuba diving mailing list
misc.fitness.weights → Body building
rec.climbing → Scaling new heights
rec.equestrian → Riding out
rec.martial-arts → Fighting forms
rec.running → Running commentary

```
rec.scuba → Underwater adventures
rec.skiing.snowboard → Snowboarding techniques
rec.skydiving → Jumping out of planes
rec.sport.baseball → Baseball hierachy split by clubs
rec.sport.basketball.pro → Professional basketball
rec.sport.boxing → Fighting talk
rec.sport.cricket → Stats, scorecards, and cricket news
rec.sport.football.canadian → Canadian football
rec.sport.football.pro → Get grid ironed
rec.sport.golf → Driving the dimpled ball to drink
rec.sport.hockey → Hockey on ice
rec.sport.olympics → Atlanta 96 . . . and Sydney 2000
rec.sport.paintball → Weekend warriors
rec.sport.pro-wrestling → Advanced cuddling
rec.sport.rowing → Gently down the stream
rec.sport.rugby → Rugby union talk
rec.sport.soccer → Footie, by any other name
rec.sport.tennis → Racket debates
```

Transport

```
alt.disasters.aviation → Justify your fear of flying
alt.scooter → Love on little wheels
ba.motorcycles → Bay Area bikies
bit.listserv.railroad → Locophile's mailing list
rec.autos.4x4 → Off-road transport
rec.autos.driving → Elbows in the breeze
rec.autos.misc → Car talk
rec.aviation.homebuilt → Ultralight aircraft
rec.bicycles.misc → General bike banter
rec.boats → Getting your feet wet
rec.motorcycles → Wild at heart
rec.railroad → All about trains
sci.aeronautics → The art of flying
```

Travel

```
bit.listserv.travel-l    → Travelers mailing list
misc.immigration.canada  → Becoming a Canadian Resident
misc.immigration.usa     → Green cards and US entry
rec.backcountry          → Getting off the track
rec.travel.air           → Defying gravity
rec.travel.asia          → Go east, young man
rec.travel.europe        → US students overcome Europhobia
rec.travel.marketplace   → Trade tickets and rooms
rec.travel.misc          → Traveler's tales
rec.travel.usa-canada    → Great American trails
```

Software
Roundup

There's no better place to find the latest Net software than on the Net itself. This chapter is a selection of the most popular and essential programs, which will get you started – and then some – on PC or Mac. Also detailed here (at the end of this introduction) are the places to look for updates on new software. The Net is constantly evolving, and you'll want to check these addresses from time to time to see that you're making the most of it all.

How to find software files

We've omitted filenames from the FTP addresses, as being mostly betas, they change often. To retrieve them, just enter the address into your FTP client. If you're using Netscape or Mosaic, you can type it in as a URL. In stand-alone FTP clients, you may need to separate the host name from the directory path.

Once you've been accepted, look around the directory for a README.txt or INDEX.txt file. Click on it to find out what's in the directory. If it's not there, have a look in other directories. Once you've identified the file, double-click to download it, making sure you've chosen "binary transfer." Once you've received it, transfer it into an empty directory or folder to decompress it.

Unless it's a self-extracting file (.exe or .sea), you'll need an archiving programming such as WinZip or Stuffit. (see page [file compression]).

When you've extracted the file, read the accompanying text files for instructions on how to install the program. It's usually just a matter of clicking on install.exe or setup.exe in Windows File Manager, or on an install icon on the Mac.

Most programs are now being released in two versions, 16 bit and 32 bit. If you're running Windows 95, OS/2, or a PowerMac, go for the faster 32 bit versions. These programs will not work with 16 bit operating systems like Windows 3.11 or with Trumpet Winsock.

To find the latest and greatest releases try the following WWW sites:

PC Stroud's Consummate Winsock Applications

http://cwsapps.texas.net/

MAC University of Texas Mac archive

http://wwwhost.ots.utexas.edu/mac/main.html

Info-Mac archive mirrors

http://www.astro.nwu.edu/lentz/mac/net/
  info-mac-mirrors.html
and: http://hyperarchive.lcs.mit.edu/HyperArchive/
Abstracts/comm/tcp/HyperArchive.html

AMIGA The Amiga Web Directory

http://www.prairienet.org/community/clubs/cucug/
  amiga.html

PC Internet Software

COMBINATION SUITES

All-in-one packages are rapidly evolving into acceptable alternatives to the eternal Net software chase. At this stage, only Emissary could really claim to have any superior components to the stand-alones, however that may change as they become more commercial.

✔ Emissary
ftp://www.twg.com/pub/
http://www.twg.com/

GNN Works
ftp://ftp.megaweb.com/pub/iw/
http://www.megaweb.com/

QMosaic Internet Toolbox
ftp://qdeck.com/pub/normandy/qmosaic/
http://www.qdeck.com/

Turnpike
ftp://ftp.demon.co.uk/pub/mirrors/turnpike/
http://www.turnpike.com

COMMUNICATION

mIRC
ftp://papa.indstate.edu/winsock-1/winirc/
http://mars.superlink.net/user/mook/mirc.html

FRIENDLY FREEWARE IRC CLIENT.

Worlds Chat
ftp://ftp.worlds.net/pub/
http://www.worlds.net/wc/welcome.html

VIRTUAL REALITY CHAT TRIAL.

✔ WS IRC
ftp://papa.indstate.edu/winsock-1/winirc/
Best shareware IRC client. Has add-on audio and video capabilities.

✔ Internet Phone
ftp://ftp.fast.net/vocaltec/
http://www.vocaltec.com/
Like a telephone or a walkie-talkie depending on your sound card.

CU-SeeMe
ftp://gated.cornell.edu/pub/video/
http://cu-seeme.cornell.edu/
Patchy Internet video-conferencing, lacks PC audio.

FILE TRANSFER UTILITIES

✔ CuteFTP
ftp://papa.indstate.edu/winsock-1/ftp/CuteFTP.Betas/
http://papa.indstate.edu:8888/CuteFTP/
Best stand-alone FTP client, allows you to stop transfer without disconnecting.

F-Prot
ftp://risc.ua.edu/pub/ibm-antivirus/
http://www.datafellows.fi/
Free, functional anti-virus toolkit.

✔ McAfee's Virus Scan

```
ftp://mcafee.com/pub/beta/
http://www.mcafee.com/a-v/pub/scan2.html
```

The best shareware virus scanner. More up-to-date than Microsoft's.

WS-FTP

```
ftp://ftp.coast.net/SimTel/win3/winsock/
http://www.csra.net/junodj/
```

Popular and proven file transfer

WS-Archie

```
ftp://ftp.coast.net/SimTel/win3/winsock/
```

Pre-configured with Archie addresses. Can launch WS-FTP for retrieval.

✔ WinZip

```
ftp://ftp.WinZip.com/WinZip/
```

Essential decompression utility suite.

MAIL

✔ Pegasus Mail

```
ftp://risc.ua.edu/pub/network/pegasus/
http://www.cuslm.ca/pegasus/
```

Feature-rich and free.

Eudora Light

```
ftp://ftp.qualcomm.com/quest/eudora/windows/
http://www.qualcomm.com/quest/
```

Lacks many of the commercial version's features.

Email Connection

```
ftp://ftp.connectsoft.com/pub/
http://www.connectsoft.com/
```

Easy-to-use mailer, but lacks advanced filtering and attachments.

NetCetera

`ftp://ftp.airtime.co.uk/pub/windows/netcetera/`

Combined mail, Usenet, Gopher and FTP client.

TELNET

✔ CommNet

`ftp://ftp.radient.com/`

`http://www.radient.com/`

Z-modem file transfer capability.

Ewan

`ftp://ftp.best.com/pub/bryanw/pc/winsock/`

`http://www.lysator.liu.se/~zander/ewan.html`

Reliable and functional Telnet client.

USENET

✔ Free Agent

`ftp://ftp.forteinc.com/pub/forte/free_agent/`

`http://www.forteinc.com/forte/agent/freagent.htm`

Queue multiple articles, automatically decode binaries.

News Express

`ftp://ftp.microserve.net/pub/msdos/winsock/`

Fast, not multi-threaded, with smart filtering feature.

WEB BROWSERS

✔ Netscape

`ftp://ftp2.netscape.com/pub/`

`http://home.mcom.com/home/welcome.html`

The essential Web, FTP, Gopher, Usenet browser. Allows multiple FTP sessions in background, seamless navigation, but falls a little short as a newsreader.

Mosaic

ftp://ftp.ncsa.uiuc.edu/Web/Mosaic/Windows/
http://www.ncsa.uiuc.edu/General/NCSAHome.html
Functional, but dwarfed by Netscape.

Slipknot

ftp://interport.net/pub/pbrooks/slipknot/
http://www.interport.net/slipknot/slipknot.html
SLIP emulation browser.

✔ Webspace

ftp://ftp.sd.tgs.com/pub/template/OpenInventor/Windows/
http://www.sd.tgs.com/~template/WebSpace/
Virtual Reality Markup Language (VRML) browser.
Possibly the Web's next generation.

WEB UTILITIES

✔ HotDog

ftp://ftp.sausage.com/pub/
http://www.sausage.com/
Superb commercial HTML 3.0 compliant authoring
program. Limited free trial.

HTML Writer

ftp://lal.cs.byu.edu/pub/www/tools/
http://lal.cs.byu.edu/people/nosack/
Can handle large Web pages. Donation-ware.

Internet Assistant

ftp://ftp.microsoft.com/deskapps/word/winword-public/
  ia/wordia.exe
http://www.microsoft.com/pages/deskapps/word/ia/
  default.htm
Microsoft's free, but cumbersome, Word 6.0a HTML
extension.

✔ Real Audio

http://www.realaudio.com/dloadintro.html
Listen to real-time Web audio broadcasts.

✔ Sesame

ftp://ftp.ubique.com/pub/outgoing/pc/
http://www.ubique.com/
Netscape extension which enables two-way Web chat in
"Virtual Places."

TCP/IP

✔ Net Dial

ftp://ftp.enterprise.net/pub/netdial/
http://www.trumpet.com.au/
Automatic dialer for Trumpet Winsock.

✔ Trumpet Winsock

ftp://papa.indstate.edu/winsock-1/winsock/
http://www.trumpet.com.au/
Reliable 16 bit TCP/IP socket for Windows. Worth getting just for Ping, TCPMeter and Hop, which are
bundled free. Will not work with 32 bit software.

Twinsock

ftp://ftp.coast.net/SimTel/win3/winsock/
http://ugsparc0.eecg.utoronto.ca/~luk/tsfaq.html
SLIP emulator. Enables limited Web browsing without
full Internet access.

VARIOUS TOOLS

✔ ACDsee

ftp://dataflux.bc.ca/pub/acd/acdsee/
http://vvv.com:80/acd/acdsee.html
Lightning-fast image browser.

Acrobat Reader

ftp://ftp.adobe.com/pub/adobe/Applications/Acrobat/
  Windows/

http://www.adobe.com/

View Portable Document Format (PDF) files.

Auto-WinNet

ftp://ftp.coast.net/SimTel/win3/winsock/

http://www.computek.net:80/physics/

Automate many routine Net tasks such as retrieving
Web pages, news articles and mail.

Lview Pro

ftp://ftp.ncsa.uiuc.edu/Mosaic/Windows/viewers/

http://mirror.wwa.com/mirror/busdir/lview/lview.htm

View and manipulate images.

Timers

Tardis, Timesync, WinSNTP

http://gfecnet.gmi.edu/software/softsync.html

Synchronise your PC's clock with another computer or
an atomic clock.

✔ VMPeg

ftp://papa.indstate.edu/winsock-l/Windows95/Graphics/

M-PEG movie player.

WS-Finger

ftp://sparky.umd.edu/pub/winsock/

http://www.biddeford.com/~jobrien/tidewater.html

Enables Finger and Whois lookups. Becoming obsolete.

WS Gopher

ftp://dewey.tis.inel.gov/pub/wsgopher/

The best specialist Gopher client. Becoming obsolete.

WST-Bar

ftp://ftp.coast.net/SimTel/win3/winsock/

http://www.infinet.com/~jdzg/
Launch Net applications from single control bar.

WS-Timer
ftp://ftp.sentex.net/pub/incoming/
Record online time.

Mac Internet Software

COMMUNICATIONS

CU-SeeMe
ftp://sunsite.unc.edu/pub/packages/infosystems/
    CU-SeeMe/ *or* http://cu-seeme.cornell.edu
Video/audio-conferencing over the Net.

✔ Homer
ftp://ftp.aloha.net/pub/Mac/
Groovy IRC client with inbuilt text to voice converter.

Maven
http://tampico.cso.uiuc.edu:80/~scouten/sw/maven.html
ftp://sunsite.unc.edu/pub/packages/infosystems/maven/
Audio-conferencing client. Listen to Internet Radio.

FILE TRANSFER UTILITIES

✔ Anarchie
ftp://ftp.share.com/pub/peterlewis/
Multi-tasking file searches, FTP-ready results.

✔ Disinfectant
ftp://ftp.acns.nwu.edu/pub/disinfectant/
Anti-virus scanner.

Drop Stuff

ftp://ftp.aloha.net/pub/Mac/

Drop file onto icon to compress or encrypt it.

✔ Fetch

ftp://ftp.dartmouth.edu/pub/mac/

http://www.dartmouth.edu/pages/softdev/fetch.html

Multiple connection, drag and drop, file transfer, automatic decoding.

Stuffit Expander

ftp://ftp.aloha.net/pub/Mac/

Decompress stuffit and Compact Pro files.

✔ Stuffit Lite

ftp://ftp.hiwaay.net/pub/mac/utils/

Selectively unstuff archives.

✔ UULite

ftp://ftp.hiwaay.net/pub/mac/utils/

Convert UUencoded files into binaries.

MAIL

✔ Eudora Light

ftp://ftp.qualcomm.com/quest/mac/eudora/

http://www.qualcomm.com/quest/

Freeware version, with reduced features.

TCP/IP

✔ MacPPP

ftp://ftp.merit.edu/internet.tools/ppp/mac/

http://macsolutions.interstate.net/macppphelp.html

Use in conjunction with MacTCP to enable PPP connectivity.

MacTCP Monitor

ftp://ftp.utexas.edu/pub/chrisj/
http://gargravarr.cc.utexas.edu/mactcp-mon/main.html

Graphical display of TCP data flow.

✔ MacTCP Updaters

http://www.info.apple.com/

Update MacTCP to the latest version.

MacTCP Watcher

ftp://redback.cs.uwa.edu.au/Others/PeterLewis

TCP testing tools such as Ping and DNS lookup.

TELNET

Comet

ftp://ftp.cit.cornell.edu/pub/mac/comm/

Efficient, feature-packed Telnet client.

✔ NCSA Telnet

http://www.ncsa.uiuc.edu/SDG/Software/Brochure/
  MacSoftDesc.html
file://ftp.ncsa.uiuc.edu/Mac/Telnet/

Drag and drop remote access.

USENET

✔ NewsWatcher

ftp://ftp.acns.nwu.edu/pub/newswatcher/

Automatic binary decoding.

Nuntius

ftp://ftp.ruc.dk/pub/nuntius/
http://guru.med.cornell.edu/~aaron/nuntius/nuntius.html

Easy to use popular newsreader.

WEB BROWSERS

✔ Netscape
http://www.mcom.com/info/index.html
ftp://ftp2.netscape.com/netscape/mac/
The browser of choice.

NCSA Mosaic
ftp://ftp.ncsa.uiuc.edu/Mac/Mosaic
http://www.ncsa.uiuc.edu/SDG/Software/Mosaic/
  NCSAMosaicHome.html
The shadow.

WEB UTILITIES

✔ Arachnid
ftp://sec-look.uiowa.edu/pub/demos/
http://sec-look.uiowa.edu/about/projects/
  arachnid-page.html
HTML 3.0 compliant editor.

HTML Grinder
ftp://ftp.matterform.com/matterform/www/html_grinder/
http://www.matterform.com/mf/grinder/htmlgrinder.html
Drag and drop Web page updating.

✔ Real Audio
http://www.realaudio.com/
Listen to real-time audio over the Web.

RTFtoHTML
ftp://ftp.hiwaay.net/pub/mac/html_tools/
Convert rich text word processor files into Web pages,
drag and drop multi file processing.

VARIOUS TOOLS

Blue Skies
gopher://groundhog.sprl.umich.edu:70/11/Software
Weather Gopher client.

✔ JPegViewer
ftp://ftp.luth.se:/pub/mac/graphics/graphicsutil/
View most image file formats.

MacWeather
ftp://ftp.utexas.edu/pub/mac/tcpip/
Install a global weather station on your desktop.

Network Time
ftp://mirrors.aol.com/pub/info-mac/comm/tcp/
Synchronize your Mac clock.

Sound Machine
ftp://ftp.utexas.edu/pub/mac/sound/
http://www.znet.com/mac/soundmachine.html
Play .au sound files, works well in conjunction with
Web browser.

✔ SoundApp
ftp://ftp.utexas.edu/pub/mac/sound/
Play most sound file formats.

✔ Sparkle
ftp://ftp.sunet.se:/pub/mac/info-mac/grf/util/
http://www.znet.com/mac/sparkle.html
Play Quicktime and M-PEG movies.

TurboGopher
ftp://boombox.micro.umn.edu/pub/gopher/
  Macintosh-TurboGopher/
Gopher-specific client.

PART THREE

contexts

A Brief History of the Internet

The Internet may be an overnight media phenomenon, but it's not new. In fact, as a concept, it's actually older than the mean age of its users, with origins dating back to the 1960s – a very long time before anyone coined the buzzword "information superhighway." Of course, there's no question that the Internet deserves its current level of attention – it is a quantum leap in global communications. But, right now, it's more of a prototype than a finished product. While Microsoft's Bill Gates and Vice President Al Gore rhapsodize about such household services as video-on-demand, most Net-users would be happy with a system fast enough to view stills-on-demand. Nonetheless, it's getting there. Almost every day, something new is released which promises to revolutionize the Internet, and maybe our lifestyles, in some way.

The concept of the Net might not have been hatched in Microsoft's cabinet war rooms, but it did play a role in a previous conquest for world domination. It was 1957, at the height of the Cold War. The Soviets had just launched the first Sputnik, thus beating the USA into space. The race was on. In response, the US Department of Defense formed the **Advanced Research Projects Agency (ARPA)** to bump up its technological prowess.

Twelve years later, this spawned **ARPAnet** – a project to develop a military research network, or more specifically, the world's first decentralized computer network.

In those days, PCs didn't exist. The computer world was based around mainframe computers and dumb terminals. That usually involved a gigantic, but fragile, box sealed in a climate-controlled room, acting as a hub, with a mass of cables spoking out to keyboard/monitor ensembles. The concept of independent intelligent processors pooling resources through a network was brave new territory which would require the development of new hardware, software, and connectivity. The driving force behind decentralization, ironically, was the bomb-proofing factor. Nuke a mainframe and the system goes down. But bombing a network would, at worst, only remove a few nodes. The remainder could route around it unharmed.

Over the next decade, an increasing number of **research agencies** and **universities** joined the network. US institutions such as UCLA, MIT, Stanford, and Harvard led the way, and in 1973, it crossed the Atlantic to include University College London and Norway's Royal Radar Establishment. The 70s saw the introduction of **electronic mail**, **FTP**, **Telnet**, and what would become the **Usenet** newsgroups. The early 80s brought **TCP/IP**, the **Domain Name System**, **Network News Transfer Protocol**, and the European networks **EUnet** (European UNIX Network), **MiniTel** (the widely adopted French consumer network), and **JANET** (Joint Academic Network), as well as the Japanese **UNIX** Network. ARPA evolved to handle the research traffic, while a second network, MILnet, took over the US military intelligence.

An important development took place in 1986, when the US National Science Foundation established **NSFnet** by linking five university super-computers at a backbone speed of 56 kbps. This opened the gateway for external universities to tap in to superior processing power and share resources. In the three years between 1984 and 1988, the number of host computers on the **Internet** (as it was now being called) grew from about 1,000 to over 60,000. NSFnet, meanwhile, increased its capacity to T1 (1,544 kbps). Over the next few years, more and more countries joined the network, from as far afield as Australia, New Zealand, Iceland, Israel, Brazil, India, and Argentina.

It was at this time, too, that **Internet Relay Chat** – which had just been released – enjoyed its moment of fame, as an alternative to CNN's incessant, but censored, coverage of the Gulf War. By this stage, the Net had grown far beyond its original charter. Although ARPA had succeeded in creating the basis for decentralized computing, whether it was actually a military success was debatable. It might have been bomb-proof, but on the other hand, it had opened new doors for espionage. It was never particularly secure and it is suspected that Soviet agents routinely hacked in to forage for research data. In 1990, ARPAnet folded, and **NSFnet** took over administering the Net.

Global electronic communication was far too useful and versatile to restrict to academia, in any case, and it was beginning to attract the attention of **big business**. The Cold War was apparently over and world economies were starting to regain confidence after the 87 stock market savaging. Market trading moved from the pits and blackboards onto computer screens. The financial sector expected fingertip real-time data and that feeling was spreading. The world was ready for a people's network. Since the foundation of the Net was already in place, and funded by taxpayers, there was really no excuse not to open it to the public.

In 1991, the NSF lifted its restrictions on commercial usage. During the early years of the Net, its "Acceptable Use Policy" specifically prohibited the use of the network for profit. Changing that policy irreversibly opened the door to business. Before anyone could connect to the Net, someone had to sell them a connection. This in itself was big business. **The Commercial Internet eXchange (CIX)**, a network of major commercial access providers, formed to create a commercial backbone, and divert traffic from the NSFnet. Before long, budding access providers were rigging up points of presence in their bedrooms. Meanwhile, NSFnet upgraded its backbone to **T3** (44,736 kbps)

The Net had established itself as a viable medium for transferring data, but it was nearly impossible to find anything. The next few years saw an explosion in navigation protocols such as **WAIS**, **Gopher**, **Veronica**, and most importantly the **World Wide Web**, which emerged into the public domain in 1992.

The Web had been proposed in 1989 by Tim Berners-Lee of **CERN**, the Swiss Particle Physics institute, and it was initially envisioned as a means of sharing physics research. Its goal was to provide a seamless network in which information from any source could be accessed in a simple, consistent way with one program, on any platform, and encompass all existing infosystems such as FTP, Gopher, and Usenet, without alteration. It was an unqualified success.

As the number of hosts broke 1,000,000, the Internet Society was formed to brainstorm protocols and attempt to coordinate and direct the Net's escalating expansion. **Mosaic**, the first graphical Web browser, was released, and declared to be the "killer application of the 90s." It provided a foolproof point and click interface to the Net's riches. The Web's traffic increased by 2,500 percent in the year up to June 1994, and domain names for commercial organizations (.com) began to outnumber educational institutions (.edu).

As the Web grew, so too did the global village. The media was starting to notice, slowly realizing that this was something that went beyond computer nerds and science academics. They couldn't miss it, actually, with almost every country in the world connected or in the process. Even the White House was online.

Of course, as word of a captive market got around, entrepreneurial brains went into overdrive. Canter & Seigel, an Arizonan law firm, set a precedent by continuously "spamming" Usenet with advertisements for the US green card lottery. Although the Net was tentatively open for business, crossposting **advertisements** to every newsgroup was decidedly bad form. Such was the ensuing wrath, that C&S had no chance of filtering out genuine responses from the server-breaking level of hate-mail. A precedent was set for how not to do business on the Net. Pizza-Hut, by contrast, showed how to do it subtly by setting up a trial service on the Web.

By the onset of 1995, the Net was well and truly within the public realm. It was impossible to escape. The media was already becoming bored with extolling its virtues so it turned to sensationalism. The Net reached the status of an Oprah Winfrey issue. Tales of hacking, pornography, terrorist literature, and sexual harassment tarnished the Internet's iconic position as the great international equalizer. But that didn't stop the proliferation of businesses, schools, banks, government bodies, politicians, and consumers from going online, nor the major online services – such as **CompuServe**, **Prodigy**, and **America Online**, which had been developing in parallel since the late 1980s – from adding Internet access as a sideline to their existing private networks.

As 1995 progressed, Mosaic, the previous year's killer application, lost its footing to a superior browser, **Netscape**. Not such big news, you might imagine, but after a half year of rigorous beta-testing, Netscape went public with the third largest ever NASDAQ IPO share value – around $2.4bn. Meanwhile, **Microsoft**, which had formerly disregarded the Internet, released **Windows 95**, a new universal operating platform which incorporated access to the controversial **Microsoft Network**. Although **IBM** had done a similar thing six months earlier with **OS/2 Warp** and its **IBM Global Network**, Microsoft's was an altogether different scheme. It offered full Net access, but its real product was its own separate network, which could potentially supersede the Net, giving Microsoft the sort of reign over information that Coke has over tooth decay. If that does occur, it will be a significant tragedy, for whatever its faults, the Net proper is an organically democratic medium.

Whatever, now that Keanu Reeves and Sandra Bullock have starred in films about it, the Rolling Stones have played a live concert over it, Michael Jackson has used it to conduct his first open interview, and more than thirty million people have email addresses on it, you would have to concede that the Internet has finally arrived. Where it goes from here is anyone's guess. The immediate horizon promises such goodies as virtual reality browsing, guaranteed secure transaction processing, smart currencies, 64 kbps home ISDN links, and live screen data, as well as increasing government attention to international cash transactions, licentious content, and fraud. Immediate realities suggest that email will fast become as integral to business communications as the fax, and the Web as everyday as the Yellow Pages.

It's hard not to get the impression that the future has already arrived!

Net Language

The Internet hasn't always been a public thoroughfare:
it used to be a clique inhabited by students and
researchers nurtured on a steady diet of UNIX, scientific nomenclature, and in-jokes. Next door in a
parallel world, thousands of low-speed modem jockeys
logged into independent bulletin board networks, to
trade files, post messages, and chat in public forums.
These groups were largely responsible for the development of an exclusively online language consisting of
acronyms, emoticons (smileys and such), and tagged
text. The popularizing of the Internet brought these
groups together along with, more recently, the less
digitally versed general public.

Low online speed, poor typing skills, and the need for
quick responses were among the official justifications
for keeping things brief. But, it was also a way of showing off that you were in the know. These days, they're
not used quite so prevalently, but you're sure to
encounter them in Internet Relay Chat (IRC) and, to a
lesser extent, Usenet. Since IRC is a snappy medium,
and line space is at a premium, acronyms and the like
can actually be useful – as long as they're understood.

Shorthand: Net acronyms

It doesn't take more than a quick glimpse at the
acronyms below to realize that the Net is peppered with
four-letter words. We're not recommending their use – if

you don't tell people to "fuck right off" in ordinary speech or letters, then FRO is hardly appropriate usage. However, you may at least want to know what's being said. And, BTW (by the way), it must be added that a few pieces of Net shorthand are genuinely useful and/or funny, even if they don't make you ROFL (roll on the floor laughing).

AFK	Away from keyboard
AOL	America Online
BAK	Back at keyboard
BBL	Be back later
BFD	Big fucking deal
BFN	Bye for now
BRB	Be right back
BTW	By the way
FB	Furrowed brow
FRO	Fuck right off
FUBAR	Fucked up beyond all recognition
GAL	Get a life
GRD	Grinning, running, and ducking
GTRM	Going to read mail
HTH	Hope this helps
IMO	In my opinion
IMHO	In my humble opinion
IYSWIM	If you see what I mean
IAE	In any event
IOW	In other words
LOL	Laughing out loud
NRN	No reply necessary
NFW	No fucking way
OIC	Oh I see
OTOH	On the other hand
ROTFL	Rolling on the floor laughing
RTFM	Read the fucking manual

SOL	Sooner or later
SYL	See you later
TTYL	Talk to you later
WGAS?	Who gives a shit?
YL	Young lady

Smileys and Emoticons

Back in the simple old days, it was common to temper a potentially contentious remark with a <grins> tacked on to the end in much the same way that a dog wags its tail to show it's harmless. But that wasn't enough for the Californian E-generation whose trademark smiley icon became the 80s peace sign. From the same honed minds that brought numeric messages to the pocket calculator, came the ASCII smiley. This time, instead of turning it upside down, you have to look at it sideways to see a smiling face – an expression that words, supposedly, fail to convey, at least in such limited space. Just having a smiley wasn't enough though, and so a whole family of **emoticons** (emotional icons) were born.

The odd smiley undoubtedly has its place in diffusing barbs, but how many of the other emoticons you use, and how often you use them, is up to your perception of the line between cute and dorky. All the same, don't lose sight of the fact that they're only meant to be fun :-).

:-)	Smiling
:-D	Laughing
:-o	Shock
:-(	Frowning
:'-)	Crying
;-)	Winking
{}	Hugging

: *	Kissing
$-)	Greedy
X-)	I see nothing
:-X	I'll say nothing
:-L~~	Drooling
:-P	Sticking out tongue
(hmm)Ooo.. :-)	Thinking happy thoughts
(hmm)Ooo.. :-(	Thinking sad thoughts
O:-)	Angel
}:>	Devil
(_)]	Beer
\\//	Vulcan salute
\o/	Hallelujah
@--`-,----	A rose

Emphasis

Another way of expressing actions or emotions is by adding a commentary within < these signs >.

For example:

<flushed> I've just escaped from the clutches of acronym-fetishists
< removes cap, wipes furrowed brow >.

It is also common practice to use asterisks to *emphasize* words, in place of bolds and italics. You simply *wrap* the appropriate word.

Glossary

A

Access Provider Company that sells Internet connection. Known variously as Internet Access or Service Providers (IAPs or ISPs).

Anonymous FTP server A remote computer, with a publicly accessible file archive, that accepts "anonymous" as the login name and an email address as the password.

Archie A program that searches Internet FTP archives by filename.

ASCII The American Standard Code for Information Interchange. A text format readable by all computers. Also called "plain text."

Attachment A file included with mail.

B

Bandwidth The size of the data pipeline. The higher the bandwidth, the faster data can flow.

Baud rate The number of times a modem's signal changes per second when transmitting data. Not to be confused with bps.

BBS Bulletin Board System. A computer system accessible by modem. Members can dial in and leave messages, send email, play games, and trade files with other users.

Binary file All non-plain text files are binaries, including programs, word processor documents, images, sound clips, and compressed files.

Binhex A method of encoding, commonly used by Macs.

Bookmarks A Web browser file used to store URLs.

Bounced mail Email returned to sender.

Bps Bits per second. The rate that data is transferred between two modems. A bit is the basic unit of data.

Browser A program, such as Netscape, that allows you to download and display Web documents.

C

Client A program that accesses information across a network, such as a Web browser or newsreader.

Cyberspace A term coined by science fiction writer William Gibson, referring to the virtual world which exists within the marriage of computers, telecommunication networks, and digital media.

D

Direct connection A connection, such as SLIP or PPP, whereby your computer becomes a live part of the Internet. Also called full IP access.

DNS Domain Name System. The system that locates the numerical IP address corresponding to a host name.

Domain A part of the DNS name that specifies certain details about the host such as its location and whether it is part of a commercial, government, or educational entity.

Download Transfer a file from one computer to another.

E

Email address The unique private Internet address to which your email is sent. Takes the form, user@host.

Eudora Popular email program for Mac and PC.

F

FAQ Frequently Asked Questions. Document that answers the most commonly asked questions on a particular subject. Every newsgroup has at least one.

Finger A decreasingly popular program that can return stored data on UNIX users or other information such as weather updates. Often disabled for security reasons.

Firewall A network security system used to restrict external traffic.

Flame Abusive attack on someone posting in Usenet.

FTP File Transfer Protocol. The standard method of transferring files over the Internet.

GIF Graphic Image File format. A compressed graphics format used commonly on the Net.

Gopher A menu-based system for retrieving Internet archives, usually organized by subject.

GUI Graphic User Interface. A method of driving software through the use of windows, icons, menus, buttons, and other graphic devices.

H

Hacker A computer enthusiast who derives joy from discovering ways to circumvent limitations. A criminal hacker is called a cracker.

Home page Either the first page loaded by your browser at start-up, or the main Web document for a particular group, organization, or person.

Host Your host is the computer you contact to get on to the Net.

HTML HyperText Markup Language. The language used to create Web documents.

I

Image map A Web image that contains multiple links. Which link you take depends on where you click.

Infoseek Commerical Web search database located at http://www.infoseek.com

Internet A cooperatively run global collection of computer networks with a common addressing scheme.

IP Internet Protocol. The most important protocol on which the Internet is based. It defines how packets of data get from source to destination.

IP address Every computer connected to the Internet has an IP address (written in dotted numerical notation), which corresponds to its domain name. Domain Name Servers convert one to the other.

IRC Internet Relay Chat. An Internet system where you can chat in text, or audio, to others in real time, like an online version of CB radio.

ISDN Integrated Services Digital Network. An international standard for digital communications over telephone lines, that allows for the transmission of data at 64 or 128 kbps.

ISP Internet Service Provider. A company that sells access to the Internet.

J

JPEG A graphic file format that is preferred by Net users because its high compression reduces file size, and thus the time it takes to transfer.

K

Kill File A newsreader file into which you can enter key words and email addresses to stop unwanted articles.

L

Leased line A dedicated telecommunications connection between two points.

Lycos A free Web search database located at
http://lycos.cs.cmu.edu/

M

MIME Multipurpose Internet Mail Extensions. A recent standard for the transfer of binary email attachments.

Mirror A replica FTP or Web site set up to share traffic.

Modem MOdulator/DEModulator. A device that allows a computer to communicate with another over a standard telephone line, by converting the digital data into analog signals and vice versa.

Mosaic The first point and click Web browser, created by NCSA, currently (largely) superseded by Netscape.

MPEG A compressed video file format.

Multimedia The incorporation of many types of media such as graphics, text, audio, and video, into one resource.

N

Name server A host that translates domain names into IP addresses.

The Net The Internet.

Netscape The most popular Web browser – and the company that produces it.

Newbie A newcomer to the Net, discussion, or area.

Newsgroup The Usenet message areas, or discussion groups, organized by subject hierarchies.

NNTP Network News Transfer Protocol. The standard for the exchange of Usenet articles across the Internet.

Node Any device connected to a network.

P

Packet A unit of data. In data transfer, information is broken into packets, which then travel independently through the Net. An Internet packet contains the source and destination addresses, an identifier, and the data segment.

Ping A program which sends an echo-like trace to test if another host is available.

POP3 Post Office Protocol. An email protocol which allows you to pick up your mail from anywhere on the Net – even if you're connected through someone else's account.

POPs Points of Presence. An access provider's range of local dial-in points.

Post To send a public message to a Usenet newsgroup.

PPP Point to Point Protocol. A protocol which allows your computer to join the Internet via a modem. Each time you log in, you're allocated a temporary IP address. It's a more efficient system than the old SLIP connnections, and easier to configure.

Protocol An agreed way for two network devices to talk to each other.

R

Robot A "crawler" program that trawls the Web to update search databases such as InfoSeek and Lycos.

S

Server A central computer that makes services available on a network.

Signature file A self-designed footer that can be automatically attached to email and Usenet postings.

SLIP Serial Line Internet Protocol. A protocol that allows your computer to join the Internet via a modem and requires that you have a pre-allocated fixed IP address configured in your TCP/IP setup. It's slowly being replaced by PPP.

SMTP Simple Mail Transfer Protocol. The Internet protocol for transporting mail.

Spam Inappropriately post the same message to multiple newsgroups.

Stuffit A common Macintosh file compression format.

T

TCP/IP Transmission Control Protocol/Internet Protocol. The protocols that drive the Internet, regulating how data is transferred between computers.

Telnet An Internet protocol that allows you to log on to a remote computer and act as a dumb terminal.

Trumpet-Winsock A Windows program that provides a dialup SLIP or PPP connection to the Net.

U

UNIX An operating system used by most service providers and universities. So long as you stick to graphic programs, you'll never notice it.

URL Uniform Resource Locator. The addressing system for the World Wide Web.

Usenet User's Network. A collection of networks and computer systems that exchange messages, organized by subject into Newsgroups.

UUCP UNIX to UNIX Copy Program. A store and forward file transfer system.

UUencode A method of encoding binary files into text so that they can be attached to mail or posted to Usenet. They have to be UUdecoded to convert them back. The better mail and news programs do this automatically.

W

WAIS Wide Area Information Servers. A system that searches by key word through database indexes around the Net. Losing popularity to Web tools such as InfoSeek and Lycos.

Web The World Wide Web or WWW. A network of graphic/hypermedia documents on the Internet that are interconnected through hypertext links.

Web authoring Designing and publishing Web pages using HTML.

World Wide Web See Web, above.

Y

Yahoo A superb directory of Web sites located at:
http: //www.yahoo.com

Z

Zip PC file compression format which creates files with the extension .zip, using PKZip or WinZip software. Commonly used to reduce file size for transfer or storage on floppy disks.

Zmodem A file transfer protocol which, among other things, offers the advantage of being able to pick up where you left off after transmission failure.

Although the best way to find out more about the Internet is to get online and crank up one of the Web's search engines, sometimes it's simply more convenient – and, yes, more enjoyable! – to read about it in book or magazine. Among regular Internet magazines, the best are the US-based *Internet World* and cyber-style bible *Wired*, and the UK-based *Internet* and *.net*.

Net books are harder to recommend, as things change so quickly in cyberspace. It's certainly unwise to buy a practical guide published more than a year previously. In this short book, I've attempted to provide everything you need to know to get active on the Internet, and I would contend that most other books on the Net are absurdly overdetailed. However, you may want to add one of the fat techie volumes for those moments when you get stuck on something arcane like a mailing list command. And you may want a more specialized volume, if, for example, you want to create your own Web pages. Listed below, then, are a few volumes you may find useful or interesting, plus a selection of further reading on the wider Internet debate.

Practical general guides

Ed Krol, *The Whole Internet User's Guide & Catalog* (O'Reilly & Associates, US). Seminal general guide.

Adam Engst, *The Internet Starter Kit* (Hayden, US). Step-by-step guidance, plus software. For Mac/Windows.

John R. Levine & Carl Baroudi, *Internet Secrets* (IDG Books, US). Digest of useful advice from 40 Net experts.

Various, *Tricks of the Internet Gurus* (SAMS Publishing, US). Assorted nuggets from various Net knowbies.

Web site creation

Genesis & Devra Hall, *Build a Web Site* (Prima Publishing, US). CGI scripting, HTML, browser technology, and how to become a Webmaster.

Taylor, *Creating Cool Web Pages with HTML* (IDG Books, US). Mastering Hypertext Markup Language.

Other specialist guides

Maloff, *Expanding Your Business Using the Internet* (IDG Books, US). The Net in its business context.

Stallings, *The Official Internet World Security Handbook* (IDG Books, US). Keep out virtual intruders.

Jamsa & Cope, *Internet Programming* (Jamsa Press, US). Learn to create your own Internet applications.

What's on/Directories

Harley Hahn and Rick Stout, *The Internet Yellow Pages* (Osborne, UK). This is the best of a flurry of "Yellow Pages" available – and about the only one that doesn't add the meaningless tag "official" to its title.

Various, *Netguide: What's on in Cyberspace* and *Netgames: What's playing in Cyberspace* (Random House, US). Two from a useful series of TV-style guides, including online services and BBSs, as well as the Net.

Various, *Internet Pocket Tours* (Sybex, US). Another handy series of guides devoted to specific interests – music, travel, sports, games, money, etc.

Gary Wolf and Michael Stein, *Aether Madness: An Offbeat Guide to the Online World* (Peachpit Press, US). Way the quirkiest and most entertaining Net travelog to date, with both informed guiding and thoughtful writing. Also nice coverage of BBSs, large and small.

Lamont Wood, *The Net After Dark: The Underground Guide to the Coolest Hangouts* (Wiley, US). Digs into the Net's seedy, weird, and controversial bowers.

Net debates

Nicholas Negroponte, *Being Digital* (Knopf, US/Hodder, UK). MIT luminary and *Wired* columnist sets out what's in store for the future.

Bill Gates, *The Road Ahead* (Penguin, US/UK). What Bill thinks now has a certain self-fulfilling aspect.

Clifford Stoll, *Silicon Snake Oil* (Doubleday, US/Macmillan, UK). Apostasy! Stoll is a Californian geek who has decided the Net is vastly overrated.

Carla Sinclair, *Netchick: A Smart-Girl Guide to the Wired World* (Holt, US). So what's in the Net for women? A survey of the hip, feminist digitalia.

Still want more?

Well, the Net, of course, has its own directories of books about itself. The best is:

The Unofficial Internet Booklist

http://www.northcoast.com/savetz/blist.html

PART FOUR

directories

Cybercafés

One of the best ways to test drive the Internet or to pick up mail on the road is by visiting a cybercafé. As well as serving coffee and snacks, these coffee shops provide casual Internet access. Their terminals have the latest Internet software installed and they usually have someone nearby to lend a hand. You pay for the time you're online and of course the coffee and cakes you devour. Terminals are also finding their way into bookstores, computer stores, even bars and pubs.

Our listings below feature a range of cybercafés open at the time of publication. To pack them in, we've printed phone numbers only, so you'll need to call for addresses; you could even ask if they know of any closer to home – cybercafés are a growth industry. Once you get online, check out Mark Dziecielewski's superb guide at: http://www.easynet.co.uk/pages/cafe/ccafe.htm and the newsgroup alt.cybercafes which provides advice on locating cybercafés and setting up your own.

Australia

Brisbane	Grand Orbit	07 2361384
Broadbeach	Internet Quest	075 570 2322
Canberra	Internet Café	06 2621489
Melbourne	CyberNet Café	03 818 1288
Newcastle	Planet Access	049 623 862
Ringwood	Virtual Access Café	039 879 8777
St. Kilda	NetCafé	03 534 2620

Belgium

Antwerp	Wie Katoen	03 233 0587
Brussels	Internet Yourself	02 285 0500
Brussels	NetCity	02 218 0305
Ghent	Internetcafé	09 220 5602

Britain

Bedford	Cyber	01234 349 990
Birmingham	Custard Factory	0121 604 7777
Birmingham	Sputnik	0121 643 0426
Brighton	Zap Cybercafé	01273 672 234
Cambridge	CB1	01223 576 306
Cambridge	The Six Bells	01223 566 056
Cheltenham	Interact Café	01452 613 378
Ealing	Republic	0181 579 4532
Edinburgh	Cyberia	0131 220 4403
Edinburgh	Web13	0131 229 8883
Kingston	Cyberia	0181 974 9650
Leicester	The Ark	0116 262 0909
Liverpool	Café Internet	0151 255 1112
Liverpool	Charlotte's Web Café	0151 252 1150
London	Cyberia	0171 209 0990
Manchester	Wet	0161 236 5920
Nottingham	Cyberpub	0121 344 2417
Stockport	Peak Art Cybercafé	01663 747 770

Canada

Fredericton	Whitney Coffee Co	506-454 2233
Montreal	Café Electronique	613-546 5824
Ottawa	CyberPerk	613-789 7873
Prince George	The Internet Café	604-563 4583
Québec	Chez Ulysse	514-653 9344

| Trail | Java Junction | 604-368 JAVA |
| Vancouver | Cafe.net | 604-681 6365 |

Denmark

| Copenhagen | C@fe Internet | 031 427 202 |

Finland

| Helsinki | Internetcafé Helsinki | 90 685 2976 |

France

Besançon	La Web	81 812 846
Marseille	Cyb.Estami.Net	91 114 243
Nice	La Douche Cyber Café	93 923 434
Paris	Café Orbital	40 200 514

Germany

| Friemersheim | Dorfschenke | 20 654 72 79 |
| Hamburg | Elcafe | 40 389 57 06 |

Hong Kong

| Hong Kong | Cyber Café Club | 2530 9195 |

Iceland

| Reykjavík | Síbería Netc@fé | 551 6003 |

Ireland

| Dublin | Underground Club | 01 679 3010 |
| Dun Laoghaire | Café Bleu | 284 6969 |

Italy

Milan .... Cyber Café 022 730 4426
Padua .... Ossteria alla Ventura .. 049 663 023
Torino .... Virtualia 011 606 3978

Malaysia

Kuala Lumpur .. Interserve Cybercafe .. 603 719 5803

Netherlands

Amsterdam ..... Mystèr 2000 .... 020 620 2970
Rotterdam ..... Café De Unie 010 411 7394

New Zealand

Wellington ..... CyberSpace Café 04 499 8560

Norway

Bergen .... CyBergen 090 070 638

Singapore

Singapore ...... Cyber Place 734 5448

South Africa

Cape Town ..... iCafé 021 246 576
Johannesburg .. Milky Way Café 011 487 3608

Spain

Madrid .... La Ciberteca 01 556 5603

Sweden

Linköping . . . . . . BerZyber 013 207 422
Stenungsund . . . Internet Café &
PC Museum 030 369 648

Switzerland

Basel . . . . @Lounge 061 262 0830
Fribourg . . . . Scottish Bar Pub 037 268 202

United States

Allentown . . . . . . Cappuccino Caffe
Surf Station 610 395-8262
Ashland . . . . Garo's Java House . . . 503 482-2261
Ashland . . . . PaperMoon
Espresso Café 503 488-4883
Atlanta . . . . Red Light Café 404 874-7828
Austin . . . . Electronic Café
International 512 703-8922
Block Island . . . . Juice 'n Java 401 466-5220
Bloomington . . . . Original Kona
Koffee Co 812 334-1233
Buffalo . . . . Common Grounds . . . 716 633-4589
California . . . . . . DP's Cafe Costa Mesa . 714 722-9673
Cambridge . . . . . Cybersmith 617 492-5857
Dillon . . . . Caroline's Coffeehouse 970 468-8332
Honolulu . . . . . . The Internet C@fé . . . 808 735-JAVA
Matthews . . . . . . On-Ramp 704 849-2210
New York . . . . . . alt.coffee 212 946-2074
New York . . . . . . Cybercafé 212 334-5140
New York . . . . . . The Heroic Sandwich . 212 254-2944
NY East Village . @Café 212 979-5439
NY East Village . Internet Café 212 614-0747

Philadelphia	Cyber Loft	215 564-4380
Portland	Cafe Electrique	503 284-7837
Portland	The Habit	503 235-5321
Providence	C@fé Online	401 885-7555
San Antonio	The Coffee Gallery	210 226-5123
San Diego	Café Renaissance	619 297-2700
San Francisco	Cyborganic	415 553-8554
San Francisco	ICON Byte Bar	861 BYTE-2983
Scranton	Internet Café	717 344-1969
Seattle	Internet Café	206 323-7202
Seattle	Speakeasy Café	206 728-9770
St. Louis	Gothic Coffee House	314 865-BEAN
St. Louis	The Grind	314 454-0202
Venice	Cyber Java	310 581-1300
Virginia	Bogen's Blacksburg	703 953-2233

Internet Service Providers

The directories following cover major Internet Service Providers (ISPs or IAPs) in **North America**, the **UK**, **Europe**, **Australia**, and **New Zealand**. They are by no means a complete list and concentrate on larger ISPs with multiple points of presence: ie, a range of phone numbers that you can use to dial in for access. There are, in addition, literally hundreds of local access providers, catering for individual cities and/or states.

Even the ISPs listed, however, operate mostly in one country only (or US and Canada). For truly international access – if that is a priority – you will be better off with one of the major **online services**, such as **CompuServe**, **IBM Global Network**, or **Microsoft Network**; these are detailed on p.35–43.

If you can arrange temporary Internet access, you can consult a fairly exhaustive list of ISPs on the Net at the **newsgroups** alt.internet.services or alt.internet.services (these are also good places for queries about international access), or by viewing the World Wide Web site "Internet Access Providers" at: http://www.best.be/iap.html.

For more about ISPs and all the practicalities of getting connected, see p.18–34.

NORTH AMERICAN ISPs

Provider ✉ Email	ℂ Phone Points of Presence
a2i communications ✉ info@rahul.net	ℂ 408 293-8078 252, 293, 364, 408, 415, 444, 510, 707
Ans Core Systems ✉ info@ans.net	ℂ 1-800 456-8267 202, 203, 206, 214, 215, 216, 212, 303, 310, 314, 404
CAPCON Library Network ✉ info@capcon.net	ℂ 202 331-5771 202, 301, 410, 703
CERFnet ✉ help@cerf.net	ℂ 1-800 876-2373 619, 510, 415, 818, 714, 310, 800
CICNet ✉ shaffer@cic.net	ℂ 1-800 947-4754 313, 708, 800
ClarkNet ✉ info@clark.net	ℂ 410 254-0749 202, 301, 410, 703
CRL ✉ info@crl.com	ℂ 415 837-5300 213, 310, 404, 415, 510, 602, 707, 800
Delphi Internet ✉ walthowe@delphi.com	ℂ 1-800 544-4005 US, Canada, Guam, Puerto Rico, SprintNet, TymNet
Digital Express Group ✉ info@digex.com	ℂ 1-800 969-9090 201, 212, 215, 301, 410, 609, 610, 703, 908
EMI ✉ netguru@emi.com	ℂ 1-800 456-2001 202, 212, 315, 516, 518, 607, 617, 716, 914
Evergreen Internet Services ✉ evergreen@enet.net	ℂ 602 926-4500 602, 702, 801

Grebyn	✆ 703 406-4161
✉ info@grebyn.com	202, 301, 703
HoloNet	✆ 510 704-0160
✉ info@holonet.net	510, PSINet, Tymnet
Hookup Communications	✆ 1-800 363-0400
✉ info@hookup.net	519, Canada
I-Link	✆ 1-800 ILINK-99
✉ info@i-link.net	602, 801, 206, 503, 303, 213, 415, 512
IDS World Network	✆ 401 884-7856
✉ sysadmin@ids.net	401, 305, 407, CSN
iNet Communications, Inc.	✆ 302 454-1780
✉ info@inetcom.net	302, 215, 609, 301, 610
INS Info Services	✆ 1-800 5HOOKUP
✉ info@ins.infonet.net	402, 319, 515, 712, 800
Internet For 'U'	✆ 1-800 NETWAY1
✉ info@ifu.net	201, 908, 609
Internet Online Services	✆ 201 928-1000
✉ info@ios.com	201, 212, 908, 703, 800
Interpath	✆ 1-800 849-6305
✉ info@interpath.net	704, 919, 910
IQuest	✆ 1-800 844-UNIX
✉ info@iquest.net	317, 709, 313, 810, 812
JvNCNet - Dialin' Tiger	& 1-800 35-TIGER
✉ info@jvnc.net	201, 203-541, 203-338, 212, 401, 510, 516, 609, 708, 800, 809, 908
MCSNet	✆ 312 248-8649
✉ info@genesis.mcs.com	312, 708, 815

Merit Network	✆ 313 764-9430
✉ info@merit.edu	313, 517, 616, 906, PDN
Millennium	✆ 1-800 736-0122
✉ info@millcomm.com	US-wide
Msen	✆ 313 998-4562
✉ info@msen.com	313, 800, 810
MV Communications	✆ 603 429-2223
✉ info@mv.mv.com	508, 603, 617
NEARNet	✆ 617 873-8730
✉ nearnet-join@nic.near.net	508, 603, 617
NeoSoft	✆ 1-800 GET-NEOS
✉ info@neosoft.com	314, 504, 713, 800, SprintNet
Netcom	✆ 1-800 501-8649
✉ info@netcom.com	US-wide
Network Intensive	✆ 714 450-8400
✉ info@ni.net	213, 310, 505, 714, 805, 818, 909
Novalink	✆ 1-800 274-2814
✉ info@novalink.com	US, Canada
OARNet	✆ 614 728-8100
✉ info@oar.net	216, 419, 513, 614, 800
OnRamp	✆ 214 746-4710
✉ info@onramp.net	214, 817, 713
Panix	✆ 212 877-4854
✉ info@panix.com	212, 516, 718
Portal	✆ 408 973-9111
✉ info@portal.com	408, 415, SprintNet
PREPNet	✆ 412 268-7870
✉ prepnet+@andrew.cmu.edu	215, 412, 717, 814

| PSI World Dial Service | ☏ 1-800 827-7482 |
| ✉ info@psi.com | US, Tokyo |

| SprintLink | ☏ 1-800 817-7755 |
| ✉ info@sprintlink.net | Worldwide |

| The Destek Group, Inc. | ☏ 603 635-3857 |
| ✉ info@destek.net | 207, 508, 603, 617, 800, 802 |

| The World, Software Tool & Die | ☏ 617 739-0202 |
| ✉ office@world.std.com | 508, 617, CSN |

| WestNet Internet Services | ☏ 914 967-7816 |
| ✉ info@westnet.com | 208, 303, 307, 505, 602, 801 |

| YPN | ☏ 1-800 NET-1133 |
| ✉ info@ypn.com | US-wide |

BRITISH AND IRISH ISPs/IAPs

Provider ✉ Email	☏ Phone Points of Presence
BBC Networking Club ✉ info@bbnc.org.uk	☏ 0181 576 7799 Birmingham, Bristol, Cambridge, Edinburgh, London, Manchester
BTnet	☏ 01442 295828 UK-wide
Byson Computers ✉ ian@byson.demon.co.uk	☏ 01635 869480 Newbury and as Demon
CityScape ✉ sales@cityscape.co.uk	☏ 01223 566950 Birmingham, Bristol, Cambridge, London, Edinburgh, Warrington

| Delphi | ✆ 0171 757 7080 |
| ✉ ukservice@delphi.com | London and 98 UK GNS points |

| Demon | ✆ 0181 371 1234 |
| ✉ sales@demon.net | UK-wide |

| The Direct Connection | ✆ 0181 317 0100 |
| ✉ helpdesk@dircon.co.uk | Birmingham, Bristol, Cambridge, Edinburgh, London, Manchester |

| Easynet | ✆ 0171 209 0990 |
| ✉ admin@easynet.co.uk | Birmingham, Bristol, Cambridge, Edinburgh, London, Warrington |

| EUnet GB | ✆ 01227 266466 |
| ✉ sales@britain.eu.net | Europe-wide |

| Foremost Training | ✆ 0141 248 6377 |
| ✉ donald@scotnet.co.uk | Aberdeen, Glasgow |

| Ireland On-Line | ✆ 353 (0) 855 1793 |
| ✉ postmaster@iol.ie | Eire and Northern Ireland |

| Leaf Distribution | ✆ 01256 707777 |
| ✉ sales@leaf.co.uk | Birmingham, Bristol, Cambridge, Edinburgh, London, Manchester |

| PC User Group | ✆ 0181 863 1191 |
| ✉ info@win-uk.net | Birmingham, Bristol, Cambridge, Edinburgh, London, Manchester |

| Pipex | ✆ 01223 250120 |
| ✉ sales@pipex.net | Birmingham, Bristol, Cambridge, Edinburgh, London, Manchester |

| RedNet | ✆ 01494 513333 |
| ✉ info@red.net | Birmingham, Bristol, Cambridge, Edinburgh, London, Manchester |

EUROPEAN ISPs

Provider ✉ Email	☎ Phone Points of Presence
Contributed Software ✉ info@contrib.de	☎ 030 6946807 Germany
EUnet ✉ info@Britain.EUnet	☎ (UK) 1 227 266466 Europe-wide
Individual Nettwork ✉ in-info@individual.net	☎ 0441 9808556 Germany
Netland ✉ info@netland.nl	☎ 020 6943664 Netherlands
Orstom ✉ michaux@orstom.orstom.fr	☎ 067 547510 France
Switch ✉ postmaster@switch.ch	☎ 01 2681515 Switzerland

AUSTRALIAN ISPs

Provider ✉ Email	☎ Phone Points of Presence
Ausnet ✉ sales@world.net	☎ 008 806 755 All capital cities, Alice Springs, Gold Coast, Coffs Harbour, Newcastle
DIALix Services ✉ justin@dialix.com	☎ 1800 642 433 All capital cities
InterConnect ✉ info@interconnect.com.au	☎ 1800 818 262 All capital cities

Provider	✆ Phone
✉ Email	Points of Presence
OzEmail	✆ 1800 805 874
✉ support@ozemail.com.au	All capital cities, Cairns, Newcastle, Woolongong, Townsville, Alice Springs, Sunshine Coast, Gold Coast
Pegasus	✆ 1800 812 812
✉ support@peg.pegasus.oz.au	All capital cities

NEW ZEALAND ISPs

Provider	✆ Phone
✉ Email	Points of Presence
Internet Company of NZ	✆ 09 358 1186
✉ help@icons.co.nz	NZ
NZ Online	✆ 0800 732 800
	NZ
Planet	✆ 09 378 6006
✉ alan@ak.planet.co.nz	NZ

ASIAN ISPs

Provider	✆ Phone
✉ Email	Points of Presence
Hong Kong Supernet	✆ 2358 7924
✉ info@hk.super.net	Hong Kong
Axcess India	✆ 022 493 7676
✉ sharad@axcess.net.in	India
University of Indonesia	✆ 727 0162
✉ postmaster@UI.AC.ID	Indonesia

Global Online Japan	ℂ 03 5330 9380
✉ info@gol.com	Japan
Dacom	ℂ 02 220 5232
✉ help@nis.dacom.co.kr	Korea
Jaring	ℂ 2549601
✉ info@jaring.my	Malaysia
Brain Net	ℂ 042 541 4444
✉ info@brain.com.pk	Pakistan
SingNet	ℂ 7515034
✉ sales@singnet.com.sg	Singapore
Pristine Internet Gateway	ℂ 02 368 9023
✉ robert@pristine.com.tw	Taiwan
Thaisarn Internet Service	ℂ 662 248 8007
✉ sysadmin@nwg.nectec.or.th	Thailand

Acknowledgments

I hadn't planned to write a book until Mark Ellingham from Rough Guides approached me. I was organizing an overland trek from Karachi to Hong Kong – areas the Net hadn't yet reached. It was doctor's orders. I had developed an umbilical attachment to the World Wide Web. It was taking over my life. I had surfed through tens of thousands of pages, tapping in to the most diverse minds in existence. But each day, hundreds more would appear. It was endless. Even when I closed my eyes at night, I would still be feverishly skipping through the pages cached in my memory. The Net is an addiction. You'll see.

At the time, I was writing *Internet* magazine's "What's On the Web" guide – which had grown from just a few pages to half the world's largest Internet magazine in the space of only a few months – and between times explaining to countless journalists that the Internet doesn't have a public relations agency. I was living and breathing the Net from missed-breakfast to TV dinner-time. The last thing I needed was to get in deeper and try to write a compact fool-proof guide to something that no-one really understood, that changed every minute, and that was somehow related to Swiss physicists. And a book that wouldn't be out of date before it was finished. But, who was I kidding? I couldn't leave the Net and miss even an episode in the world's largest soap opera.

As a compromise, I headed to Brisbane where I wouldn't be disturbed by undue excitement or quality television, would be fed at regular intervals by my loving parents, and could still patch in. The great thing about the Internet is that it removes distance. The Net is the Net whether you're in Australia or Antarctica. No-one's more than a few minutes away. It was the perfect writing environment, but I needed the help of a small cast of heroes.

Without the generosity and inspiration of *Internet* magazine's Roger Green, Neil Ellul, and Lisa Hughes, this book would never have happened. Some of the Web reviews come courtesy of the magazine's "What's On" guide. (If you find them useful, there's plenty more each month.) And, being able to pepper old hands like Neil and Anton Leach with teasers about the ins and outs of SMTP, TCP/IP, and POP3, and get sensible answers, truncated the research curve by months.

Thanks also to: Gerry and John for bailing me out of hardware Hades after my modem, and then notebook, went pear-shaped, wobbled, fell over, and refused to get up again; Mark and Henry for not making a fuss about missed deadlines and for flooding me with daily clippings, books, and advice; my parents for passing fresh avocados, custard apples, and passionfruit through the cage bars; Jane for patiently waiting; *EasyNet* for a perpetually fast and reliable POP mailbox; *CompuServe* for Net connections everywhere from Hong Kong to Surfers Paradise; Jonathan Richman for what he said about the modern world; Jo for her help with hard words; and Murray and Simone for tip-toeing around the house before mid-day.

But most of all, thanks to the unsung Webmasters and freedom-of-speech fighters who make the Net the last bastion of independence, equality, and higher thought. May you join their ranks.

Angus J. Kennedy (angusk@roughtravl.co.uk)

Index

O

P

R